SHOW OF
HANDS

ALSO BY ANTHONY McCARTEN

NOVELS

Spinners, 1999
The English Harem, 2002
Death of a Superhero, 2006

PLAYS

Cyril Ellis Where Are You, 1984
Pigeon English, 1986
Yellow Canary Mazurka, 1987
Ladies Night (with Stephen Sinclair), 1987
Weed, 1990
Via Satellite, 1991
Legless (with Stephen Sinclair), 1991
Let's Spend the Night Together, 1993
Ladies Night II (with Stephen Sinclair), 1993
F.I.L.T.H.—Failed in London Try Hong Kong, 1995
Four Cities, 1996

FILMS

Pumpernickel (short), 1989
Rodney & Juliet (short), 1990
Nocturne in a Room (short), 1993
Fluff (short), 1995
Via Satellite, 1998
English Harem, 2006
Show of Hands, 2008

SHORT STORIES

A Modest Apocalypse & Other Stories, 1991
Vital Writings, 1991
Introductions: First Fictions, 1992

SHOW OF
HANDS

A Novel

Anthony McCarten

WASHINGTON SQUARE PRESS
NEW YORK LONDON TORONTO SYDNEY

Washington Square Press
A Division of Simon & Schuster, Inc.
1230 Avenue of the Americas
New York, NY 10020

First Washington Square Press trade paperback edition February 2009

WASHINGTON SQUARE PRESS and colophon are registered trademarks of
Simon & Schuster, Inc.

For information about special discounts for bulk purchases,
please contact Simon & Schuster Special Sales at 1-800-456-6798
or business@simonandschuster.com

Designed by Davina Mock-Maniscalco

Manufactured in the United States of America

1 3 5 7 9 10 8 6 4 2

Library of Congress Cataloging-in-Publication Data

McCarten, Anthony, 1961–
Show of hands : a novel / Anthony McCarten.
    p.   cm.
1. Automobile dealers—Fiction. 2. Selling—Automobiles—Fiction.
3. Publicity—Fiction. I. Title.
PR9639.3.M195S56 2009
823'.914—dc22
2008044714

ISBN-13: 978-1-4165-8607-4
ISBN-10:   1-4165-8607-5

For Margaret Mary McCarten
1921–2007

SHOW OF
HANDS

The Contenders

ON THE MORNING before the contest, Tom Shrift watched from his upstairs window as his neighbor mowed a little lawn, the man lapping back and forth until he had achieved six parallel stripes, which alternated in intensity—green and dark green—a tweedy warp that produced in Tom alternating feelings of envy and rage, envy and rage.

> *And did those feet in ancient time*
> *Walk upon England's mountains green . . .*

Where were Tom's green mountains? Where were his feet to walk free? Quarantined in his first-floor apartment, denied an outdoor space of his own (he'd wanted a small Juliet-style balcony, but his neighbor had successfully objected to the council), Tom observed this lawn painfully not his own, then opened his front window slightly, so that the canted glass lifted into his face a breeze strong with an exhalation of cut grass.

Loss, this was what he felt. Loss and deprivation. One man owns, another man craves—the craving far more passionate than the dull pleasures of ownership. How galling not *to have* when you were the type who deserved to have—yes, *deserved*.

He turned from the window. Three clocks told him he was late, was behind schedule already.

He must not let the petty feud raging between himself and his neighbor detain him today. He had a job interview downtown. He dressed quickly and with close attention, choosing a bold silk tie to augment a white shirt. Ready to do battle, he drove sharply, with the aggression that London's hustling, asphyxiating traffic required.

He parked hastily, found the building he needed, then rose, rose, rose up in a glass elevator traveling up the outer shell of the skyscraper. Immaculate in his suit, he soon sat before a corporate human resources drone—Tom's mortal enemy—the kind of specimen who, everywhere, stood between him and the life he deserved.

A transcript of this exchange would later read:

Interviewer: You've worked mainly for yourself.

Tom: Mm-hmm.

Interviewer: You prefer that? Okay. So, then, what's changed?

Tom: I had some bad luck.

Interviewer: You sold . . . I see, birthday cards. Cute.

Tom: I owned and ran a highly successful greeting card company, with contracts in four countries, whose hallmark was quality reproductions of art masterpieces. You have to know a lot about art and I do.

Interviewer: You've ceased trading?

Tom: I spent a lot of money trying to license images from the Hermitage in St. Petersburg. I was cheated.

Interviewer: Any other reasons for the collapse? Do you bear any responsibility yourself?

Tom: I was lied to. Swindled, basically.

Interviewer: And but for that, you'd still be trading? Fine. Okay.

Tom: Look, where are you going with this? I lost a lot
      of money. Maybe I . . .

Interviewer: You . . . ?

Tom: I may have been too ambitious, but that's all.

Interviewer: You want to take the world by storm.

Tom: I want the universe to know I've been here, yes.

Interviewer: A quote?

Tom: Forget it.

Interviewer: So, maybe you're not so good on the
                  details. Are you still carrying debts from
                  that time?

Tom: Let's just say it's made me available for this line
      of work.

Interviewer: You're probably more used to being on
                  this side of the table, then?

Tom: Well . . . you said it, not me. I shouldn't . . .
      I shouldn't really be in this sort of situation.

Interviewer: Okay, so let's see. Single. Unemployed.
                  Mm'kay. Kids?

Tom: No.

Interviewer: No kids . . . mm'kay.

Tom felt his hackles rise. Later, he would fume about why the guy
had dwelled only on the negative. *Praise me, you wanker! How
come you don't read out "Member of Mensa" from my résumé?
Praise me! How many job applicants have you seen lately who
think of turning the dead Russian collections into beautiful daily
things? How many, fuckface?*

Interviewer: Forty-two years old. You don't look forty-
                  two. What's the secret? Being single?

Tom: It's a secret.

Interviewer: A lot of our team are considerably younger than you. This is a high-pressure job.

Tom: I don't view youth as an advantage. I'm forty-two years old. I bring a lot to the table. My CV speaks for itself. Can we move on?

Interviewer: Would you . . . would you say you're a team player, Tom?

Tom: A team player? No. I wouldn't say I'm a team player. Can I ask—have you ever interviewed anyone before? Seriously. Just a question. Because having looked into your "team's" performance in the last two years, I think the *last* thing you should be looking for is "a team player."

He'd blown it. At this point the man told Tom he had "an aggressive character," before declaring the interview over. Tom was soon back on the street, inhaling the carbon air, and battling the crowds once more.

Reaching his car—he'd parked wantonly in a private parking lot behind the Odeon Cinema—he was horrified to see a female parking warden standing beside it.

He ran. *Oh please, no.* He rushed forward, clasping his hands together, begging the small, white, uniformed woman with a small, pale, child's face to give him a break.

"Hey, hey . . . whoa, whoa. I'm here." Shouting, holding up his arms in surrender: "It's okay. And this is free parking, right? It's *free* parking. I use this all the time. Whoa, whoa, whoa. Stop that. I'm going *right now.*"

Refusing to look at him, the parking attendant replied, "It's not free parking, sir."

"Where? Where is the 'no parking' sign? Where is it? Tell me. Go on. Tell me."

"This is not free parking, sir. This is . . ."

"Oh come on!"

". . . this is private."

"Private? . . . Where? Where does it say 'private'? *Exactly?*"

"It's the property of Odeon Cinemas, sir, and is reserved for use by their staff."

"Since when?"

"It's a gated area, and I can only assume you accessed it by mounting the pavement on High Street and entering it that way, which is another offense."

"And this is your jurisdiction? Are you allowed to enter private property and adopt overzealous commission-seeking tactics? Oh, man. You people. I can't afford this. Okay? You want the truth? This makes a difference to me. I can't pay this. Please." He held wide his arms, cruciform: the Kensington Christ. "I'm serious. Give me a break here. I'm . . . I'm going through . . ." His arguments petered out. "I don't believe this . . . what a bitch."

Silence from the parking warden at this, a professional reserve.

"You're kidding me, right?"

The attendant continued entering her data.

"You're writing me a ticket? You're writing me . . . ? I don't be— Fucking unbe— What are . . . you people? Blood-sucking leeches. Vampires. . . . Know what you are? Satan's concubines!" At last he elicited a glance from her—he'd got through at last. He quickly exploited the weakness. "Should be ashamed of yourselves. How you live with yourself is a mystery. So . . . so how much is that for? The ticket? What's the fine?"

A level voice. "Hundred pounds. Unless you pay within fourteen days."

"And what's your cut? Your cut of that? Fifty percent? Exactly! No wonder you won't let anyone off. What a bitch. You people are the scum of the earth."

Barely audibly, the woman replied, "You're entitled to your opinion, sir."

Her handheld ticket machine then made a succession of *brrrrrrs* and clicks before producing Tom's fine, which, when he refused to take it, she bagged and stuck to his windscreen. And with that, she was gone.

In a radical change to his plans—one had to react quickly in a big city—Tom drove straight for a garden-supply outlet near his home. With his blood still boiling he walked the aisles of the superstore, locating several plastic bottles of the brand of weed killer he wanted. On the label, a skull-and-crossbones symbol, plus the words *extra strength*. Yes. He was happy to pay the steep forty pounds they wanted for this toxic product—it was a very small price to pay to end a feud, once and for all.

With an extreme action in mind, and when he really ought to have been fast asleep in preparation for the contest, he stayed up after midnight, waiting for his neighbor's noises to subside and cease.

At quarter past the hour he received an incoming call on his mobile phone. The LCD screen revealed it to be his aged mother. Grateful for the way modern phones alerted you to the identity of the caller, he turned the device off, screening the old lady out. Tonight was no time to go over all their grievances once more—her failures as a mother, Tom's as a son, et cetera. Only at 1:30 did he dare creep down the stairs and quietly open his door's triple locks—*clack, cluck, click*—before passing through the shared lobby and out of the communal front door into the night.

The city. Electrically aglow; the glow unable to rise beyond the monoxide lid of gases so that it bounced back. Down upon a lawn. Green grass. His enemy's field. And Tom was going to kill it.

And did those feet in ancient time
Walk upon England's mountains green . . .

His feet tingled upon the cold wet blades, increasing his sense of trespass. Should he rethink this action? What future madnesses would this lead to? He looked toward his neighbor's darkened windows, hoping to summon the old enmities that had led him here—those tit-for-tat reprisals dating back two years now—hoping once more to envisage the leery face of his tormentor peering between the sun-browned curtains, those stupid, clotted facial features, that aggressive glare, but the window only gave him back himself—just Tom Shrift, a cat burglar with a watering can, forty-two, unshaven, a moonlit ghost.

Only the weight of the watering can drew him back to his mission, and with half a heart he poured the poison as planned. Killing grass. A terrible crime. Really a madman's response. The potion flowed unbroken as he moved about the lawn until the can couldn't produce another drop. Now, he thought, as he slipped back inside and sealed the door again on his actions and on the city that held him captive, he could once more get on with his life, his real one.

THE DAY BEFORE the contest had been a nasty one for Parking Warden 2061, Jess Podorowski. Of those people she'd penalized, more than the usual number had been especially vile to her, some saying terrible things, one man even shouting so loudly that his spit had flecked her face. Hatred, this she was more or less used to. But spit, that was uncommonly foul.

Throughout it all she'd been unable to answer back. The rules of her job were very clear on this point: she was to remain mute, withstand the abuse and tirades, silently go about her work, enter the correct details, press the submit button on her ticketing machine, issue the ticket and then walk away—in many ways, it really was the perfect job for someone like her.

She paused to stretch her lower back, her weak point. This job did her no favors in the lumbar department. Nine and a half hours took their toll. In her logbook she noted her position, details of charge notices issued so far. And that's when she looked up and saw him.

The sudden delight in just seeing his face again, coming up the crowded street toward her. Her heart received a small electric jolt as his name leaped back to her tongue. Her beloved. Maciek. How extraordinary, on the same street where she was working, the one face she most wanted to see. But then again, they had always had a way of bumping into each other in a crowd. From the very start, coincidence and chance had informed them that they were destined to be together.

The only problem: Maciek was dead. Two full years. So it didn't take very long for the approaching face to take on the blank meaninglessness of a stranger who bore less and less resemblance to her late husband, and then no resemblance at all.

Her heart collapsed. Tricked again, she shook her head, clamped her feelings down and went back to work. She must move on and not fall prey to sentimental delusions. More cars awaited her, standing in violation. She returned to her beat. Had to.

Jess Podorowski. Her vital statistics? Widowed. Thirty-nine. Five foot five. Pale Slavic face. Her mother, a Polish immigrant from Lodz, her father from Milton Keynes. Born silent. Learned to cry three hours later, alone in the postnatal wing. As a kid, quiet, overlooked. Destined to be plain. Tolerated too much. Dwelled on things. Bit her tongue. And the reward for such meekness? To grow up taking hell from all quarters. *The Lord works in mysterious ways,* she prayed, as she walked the streets of West London.

Thank God it was Friday at least. At the end of her shift she hurried homeward in her civvies, catching the bus to her front door just in time to rendezvous with the Social Services minibus as it off-loaded her darling daughter, Natalie—little Nat, a tetraplegic cripple, eighty percent helpless, happy in her chair anyway: *God bless this little girl*, Jess prayed daily. God protect her.

Pushing Nat to the local Tesco Express for supplies, Jess then mobiled ahead so that her Polish mother, Valeria, the old-world matron, would come up to the street and help her get Nat down the wheelchair ramp to their basement flat's side entrance.

After a supper quickly consumed, and following the big heave-ho to get Nat into bed—a nightly contest—Jess joined her mother at the dining table. Lit a cigarette. Picked up a blouse, a button, a needle, a thread.

"Oh, put that out, darling." Val shielded her face dramatically from the smoke.

Ah Mumia, Jess thought, *always the actress*. Should have been on the stage. In her late sixties she remained a fierce ball of maternal energy. Tireless always in her service to Jess and Nat, existing on two hours of sleep a night, Val sewed, baked her babka breads through the night, lit candles to the Black Madonna of Częstochowa in her one-bedroom studio flat above a betting shop, staying on call twenty-four/seven, on red alert, convinced her descendants weren't half as strong as she was, and that at any second she would be needed. And she was right. Her phone rang and rang.

"My lungs. It's starting. Oh no." She coughed. Coughed again, one hand on her chest. "Please—please—*kochanie* . . ."

"Mumia, there's nothing wrong with your lungs."

Cough, cough, cough. Jess sighed at these familiar dramatics. "Okay, okay, okay," she conceded, crushing out the butt in a saucer. Silence for a while then, enough peace so that Jess felt finally able to ask, "Can you—could you look after Nat for a day or two?"

"When?"

"Tomorrow, and Sunday, maybe Monday."

"But you're not working tomorrow or Sunday . . ."

"There's . . . . there's a competition. A contest. To win a car. You have to put your hand on it for longer than anyone else. The winner gets a brand-new car."

"They give you a free car?"

"No. You have to win it. I've been thinking about doing it."

Valeria slowly shook her head. "This is crazy. Stand around? Two days? With your hand on a car, like a *glupiec*?" Val could no longer stand to watch her daughter's inept attempt to sew on a button correctly. "Let me do it. Give."

But Jess ignored her and took from her handbag the glossy Land Rover brochure she'd picked up from a car dealership in Olympia during her shift. "Look at it. It's big enough for Nat's wheelchair in the back. I could drive her to the new school. She wouldn't have to be a boarder."

"Natalie needs a home. Not an expensive school." Val's face settled into her old look of resistance.

"It's free."

"She doesn't want to live there, she wants to live here."

"But she's getting too heavy for me to lift in and out of bed, let alone the bath."

"We do it together. We manage."

"You're getting older, Mumia. How much longer can you manage on your own when I'm working?"

Valeria shrugged. Old guidelines came to mind. "You manage until you cannot manage and still you go on!"

But none of this was new. Both women had been over the same ground many times. Both knew that this special school in Hampshire for girls with physical disabilities lay beyond the daily range of the Social Services minibus that Nat relied upon at present. The alternative of using taxis would mean wasting all the precious Disability Living Allowance that kept them financially afloat. Fortunately, the Local Education Authority had agreed to cover all Nat's tuition costs if Jess could somehow get her daughter there and back every day. The solution was a large vehicle that Jess could drive. Both women knew all these facts, but the argument was a drama they continued to rehearse over and over.

"With a car, she can go there and still live here. I just have to win this car."

"Jessie, you don't win things." Val reached out again for the mending. "And you're doing that wrong. Wind the thread around it."

Jess glared at her mother. Why, why did Valeria always have to be like this, one hand giving, the other taking away; always charging her tariffs and these deducted from Jess's nerves?

"Stop telling me what to do! Will you please just—" But she bit her tongue as usual. Forbade herself from speaking her mind fully. "I've got to do something, okay? I can't go on like . . ." She gave up. No point. Never any point. "You know—it's late. You should be heading home."

"Oh, when you need my help, fine. But when I want to say something . . ."

"Are you going to help me? Or not? Yes or no?"

"Who else helps you? Just me."

Jess, in frustration, tested the button too heavily—it popped off. The two women looked at each other, both pressed between love and frustration, between loyalty and unspoken fury. In the end Val reached over, took the garment and needle from her daughter and started to sew the button correctly.

Half an hour later, with fatigue brokering an uneasy truce, Valeria rose on her strong piano-stool legs, lifting her cardigan off the back of the chair.

"Call me when you arrive," Jess said, "just to let me know you got home safe. Three rings. I won't answer."

"I'm fine."

"Three rings. Don't forget your shawl."

"I have it."

"Love you. Three rings, Mumia." Jess kissed her mother's cheek. Val was beginning to get that old person's smell: of stale air, of sour milk in a closed room. The front door closed, and Valeria, now shawled and hatted against the wind (protected also from more occult forces by a St. Christopher medal sewn into the hem of her coat), appeared briefly through the kitchen window, rising, rising, up the wheelchair ramp toward street level.

Jess turned and stared at the uncleared table, the gravy-painted plates, the intersecting milk rings stamped by Nat's wet glass almost Olympic in configuration—and one word returned from the day gone by. It dropped now, dropped like a coin into a slot:

Submit.

The Contest

1

THE CONTENDERS BEGAN to gather on the car dealership's forecourt two hours before the official start time. Among the first was a vagrant, fresh from sleeping under a bridge, whose very proximity to the yard's gleaming, multi-thousand-pound fleet seemed a breach of the peace and an act of vandalism.

Elsewhere, a solidly fat man came onto the forecourt pushing a supermarket trolley full of supplies: clothing, cushions, food-stuffs and very many cans of beer, all he'd need—or thought he'd need—to secure the grand prize.

Then came a third person, and then a fourth. Soon there were ten, next twenty, thirty, forty, by 8:30 more than eighty. Even the well-to-do had shown up, proving once again you can never have too much. By 9:00 a.m. at least a hundred and twenty people stood among a fleet of unsold cars below the WIN A NEW CAR blimp bobbing high overhead, tugging on a fixed wire. Ten minutes later this number had climbed to a hundred and fifty, and soon beyond that, clockwise circling an opalescent blue and ultradesirable Land Rover the way dishwater swirls before it goes down the drain.

The owner of this Land Rover was Terry "Hatch" Back, from Back-to-Back New Cars (Olympia, Ltd.). He moved among the contestants, clapping strangers on the back, saying delightedly,

"Hi. Thanks for coming," and "We're going to explain everything soon," or "Hi. Welcome. Great weather," before returning to his assistant, Vince, who was just then trying to conduct a rough headcount.

"Numbers? Any idea?"

"Yeah. Too many." Vince shook his head. "More every second. What are we going to . . . I mean, what do you want to do? It's out of control."

By way of answer Hatch unhelpfully observed, "Something for nothing, it's incredible. People go mad." He ran a slow hand through a hairline with a pronounced widow's peak or vampire V, which, when joined with the twin receding arcs over the temples, produced the scalloped rim found on the head of a sharpened pencil. "Completely mad."

Vince, persistent in his concern, followed Hatch back to his office, repeating three times, "We've got a problem here." But when Hatch went up to the large window and looked out at the bustling yard he saw only beautiful solutions to all his financial woes.

"I *told* you. I knew they'd come. I *knew* it!" The small, bunched fists at his sides flexed alternately, two pumps augmenting the work of the heart. "And if it's like this already, then what's it going to be like in . . . in"—he glanced at his watch—"a whole hour still to go." He let go a laugh; an anxiety-discharging laugh. "I knew it! I told you!" Oh, the relief—the financial weight of the last two years lightening by the minute. "It's gonna be . . . look! *Huge!* Look! You can't *buy* publicity like this. Can't buy it." He turned back to his junior salesman. "Well, I can't. Maybe Coke or, or Shell or Tesco can, but . . ."

"But you *are* buying it," Vince countered. "Buying it is exactly what you're doing. By giving away a free car. All those people out there, you're paying for every single one of them."

This comment was ignored; Hatch refused to trade down his high mood. "Might even make the evening news at this rate. What do you think?"

But before Vince could answer, the dealership's third-tier salesman came in looking even more bewildered than he normally did. Dan, big-timbered, midthirties. As slow and muscularly over-developed as Vince was thin and nervy. (Neither of Hatch's two employees was a genius, and whenever Hatch asked either of them a question it was with no real expectation of a workable answer.)

"Dan, good. Close. Close the . . . great. Now listen. The press. Listen. When they *come*, okay, when they come . . . if they ask you for comment, for anything, refer them to me, understand? Refer them directly to me. I'll handle all the—"

Vince tried again. "But what are we going to . . . ?"

"All the . . . all publicity. To me." Hatch tapped his own chest. "Understand?"

"But we still have to get the numbers down, Hatch. We can't stage it like this."

"Fine. Take care of that." Hatch rechecked his mobile phone. No messages. "But refer any journalists to me. Three things: pub-licity, publicity, publicity."

"I have an idea," Vince continued. "A ballot. To pare the num-bers down to something manageable."

"Sure." And then the smile returned. "We get rid of a few but not too many. We want to make a statement here."

Vince held up pads of Post-it notes. "We write tickets. Forty, say. This is what I'm thinking. We limit the number to forty. Give everyone a number—"

But Hatch had already turned to look back at his crowd, this great, hoped-for, four-by-four-crazy crowd. "Something for noth-ing, ha! Look what happens."

Vince: "And we need to control this traffic or we'll have the police down here."

"Fine. Great. Handle it. Let's get moving. This is gonna be great."

The two junior salesmen walked out, leaving Hatch at the window. "Excellent," he muttered to no one, and then, "Come on, my lovelies," and finally, "Look at them. Something for nothing, and just *look*."

When he saw his wife, Jennifer, and his four young children pushing through the crowd, he turned, sat and waited for them. His right knee bumped against the World War II service revolver taped to the desk's underside—he had never used the gun, but if the current spate of sporadic vandalism continued, then he'd have no hesitation in frightening someone with it, sending out a message to the neighborhood underworld that he was prepared to defend what was his.

While he waited, he pulled close the brand-new megaphone resting horn down on his desk: flared at the base, the red lighthouse stripes hooping it; atop it a mouthpiece awaiting his first instructions to the contestants outside. He gripped the loud hailer and flicked it on. It barked with electricity so that he held it again at arm's reach until the squeal of feedback died down. Only then did he move the contraption back to his mouth and speak experimentally, in a low, humid voice, the words: "On your marks, get set, go."

TOM SHRIFT SLOWED his car and from a distance eyed the bedlam on the forecourt. What a joke! For a second he thought, *How unbelievably pathetic they all look, how sad, desperate, how tragic,* until he remembered he was about to become one of them.

He'd come down early to get the jump on his fellow competitors, determined to win this free car, but he hadn't foreseen *this*.

Who could have guessed: so many lost souls. *Jesus Christ, the place looks like some compound for every Londoner in extremis.* Riffraff. In bargain clothes. Unshaven men. Unattractive women. The struggling classes. Musclemen in their forties, potbellied, flip-flops on their feet. Level-headed mums in cheesy sportswear clutching water bottles, primed for combat. The old. The young. Workaday victims of brute reality. And now, here he was too, Thomas H. (for Horatio) Shrift, about to stand shoulder to shoulder with these *have-nots,* fight as they fought, hand to hand. He gripped the wheel of his misfiring Fiat Punto (he'd recently had to sell his beloved smooth-running Volvo). What a numbing and humiliating thought.

But Tom deserved to *have* once more. And when he'd won this car—and he was more or less certain of his ability to win it—then he'd waste no time in making up the ground he'd so recently lost. He'd bounce back. As he'd always done, he'd bounce back once again.

He turned off the car and angled the rearview mirror toward himself, checking whether he still looked like the type who could beat so many others. Yes, he didn't look a million miles from being such a person. His bushy eyebrows could use some attention, the odd hair curling into a sigma, but apart from this, he identified a well-groomed man, a man who mattered—or, at least, one who soon would. A special person. Living to some schedule of achievement. A man of unique skills. Tom Shrift still had that winning look—alert eyes, a decent smile, a wide jaw, below it a crisply ironed pure-cotton shirt and the broad shoulders of a tall man . . . yes, he was still the type to make a stranger think, *I'll put my money on him.*

With his forefinger he wet and smoothed down the eyebrow hair. Bachelors often missed such details. With no one to tell them, their breath offended, their underarms stank. Tom was careful not to fall victim to such traps, knew how to breathe into his cupped hands to test for bacterial breath. Perspiring heavily of late, displaying andropausal symptoms already, he washed perhaps too often, used aggressive amounts of aftershave and always took pains to deport himself as someone well loved. A fresh shirt every day. He shot the cuffs. Collars were stiffened by plastic strips. He simply refused to become pathetic. Below his now tamed brows, and separated by the long-profile Shrift nose, were two brown eyes that showed on closer inspection to be hazel—the eyes of his mother.

Should he return her call, the one he'd refused to take the night before? A daily question. No, to hell with his parents. His father or, as Tom called him, "the Void," had walked out when he was under a month old, and Tom never had a chance to ask him anything. His mother, now in an old people's home, accusing him over the phone of betrayal, had been a reluctant mother, all his youth a selfish woman. Only now that she was old and lonely did he hear from her. Daily she tried to reach him, and more often than not he refused to take her call. She had done the bare minimum as a mother; now he would do the bare minimum as a son.

Just as he cleared his phone of alerts and messages, he now cleared his head. The car's mirror had told him that, in appearance, he had everything he needed to go forward. If he had any problems—and he admitted to only one or two—they began when he opened his mouth. Provocative things always flew out. Fast-talking and sharp-witted, he spoke too candidly, couldn't stop himself. Perhaps he knew too much. Was this possible? A big reader (his small but immaculately kept bachelor pad was packed with books, the TV aerial sat on a pile of paperbacks, reference works jutted from the shelves, one corner of the broken couch rested on Churchill's intellectual labors), he refused to hide what he knew—why the hell should he? Why stay silent when a historical date is given in error, a piece of logic flabby, a quote falsely attributed, the wrong actor named in a movie? Who benefits if the foolish are allowed to go uncorrected?

And so he let rip. Tom had a head full of premium gasoline and out poured his knowledge: names, quotes, the pertinent facts. He couldn't resist setting people straight, or helping them out of a lifelong delusion. While this was damaging to his dealings with ordinary others, it was especially disastrous romantically. What woman wanted to be lectured? Told she was wrong, on the wrong track, and by a man so certain he knew what was right? Yes, he'd talked himself out of more fucks than he cared to remember, but what could he do? Dumb down, just to get a woman into bed? If this was the smart game, his mind was too rare a gift, and it wouldn't be sold short.

Back in his twenties Tom had sat a Mensa test, pitting himself against geniuses. The test confirmed that *upstairs* he was no dunce. Far from it. The score put him in the top one percent of humanity, among the elite! So how was it possible that a brainiac, that a true *bel esprit*, should be under such incredible pressure simply to survive—and be reduced to such solutions as this?

The Russians. Yes, they were to blame. Just back from St. Petersburg, a major business deal had gone sour thanks to them. Tom had excitedly flown east, planning to license images from the Hermitage for use on his Masterpiece Cards— a young but sufficiently liquid business (he knew a lot about art too)—except that he couldn't convince the apparatchiks to release reproduction rights to the old Russian masters, or at least "not to an unknown." The Russkies screwed him badly in the end, suggested there wouldn't be a problem, made him front everybody's expenses and then dropped him like a hot potato. He now owed sixty-seven thousand pounds to his banks and credit card companies, more in debt every day. The barbarity of the business world was stunning, even to a natural pessimist. He'd thought himself a good businessman, but his IQ proved no protection against lies, sharp practices, low cunning and samovar tea that was surely drugged.

He started his car again. Ignoring the waving marshals who were turning vehicles away, he crept forward and found a superb spot in a residents-only lot for which he had the correct permit. But as he reached out to open his door he hesitated. How terrible to descend so low in society as to enter an endurance contest. Perhaps he could sell this old Fiat Punto instead? No, it would *cost* him money to have it destroyed. What else could he sell? His ideas? Ha, some joke—where were the takers for these? How about his extensive library of books, then? Sell them? Negative. Near worthless— who wanted the collected writings of Winston Churchill these days, especially with their margins defaced by his own verdicts of "bravo" and "big mistake!"? How about a regular job, then? Why not just try again to find one? Strike that too. Yesterday's interview had confirmed once again why he must work for himself. So what was left? Sell his blood? Not tradable in Britain. And so, with Sir Bob Geldof not likely to stage a relief concert for him, he was stuck with this option—with this cheap, debasing, but richly prized option.

His eye rose reluctantly to the advertising blimp floating high over the dealership, the words vivid from this range: WIN A NEW CAR. Yes, he would do just that. Win it, then sell it quickly, netting him twenty to thirty grand. Lowering his eyes once again, counting the (hundred or so) people already swarming in the dealership, he decided he would send someone to oppose them. That person? *Himself.* One against the many, as usual.

And so, from his trunk he gathered up his gadgets, the provisions he'd need for this campaign—clothing, reading materials, a few medical supplies and personal effects, all meticulously selected and double-checked. He recalled the British military's term for urban warfare: FIBUA (Fighting in Built-Up Areas) or, unofficially, FISH & CHIPS (Fighting in Someone's House and Causing Havoc in People's Streets). Well, Tom was ready to fight in this built-up area now. He walked toward the car dealership with a full backpack, shaking his head, amused at the sheer mathematics of the task ahead.

Reaching the yard, he avoided eye contact. It was clearly already a case of every man for himself, and every woman too. No smiles. No nods of recognition. So be it. The war had begun, and he knew already that it would end up being a mental war. Yes, the fittest, most resilient mind would take the car. He'd done his research on this—read about how psychological these contests were. Minds cracked quickly under the strain of going without sleep, soon fell prey to delusions, absentmindedness and negative thinking. Yes, where you placed your thoughts was the big key, how well you marshaled their patterns, how well you prevented malfunctions and how deep the reserves of calming, steady, stabilizing thought. Well, he doubted this crowd could contain a tougher or steadier mind than his. Whatever qualities a person needed to outlast their rival, he had it, and in spades. His counteroffensive had begun.

JESS PODOROWSKI FROZE the moment she saw the size of the crowd. "Oh my God."

Second thoughts arose. Many of them, suddenly. With her dodgy back—the L2, third-lowest vertebra was giving her pain already—plus a slight fever (she must have taken something foreign into herself), how was she possibly to win?

She made a short silent urgent prayer: *If it is true, Lord, that there are only those who get, and those who miss out, then for once, just once, let me be on the right side of that line . . .*

Jess was prayerful; a solid, throw-everything-in-the-pot petitioner. Everything got laid at the feet of the Lord. And as a widow with a disabled daughter, poorly paid to schlep the city and suffer the very worst forms of verbal abuse, well . . . there was much, much to lay down.

But she didn't protest.

In the delivery room, when she was born, the obstetrician had pronounced her mute—three hours later the infant Jess had surprised a nurse with a low-level whimper. As a kid growing up she'd perfected this curious quietness. Dwelled on things instead. Made a martial art of forbearance. Now a pro at withstanding the rage of the people she fined, she kept a light smile on her face and prayed instead. Thought only: St. Paul was despised for his tax collecting, people threw stones at him, and yet God had looked o'er him. *Then let God look o'er me too.* Her Catholic faith armored her. She attended church on Sundays, faced an altar with an underworshiped Christ raised high on a cross, a splayed symbol of victimhood—well, her job invited its own minicalvaries also. Verbally attacked, aching to respond, she buttoned her lip instead. *Who do you think you are? What a bitch! Get a life, you whore! You cow!* In, in went the nails.

After two years she was now a veteran of roadside abuse, doing a job few other Englishwomen wanted to do. In a silly uniform—a peaked hat, a black-cloth suit and over this a Day-Glo green tunic to make her visible from Mars—she approached expired meters up and down both sides of her streets. People and their cars, dear Lord. Walking her beat she often sent this thought to God: how alike people and their cars were. A Mercedes C-Class and its owner; the stockbroker behind the wheel of that BMW 3 Series; the classy woman centrally locking her Jag sports car, both vehicle and driver immaculate, quiet running, safe, well maintained, with power in excess of their actual needs, good things happening automatically, at the touch of a button. She envied them their luxuries, their Lexus freedoms! Imagine: to not care if your meter had expired.

But the meters of the poor—gosh, a totally different story there. The owners of rusting Renaults—their cars entirely manual, underpowered, running on empty, on the cusp of needing emergency assistance at any minute—these people ran toward her, panic on their faces, holding up a solitary coin as if she were some devil and their offering a kind of talisman—desperate to drop their coin into the slot and so escape a week's bankruptcy.

Guilty, always so guilty about forcing the downtrodden lower still, Jess often showed compassion. Let them off. Her heart was with them. She counted herself among these near poor. No Lexus freedoms for Jess Podorowski either. She knew what a difference an eighty-quid fine would mean in a given week.

Daunted by the size of the crowd, her stomach tightened. There were even a couple of faces she recognized. "Oh my gosh. There's . . . oh my gosh . . . remember that guy?" Jess said to her mother standing at her side. "That guy from the bank. Remember? I thought he must be doing well. What's *he* doing here? And there, there's"—pointing elsewhere, at a man erecting a nylon windbreak as if he were camping on a beach—"he's from our church, passes out the offertory plate. I *know* some of these people." And then she began a head count. Reaching fifty, she gave up and just doubled that amount. A hundred at least. Way too many for her to win.

"Oh my God, I didn't think there'd be this many people. I thought there'd be only a few."

"Good. Then we go home then," Val chimed in, relieved at her daughter's tone of surrender.

But Jess gripped her mother's arm strongly. "No—no—I have to try, at least."

"What?"

"I'm going to do it. I need to do this."

"Why?"

"You know why. I told you why."

Jess's eyes flicked to her wheelchair-bound daughter, who was excitedly surveying the action a dozen steps away, her head swiveling this way and that like a Ping-Pong umpire. Jess and Val had taken turns pushing her down here and there was no way Nat was going to let anyone make her miss out on this.

"Why?" Val insisted.

"Please, Mumia. I can't go over it all again."

Jess turned back to Nat. Useless from the armpits down, eighty percent incapable, the girl wore diapers under those black Adidas trackpants. Severely hypothermic since the road accident that had also taken her father (a double disaster), somehow Nat maintained a happy exterior. How? By what mechanism? If Jess ever doubted that she herself had the strength to go on—and every second day she did so—then she always had the shining example of her own daughter to make her snap out of it.

Valeria was slowly shaking her head. "This is madness. I tell you, this is a mistake. The Wisnewskis do not put out their hands and beg. They do not. Look at these people. Beggars!"

"You know, you should be heading home, Mumia. Take Nat and go. I'll be fine on my own." With this, Jess walked over to her daughter and kissed her on one pale cheek. They hugged each other. With Nat giving her mother two thumbs-up, Jess waved good-bye to Valeria and joined the queue to register her name.

OUT IN THE yard, Tom ignored the long, unmoving queue that had formed in front of the registration table. Marched instead to the yard offices, tapped once on the glass, went inside. "Excuse me."

Tom interrupted a frazzled-looking man—of average height, in his forties, raven-haired—scribbling sequential numbers on consecutive pages of a little Post-it pad, then tearing them off, while saying to a younger man, probably an employee, "What I want you to do is pass these around, one each."

Both salesmen looked up at Tom, standing there in the doorway. Two children reading books on the floor also gave Tom their

attention. "Daddy?" called the older one. "What's a golden plo-
ver? It says here it's the fastest game bird in the world."

Tom glanced down. Spotted the *Guinness World Records*
book open on the floor.

"Who are you?" the older man asked Tom.

"Tom Shrift." After a pause: "Your winner."

This got their attention, nicely.

"What do you want?"

Tom spat it out: "Before we begin, and put ourselves through
hell, I just wanted to make sure you're going to enforce the rules
here, be consistent, run an even contest and not get soft on cheats
or back your own favorites. A fair contest, that's all I ask. Either
it's the rule of law or it's a shit fight. Let's not make this any
seedier than it already is. Sorry to interrupt. See you again when
it's all over."

And with this, Tom left the office.

JESS FOUND HERSELF in line between two men—a preppy,
affluent-looking twentysomething and, behind her, a tall, slim African. She made no effort to talk to them, or anyone else, and kept
her eyes mainly on her hands, that is until the young man ahead of
her shifted backward and stood on her foot. It really, really hurt.
But Jess—what could you say?—began to apologize before he
could even get a word out.

"It's my fault. It's fine," she blurted. "Really."

"I'm so sorry. Are you okay? I lost my balance."

"No, no. It's me. I'm . . . I . . . I push up too close to people.
Happens all the time. My fault."

Her foot stung. The young man was tall, heavy; his shoe heel
was of hard leather and he'd come down crushingly. But still Jess
managed to hide her agony, kept an apologetic smile, even offered
the guy a final "sorry." *He must feel awful about it,* she thought.

Voices farther up the queue discussed the weather reports. "Blue skies all week. . . . No, I heard rain. . . . No, gray." One person mentioned that there was a Guinness World Record for this kind of contest. Another refuted it. Though not quite sure what the world record was, the first insisted it had been set in Prague: was it in 1970? A bunch of Czechs had held out for over five days.

Five days! The concept sounded surreal.

"Five days?"

A transvestite: "No, sorry, that's too depressing to even *think* about."

"My God, those poor people," Jess found herself gasping to the African man behind her. "They must have been *so* desperate." And then another concern shot through her: "This one won't go on for that long, will it?"

The African shook his head. "No. Not possible. This country is too pampered. People don't have the stomach. You need a brutal country to go on for five days. People with no hope."

Pampered? Was it really? And was Jess one of the pampered, at least from an African's point of view? A new prayer formed inside her, a small refinement of her earlier one. *So . . . if it's true, Lord, if it's true that there are only those who get, and those who miss out, if it's true that there are only those who never need to struggle and those who always will, then surely, Lord, one of these groups must be missing the purpose of life. The real purpose, I mean. Surely both can't be tasting the essence of our being here . . .*

She took another short step forward. She was advancing slowly to the front of the queue but by such very slow degrees that it actually felt like no progress at all. By now, the official start time had already been reached.

The transvestite farther up the line declared, "I've never seen so many desperate people in all my life. It's quite fabulous."

Behind her, someone said, "Most people will only last a few hours."

"Oh, don't you believe it, honey. People are freaks."

And then, suddenly, a gun went off. Or something like a gun. People jumped, turned their heads. Was it a gun? If so, what did it mean? One person screamed. Was someone firing on the crowd? This possibility couldn't be dismissed.

"Oh Jesus!" the transvestite shrieked, loudly enough to put people further on edge.

"That was a gun!" the African confirmed.

And then one voice, above the others, was heard to declare: "It's started!"

These words did it. A frenzy erupted as the first few people rushed to set their hand on a car, any car. These isolated reactions created a general belief, and soon everyone was pushing forward, vying for position, treating neighbors as aggressors, and shouting, "It's started! It's started!" The idea was now concrete. The contest had begun. And anyone not obeying the starting gun would be disqualified. Not everyone could find a place on the Land Rover to lay a hand, and a few people even fell and were hurt. Cries of pain and protest rose up. Had someone been wounded by the gun? Was the yard being fired upon after all?

Hatch, meanwhile, who had been taking care of business outside and was as much taken by surprise as anyone else, had turned at the sound of the gun to look at his office. A private thought tore through his mind. It set him running through the showroom, and into the office, already more or less certain of what he'd find. He fell to his knees at once and crawled toward his younger son, who was cowering under the desk, his mouth hanging open—the expression of a five-year-old too scared to cry.

Hatch shoved the warm gun aside, sliding it across the floor into a far corner, and took his child in his arms, squeezing tight,

forcing the boy to breathe again, while his other son stood petri-
fied on the other side of the room. A bullet had just shattered the
doorframe to the left of his head.

"It's okay, it's okay, Ronny," Hatch said to the younger boy.
"It's okay. Daddy's here. Good boy. Oscar, come here too. Oscar?
Come here too. That's a boy."

And Oscar, standing by the door, oblivious to how close a bullet had come to cutting down his life, slowly obeyed and, as his
father had done, crawled toward the den under the desk to be
embraced.

VINCE'S WRISTWATCH SHOWED 10:10. Newly deputized by
his boss, he spoke into a megaphone, which merely served to am-
plify his nervousness.

"Firstly, I . . . I want to . . . I'd like to welcome you all to . . .
can you all hear me? To Back-to-Back New Cars, Olympia Limited. Now I'm sorry to tell you this but we have a problem."

A problem? The public groaned.

Too many people, said Vince, had shown up for the event, and
the number would have to be reduced by a poll, a ballot, a lottery,
which would take place in roughly forty-five minutes. In the meantime the management invited the contestants to disperse, wander
down the road to enjoy a refreshment at Starbucks or Burger King
before reconvening at 10:55 sharp for the draw.

For some it was the last straw. Many walked off, deeming
this whole event a fiasco. The rest—still over a hundred or so—
sauntered down the street as they were told, obliged to take a refreshment they didn't yet need.

Coffee always made Jess jumpy, almost irritable, but she fig-
ured she'd soon have great need of the stimulus. She grabbed her
double espresso and wedged her way through the seethe and chat-
ter of the crowd, taking a seat on a window ledge in a sunny bay

while the others around her, the great surge of strangers, pushed and shoved and tried to place their orders with the sole waitress.

A much younger woman with a bush of blonde hair sat beside her and introduced herself as Betsy. "Are you in the car contest?" Jess nodded. "Me too. Are we mad, or what? I don't even really *want* a car." Betsy laughed, then looked round the room and sighed. "It's crazy, I don't know what I'm doing here really . . . no idea . . . none at all. Oh, he's cute." She'd spotted an attractive young man, well over six feet tall, preppy looking. Jess followed Betsy's gaze and recognized at once the man in the queue who had stepped on her foot. Only out of politeness did she murmur, "Mmmm."

"Anyway," Betsy continued, only half recovering her train of thought, "what was I saying? Oh, I remember. The car. I think I'll probably sell it if I win it. Which I won't. But. You know. Seems like a fun thing to do, right? This contest?"

Jess shrugged. Fun? "Not too sure about that." She took in the crowd. "A lot of these people look pretty serious to me." And indeed, there was not one smiling face; everybody looking almost lockjawed, their chins set as if to sustain blows.

Tom Shrift entered through the front door of the crowded coffee shop. "Great," he sneered, then lowered his shoulder and applied it to the first chink in the crush, leaning forward, repeating "excuse me," as he veered and wove, pushed his way right to the front where, at the counter, he held up his hand more actively than anyone else already waiting, thereby catching the eye of the girl making the coffees. Her cheeks scarlet from the exponential demands, she shot him a harried glance. "Others before you."

Others? Of course there were others. What a lame thing to say. Nearly seven billion people now walked this planet—*and about five hundred more of them since I came into this coffee shop, you twit*—so of course there were "others" before him. He lowered his hand. This pea-brained young lady must be from some docile northern hamlet where politeness in the street was so routinely repaid that it formed a currency still worth trading in. But in a city like this, where you seldom saw anyone twice—let alone saw kindness repaid in a dependable way—such codes of politeness were worthless. *Everyone* pushed in. Cut corners. Eyed the horizon constantly for individual opportunity. This left you with no option but to act the same way, to raise your hand higher than your aggressor, hail for attention louder than your neighbor: how else to survive? Turning to look behind him, at those he had just bypassed, Tom found the usual angry faces, most of them disfigured—he was sure—by envy for the coffee order he'd just secured, rather than annoyance at a breach of etiquette. Yes, they were all merely kicking themselves for not being as assertive as him.

His gaze finally settled on a face no more than six inches from his own. This close-up face was glowing with good health and almost alarming youth. "Hi."

Grumpily, Tom replied, "Hi."

"Competing?" the cheery youngster asked, with a cultivated accent. "Me too. Looking forward to getting started, actually. Feel I've used up an awful lot of nervous energy already. Anyway. Won't be long now."

In the kid's high-born accent and diction Tom instantly heard pedigree schooling, a place on the rowing eights, a nanny to meet him at the station, real tennis, ski holidays, an out-of-season tan, a big estate with tenantry to care for, all this and more, while his own accent—he knew, and had always known—betrayed the correspondence school, the night course, the resoled shoe, the cheap underwear from Primark, the low-cost Neilson package holiday to Marbella, the season bus ticket.

"I was ahead of you," he said.

"I'm pretty sure *I* was actually . . . but . . . no, fine, go ahead. You go."

Typical of the rich, thought Tom, an indifference to opportunity. Such glib graciousness could come only from a struggle-free existence, a life of cloudless entitlement. What was this kid doing here anyway? It was an insult that the elevated should send their glowing progeny to walk the rows of the battery sheds, trying to make off with the last few eggs they'd not already claimed. Everywhere these wealthy types turned, their gaze proclaimed: *Mine.*

Tom turned back to the counter and slipped an earbud from his portable radio in place. He needed to tune out and preserve his energies. His favorite talk show host, Alex Lee Lerner, a fifty-thousand-watt blowtorch, was handing the mike over to his regular sexologist. This show was hysterical. The questions the general public wanted answers to! *What should a woman do with a man who does not gratify her? Is intercourse between brother and sister punished in Russia? What should one do if one wants to make love, and several other people are sleeping in the same room? Man was basically of a polygamous disposition, and woman a monogamous one, is this correct? What should a lonely woman do to find love? Obviously she can't* offer *herself to a man.* . . . Tom had long since concluded that people were stupid—not just individually, but collectively. How could someone be so ignorant as to not even know if it was wrong to fuck someone else while others lay sleeping in the same room?

The young man offered his hand. "Matt Brocklebank."

Tom shook it reluctantly, took out his earbud and gave his name.

"So what brings you down here?" the kid asked.

Tom took out his earbud again. "Excuse me?"

"Just wondered what brings you down here."

"A free car. What else is anyone here for? Unless they're giving away free buckets of fried chicken."

"I know. I mean . . . I guess we're all doing it for different reasons, I suppose."

"Well, I'm doing it for a free car. Do you mind?"

"I know, I just meant . . . sorry, you know . . . the reasons why we want a car. It's interesting."

"Your turn. Coffee. Go."

"Are you sure?"

"Go ahead."

Tom waited as the young man flirted with the Starbucks girl. He drummed his fingers on the counter until he got his chance to order—coffee, black, two sugars—then waited an eternity for it to arrive. Turning, he fought his way back through the crush, holding his piping-hot cup high up above the jostle.

With no free tables he was forced to sit at one already used by two people: a massively overweight but cheerful black kid, who was happy to reveal he'd been sleeping rough on the streets all night and thought that the contest wouldn't make any unusual demands upon him, and an aged pensioner, who said he also had an edge in this event in that he'd been a night watchman for thirty years. Tom sat and heard the old man's saga. The Autumn of Your Life Equity Release Scheme had seemed a good idea at first. The old boy had signed the title of his flat over to these rogues for a tiny amount of cash to see him through his twilight years, only for a poor bout of health to see all the money go on private hospital care. If he'd had no cash reserves the hospital treatment would have been free. Now, the Autumn of Your Life people were waiting for him to die. He felt unwanted in the house he'd worked a lifetime to own. "I'm Walter. Pleased to meetcha. And this here, this is Tayshawn."

Tom looked over at the grubby street kid and nodded.

Walter smiled. "In for a penny, in for a pound, Tom?"

"I suppose so."

"Into the valley of death rode the brave nine hundred, eh?"

"Six hundred. Rode the six hundred," Tom amended.

"Is it? Yeah? Always thought it was the brave nine hundred. You sure?"

"And there's no 'brave' in it. 'The Charge of the Light Brigade.'"

"Yeah? You sure? Not sure you're right there. I always thought—"

"'Theirs not to make reply/Theirs not to reason why/Theirs but to do and die: Into the valley of death/Rode the six hundred.' Alfred, Lord Tennyson."

"Shit." Walter whistled. "Not gonna argue with that."

Even Tayshawn grinned. "Cool."

"Real fizz popper, eh?" Walter added. "Lucky this is not an IQ contest, eh? Ha! Ha!"

But Tom rose, excused himself, eager to escape to the sunny bay window. There he stood, very still, trying to avoid further interactions until he saw that he was being scrutinized from a distance, drawn in once more, this time by a woman. He looked at his own shoes, then over at her again. In her late thirties, seated on the nearby window ledge, brightly lit from the side, she reminded him of a certain Vermeer to which he'd not so long ago owned the UK rights—the kind of woman who looks as if she has been loved by many men but at the moment isn't loved by anyone. She had a mournful quality about her. Thin wrists that you could slip a bagel onto. Eyes an uncanny aquamarine. In a painting you might fault the artist's decision here, deem the eyes artificial, but not in real life.

He smiled at her. He was still able to convince himself that women were superficially attracted to him for his looks alone. She smiled back, and Tom was happily surprised. This was increasingly rare. So often his efforts produced a zero response, or less than zero, but this woman's face, which had been sad and lonesome looking, suddenly had many bright things in it. Was she a contestant? Perhaps an office worker on a break, a high street shopper, even a tourist. She was too relaxed to be in the contest. Lacked the killer look.

What does a lonely woman do to find love? The radio questions came back to him. *Come to Starbucks.*

He inserted his earbud once more—just in time to hear himself (almost!) being spoken about on air! Was this a fantasy? No. Lee Lerner was fired up. He'd heard about the contest—*their* contest, Tom's contest!

> *. . . Okay, listen up, Back-to-Back Cars, in Olympia. A contest starting at ten a.m. today to give away a new car to whoever can keep their hand on it the longest. Be in to win. Call me and let me know what you think of these sorts of contests. Personally, I'd rather watch a beheading, but if you're keen to own a gas-guzzling four-by-four with the carbon footprint of . . . well, frankly, of a Sasquatch! Or if you think sleep is overrated, then get yourself down to Longview behind High Street Kensington, and give us all something to talk about.*

Never before had Tom registered on Lee Lerner's excoriating radar! Not as a topic, at least. Sure, the two men had talked several times when Tom had phoned in, got his call through (driven by a need to correct some trafficked idiocy), but this was the first time he'd ever been the subject of a Lee Lerner diatribe. How eerie. Tom had suddenly become central to the larger story of this city. Well, how about that . . . Lee Lerner had taken a dislike to the Hands on a New Car contest. This didn't surprise Tom—the contest *was* low-grade, Lee Lerner was right. It *was* the bottom of the pile, a low watermark culturally. As Tom sipped his coffee he felt his own contempt for the contest once more ripple up from his stomach toward his throat in the reverse of peristalsis—he had to swallow hard to keep it down.

When he looked back to the window ledge to find the woman who had interested him, he saw, with the merest twinge of loss, that she was gone.

"SEVENTY-FIVE!"

The apricot-colored piece of notepaper in Tom's hand read 14.

Disaster. He was out. What were the instructions again? Weren't the forty numbers *above* the "drawn" number the only ones to be left in? Was it really over for him? Had this happened so quickly?

"Seventy-five," the dealership owner, Mr. Back, repeated through his squawking megaphone to a crowd fumbling with their ballot papers. Many of these ballots, drawn blindly from a cardboard box minutes earlier, in the next moment were blowing in the wind, torn into confetti strips, tossed high in the air with disgust, a gust carrying away the shredded hopes of the majority, while those few holding numbers seventy-five to one hundred and fifteen sighed with relief or raised one triumphant fist in the manner of tennis players and freedom fighters.

Jess opened her own ticket. She could hardly bear to read it: 107. Was it really a lucky number? She had a sudden premonition of happiness. It flowed through her. She was still in! An unlucky person had just been lucky. A miracle. *Thank you, Lord. Thank you, Mary, Jesus and Joseph.* Not used to surviving into the second round of anything, she grinned, tightened the arms of her sweater, which were tied around her waist, strapping herself in, mentally, for the very long ride ahead.

Tom, however, couldn't take his eyes off his own ballot. He

kept folding the fucking note and then reopening it as if by some enchantment the number would inherit an extra one before the four. No dice. His head flooded with postdated checks, his killing overdraft, but, most of all, the lost opportunity to win. "This is . . . this is bull . . ." he muttered, first softly then loudly, "Oh come on . . . what the . . . you can't . . ."

But at that precise moment, and before he could even plan a fightback of some description, a protest, or an appeal, he felt a tap on his shoulder.

The car dealer's assistant, whom he recognized from the office, discreetly inserted a second slip of paper into his hand, then winked. "Ssshh," he said, before walking off into the crowd.

Confused, Tom opened this second note. Read on it a number: 96. He looked around, astonished. No one seemed to have noticed this secret exchange. What on earth was going on? Why had he been given this preferential number? He'd just been handed a reprieve from nowhere. But why? And then he realized. He'd been handpicked, selected, saved intentionally. The organizer had seen and understood that there was something unique in him, something dramatic and impressive, without which the contest would be a lame affair. And with this realization a great relief and peace and sense of worth descended upon him.

ACROSS THE YARD, Dan, the junior salesman, returned to his boss's side.

"You get everyone we want?" Hatch asked.

Dan nodded. "I took out five numbers from the box, and then selected another five. We've got forty."

"Good. We've got a world record to break. Let's get on with it."

Hatch took the megaphone, walked to the center of the yard and addressed the remaining contestants. "There'll be no bending of the rules. This event has been sanctioned by the book of *Guin-*

ness World Records." He let this impressive fact sink in generally before continuing. "For now you will all be divided up onto two cars until your number reduces sufficiently to put you on a single car. Those two cars will be the blue Land Rover Discovery to your right, which will be the eventual prize, and the red Subaru Jeep to your left, which will not be a prize. The rules are as follows . . ."

Forty faces inclined toward him. Beyond them, in a crescent, loitered some of the earlier hopefuls, now exiled, unwilling to depart without some slight taste of what might have been.

"A five-minute toilet break every two hours. No sleeping allowed—you snooze, you lose. And finally, no competitor is to physically or practically assist another competitor from the moment the competition begins. You're entering a new universe. Each player is *on their own.* That means *on their own*! From now on you are each only as strong as you are independently capable of being. No helping each other. Those of you, those of you who hold on to others to get by, *will be disqualified.* Is that clear? *You will be disqualified.* Find the strength you need inside yourself, or walk away now."

Hatch theatrically held the loud hailer aside to give the weak a chance to defect, but when no one did, he concluded: "And finally, to the very best and strongest among you, whoever you are, happy driving, courtesy of Back-to-Back Cars. I'll pass you now to my assistant, Vince, who will be one of the marshals. He'll explain the rules to you again in greater detail."

From the rostrum Vince continued his boss's speech, much less forcefully.

1. A marshal will blow a whistle like this to signal the start and end of each rest stop. (Dan blew his whistle.) Three Portaloos have been provided free of charge, many thanks to the Third Company of Dublin.
2. Food can be eaten at any time.

3. The palm of at least one hand must be in contact with the car at all times, with the exception, obviously, of the toilet breaks.
4. No leaning or resting on the car. And no sitting on the ground.
5. The winner will be blood tested to make sure no artificial drugs or stimulants were used.
6. As well as marshals, several closed-circuit cameras will record the event in order to prevent foul play and cheating. But as cameras can't see around corners or through people, the contestants themselves and their supporters will all have to act as informers. If you see another person take their hand off the car, you may report them. Anyone can inform on anyone, but bear in mind that false accusations will result in disqualification. If you see something you want to report, you should first nudge the person next to you and get someone else to corroborate what you've seen before you act. One contestant's word against another will not be sufficient. Repeat: one contestant's word against another will *not* be sufficient. Once you've found a corroborator then you can draw our attention simply by raising a hand, and make sure it's your free one. (Laughter.) Or you'll be out too. A marshal will come over right away and disqualify the guilty party, whoever it may be. And that's about it.

With this, Hatch took back the megaphone. "So let's see who's got the better engine. Place your hand on one of the two cars. *Nine, eight, seven . . .*"

A last-second scurry saw forty hands flatten and slither and stick upon sun-hot metal. "*Six . . . five . . . four . . .*" At first touch this heat was painful and the instinct was to lift the hand away, but after the first sting had been endured the pain dissipated.

"*Zero!*" Dan blew the whistle.

The contest was under way. And within seconds a few free hands were waving to the marshals in protest. Mistakes had been witnessed already. Someone had pushed in. Another had been unfairly forced out. Dan and Vince hurried toward the informers and quickly began to disqualify those who had slipped up.

"*Bullshit,*" came the protest from the first eliminated man, but five people verified that he'd been a moment too late to press down his hand and he had to go. His nose entirely caked in zinc ointment in preparation for many hours, perhaps even days, under a hot sun, he now had to slope off home empty-handed.

As for Hatch himself, he slipped inside the Discovery, shut the door and took a series of photographs of the hands pressed on the glass from inside the car, translucent flesh pressing like coral-pink starfish to the side of an aquarium.

The first half hour slid by. Despite the peculiar circumstances—forty sentient adults standing around with their hands on two cars—the talk became as civilized as you would expect to hear at any bus stop. As the sun beat down the contenders gradually introduced themselves. Slowly they gave up their personal details and stories: an ex-munitions man was just back from serving in Afghanistan and said it was "hellish"; an insomniac from Billingsgate with a slight stutter who thought his sleeplessness might help him during the long nights; a Romanian man with an EU work visa, who was sleeping ten to a room and unable to afford even the cheapest room of his own, saw the prize as a mobile home in which he might eat, sleep, conduct a life; another, a woman, had lost a child in a big wave in Wales and had her own private reasons for being here; a FedEx driver who strangely wore only one glove and had one week off work and nothing better to do; a child of fourteen had come without her parents' permission; a drummer from a heavy metal rock group was trying to win the seven-seater so the band could accept touring engagements; a car thief with multiple convictions made no bones about his illicit attraction to cars but wanted to own one legitimately at last; an asylum seeker from Zaire wanted a cornerstone upon which to build a new life; an ex-semiprofessional footballer who now lived in Swindon and delivered furniture for Ikea thought his fitness would shine through, and he could use the brass; a father of two from Hounslow had come down after a bet with a pal, bringing a hundred and twenty cans of beer with him and wagering three hundred pounds that by beer and pizza alone he'd be victorious; an NHS midwife, who worked at St. Mary's Hospital and who banshee laughed at anything even vaguely amusing, believed that her choice of footwear would prove decisive and wore trainers that an Olympian would be proud of. These and many more confided their stories across the two cars, all of them possessing some special advantage but equally some hidden deficiency that might either win or keep them from winning the prize.

Tayshawn, the street kid, made everyone laugh. "I'm definitely going to win. No question. The only problem is I . . . well, I was so excited about winning a new car that I . . . well, I haven't been able to sleep for the last two nights already, know what I mean, so this is my third day already without sleep."

Walter Hayle, the old man, cracked up. "You're joking! You—ha! Ha! You haven't slept for two days?"

"Uh-huh."

"And how's—ha! Ha! Oh boy. How—ha! Ha! How's that feel? Jesus."

"Like shit." Tayshawn grinned widely along with the others. "Ha! Ha! Like real shit actually. Yeah. But I'm still gonna win, see. Because I'm determined, know what I mean? I got me mind made up." And then the young man became serious again. "'Cos

I believe, yeah, that if your will is strong, yeah, you can do anything. And my will is strong. It's real strong. Ask anybody who knows me. I've got a real strong will. And that's why I'm gonna win this car. I can't be beaten. And I don't care how many days I go without sleep. Just don't care. Or how bad I feel. Don't matter. I'm just gonna go on and on and on and on. You watch me. Mental strength."

Jess, standing there, silent, abjuring chitchat, her left hand on the passenger window of the Discovery, saw no particular reason to feel either optimistic or despondent about her eventual chances. This contest remained a long shot, but what had she to lose, other than a few hours' sleep? Besides, other people got lucky—why not her? The twenty-odd people on her car, plus the twenty-odd on the other, might consist of many who were younger, fitter, more rested, but how many had Jess's level of need and self-martyring determination to win? Who could say what anyone is truly capable of?

Tom Shrift, meanwhile, pressed his hand on the front hood, which threw back a depraved distortion of his face. The overheard talk depressed him, not because he'd heard anything to make him think these people could beat him, but rather because he'd begun to hate himself with new vigor for being among their ranks. *My God, I should be a CEO by now, living in a house approached by a hundred yards of washed gravel.* It choked his lungs to think of how far behind schedule he'd slipped. He was the type of person who could descend into the heart of things and see 360 degrees of reality. And yet . . . where was he now? Laying his own life bare, hanging off the front of a car with deadbeats and dropouts, degenerates and debris, the last remnants of some kind of unconfessed Great Anglican Dream gone sour. What a travesty.

His eyes turned to the sad-eyed woman from the coffee shop who was now standing beside him. So, he'd been wrong about her. She *was* a fellow contestant. Not a tourist, not a shopper at all.

He'd noted that she didn't engage in conversation either and, like him, hardly raised her eyes. He liked this; a private person, one who perhaps had also lowered herself to be here and who probably, like him, had continually to fight the urge to lift the touching hand and walk away.

THE FIRST HOUR passed in stupendous inactivity, the formless suspense of the morning stretching into a second hour in which all thirty-nine, then thirty-eight (a poor changeover of left and right hands by a Chinese man), then thirty-seven (a teenage girl's left foot getting stomped on, making her back away), then thirty-six (a woman's elbow slipping off the hood) began to anticipate a time when each of them—as the winner—would be able to release their hands for good and return to their normal lives.

The boasting, meanwhile, was incessant, proving itself a kind of weapon.

"I'm going to win this, no question."

"I can go on for five days without sleep. Done it before."

"Wrap it now—it's mine."

"I'm gonna have it repainted. Blue is so boring."

"My husband had a dream. It's fated. I can't lose."

"God wants me to have it. He spoke to me."

"I feel great. Never felt better."

"My star chart this morning said . . ."

"It's all in the mind, this kind of contest, and my mind's made up."

When a man to Tom's left said, "Footwear. You wear the wrong footwear it's over," Tom could stand it no more and slipped in his radio earbud.

On air, another talk show in progress. Not much relief for Tom here. You turned on the radio these days and the ether disgorged its latrine slush. Enraged voices issued naïve opinions, uninformed views, crank ideas, misprisions and tailored truths. He turned the radio off. Where did you go to find relief? He looked at his watch. Twenty more minutes to go before the first break.

LOOKING OUT THE picture window, which allowed an almost scientific view of proceedings out in the yard, Hatch wound up his phone conversation with the local radio station. "Listen to me . . . no, no, *you* listen. I paid for, I paid for radio *advertising*, okay, not *criticism*. He's crit—Listen, I heard him. On air! I just heard him. He's crit—Yes, he is. He crit—Just tell your . . . yes, resident loudmouth over there . . . if he continues to bag this thing, then I'll cancel the contest and pull the advertising spend. Forty people will miss out on getting a car. And I won't mind telling the press who was responsible when they ask me. Okay? Fine. You go and talk to him. Thank you." He dumped down the phone and turned to Vince. "Some talkback shock jock. Unbelievable. Putting us down when I'm spending . . . unbelievable. That means, worse than no publicity, *negative* publicity." His frustration then fixed on Vince. "Where are the photographers? The press? I asked you to organize publicity, Vince."

"I did. They weren't interested. You're not really gonna call off the contest, are you?"

"This whole thing is about publicity. No publicity, no car sales. I'm giving away a free car here because I'm a nice guy." He sighed, slipping under like a ship, hull breached. "Get the fucking message out. We're breaking a world record here—five days, nine hours. Come on! We're sanctioned by the Guinness people . . . this is official. Someone's gotta be interested."

On saying the word *Guinness*, Hatch pointed to his bookshelves, which contained the complete series of those famous annuals dating back to their inaugural edition in 1955, but he might also have been pointing to the photo on the wall of a car flanked by eighteen young people—among them himself and Jennifer, not yet introduced on that bright day thirteen years earlier—who had narrowly missed, by two bodies, breaking the Guinness World Record for how many people you can squeeze inside a Mini Minor. (It was inside this moaning press of bodies that Hatch had warmed the body of Jennifer De Havres for the first of many times, enormous social pressure fusing them into the single conglomerate they were today.)

"A lot of people think it's in poor taste, that's all."

"Poor taste? What poor taste?" argued Hatch. "We're gonna change someone's life!"

"What do you want me to do then?"

"Do? Do? What do I want you to do? Go out there and call it off. Or else get some press down here." Hatch went limp, slumped into his chair.

"You okay, Hatch?"

"I'm fine." A second later, "I'm fine."

"'Cos Dan and me wanted to talk to you about our unpaid wages as well."

Hatch started saying, "Not now, Vince" and begging "Please" and "Now, now" and "I said not now!" while Vince tried to point out that it had been three weeks since they'd been paid.

"Three weeks is a long time. And we can't keep working unless we get paid and it isn't fair not to pay people, especially when you're expecting us to work night and day like you are right now with this thing out there."

Hatch: "We'll talk about it later. Not now. Okay? We'll do it later."

Vince shrugged his high eagle shoulders, accepted this rebuff in silence, then walked out.

Alone behind closed doors—one door leading to a greasy garage, the other to a yard full of red-eyed riffraff—Hatch looked to the far wall where his late father's framed eyes stared at him with timeless concern.

. . .

MATT BROCKLEBANK, THE preppy-looking young man, turned to the old man. "Ten minutes to go, our first rest stop. Didn't feel like two hours, did it?"

"Did to me, son." Walter Hayle straightened the stiff bones in his spine.

The attractive young woman, Betsy Richards, concurred. "My legs hurt already. I'm not gonna last long."

As for Jess, the walk-weary traffic warden, her feet were giving her the worst bother. For these to be aching already was a very bad sign. She was furious to receive such information from her body so soon. Her feet never hurt like this when she walked the beat, so why now?

"Be the first to the toilets," Tom Shrift was telling her now. "There'll be a queue. You don't want to be the last to line up. Two toilets can't serve all these people and a full bladder will make you not want to go on."

"Thanks. But I can look after myself."

Why does he tell me this, this strange man? And what on earth makes him think I want to go to the toilet? She hated men talking to her. Didn't want anyone to be interested in her in that way. Men—any other man than Maciek, basically—were a leg-crossing thought. And yet, at the same time . . . it had been two years. If she didn't soon force herself to pretend to be a normal-functioning and available woman then she'd turn into her own mother—and be out of the sexual game forever.

Was Jess poor looking? Her own view? Not exactly pretty, but not bad looking either. Her Slavonic face was okay, she had an ordinary figure—and most people had to be satisfied with that, or worse. And as for what other people thought of her, well, she believed they might say that she was a distraught-looking woman with striking eyes. Yes, they might say something kind about her eyes. But what man was looking for such a package? *Wanted: F, 40, GSOH, ordinary, penniless, bereaved, wheelchair-bound daughter, worried looking, with nice eyes.* Did she have no other physical assets? Her hair? Light brown, too thin; even hairsprays didn't make it bouffant. Her skin? Too pale, prone to moles, her blue veins visible underneath in places. Her breasts? Too flat. Her smile? Yes, perhaps this was her other drawcard. To receive her smile, Maciek had once said, was like God pressing a coin into your hand. Her stock rose sharply when she showed that she was happy.

Jess decided that after the next rest stop she would move to another part of the car, farther away from this man who might try to talk to her once more.

BUT THIS WAS not to be. After a failed attempt to go to the toilet—the queue had been too deep—she returned with thirty-five others and even switched to the Subaru this time, only to notice Tom appear beside her. Her heart sank. He would try to speak to her immediately, she knew it, rub in the fact that he'd been right—she and twenty other people had missed out on the toilets and must now cross their legs for the next two hours—but when she sneaked a glance at him he seemed distracted and made no attempt to crow. Had he even changed cars to escape *her* and been dismayed to find she was standing right by him? His manner suggested it. If so, what had she done? Had she been too rude? She almost wished for his attentions back. As usual, she ended up concluding there was something wrong with her.

Over the next half hour she dared glance several times at this strange man next to her. With an earpiece in place and a thin wire leading to a small radio in his pocket—he sometimes took it out to adjust the tuning or volume—he muttered to himself, perhaps disagreeing with something he heard, shaking his head, irritated. Maybe he was listening to a talk show? She had no time for these herself. None. Ideas and their exchange were for those without disabled daughters and jobs like hers. Finally, as she watched, he took the earpiece out completely, saying "idiot" quite audibly, then took a neatly folded newspaper from his breast pocket, a pencil from another pocket, and began, at lightning speed and with one hand, to solve a *Telegraph* crossword.

What a curious character. There was something of the stalker about him, she decided, but he wasn't bad looking. An attractive stalker. One who came across also as superintelligent. She waited until he was done with the crossword—he'd filled every square after barely more than ten minutes—before she spoke.

"You were right."

"About?"

"The toilets."

"Oh."

He shrugged, even smiled. No rubbing it in. No hint of an I-told-you-so. And when this man looked at you, he really looked at you.

"So, do you think you're going to win?" she ventured.

"Relatively certain, yes."

"How can you be?"

"If you don't think you're going to win you shouldn't be here."

She nodded—this made sense to her.

"Plus, I've got an edge, a secret advantage." He tapped his temple once.

"How secret?"

"Secret."

She smiled, waiting for more. But he gave nothing more away. "You're really not going to say?"

"No."

A weirdo, she concluded. He began to put his earpiece back in. She stopped him by asking, "Who comes second, then? I suppose *I* come second, do I?" A smile played on her face.

"No," he abruptly replied. "You're not second."

Her smile slowly faded. "I know I'm not going to be second because I'm going to be first."

"No. You're not going to be first. I don't see you making it. Sorry."

Offended, her astonishment at his rudeness almost making her speak out, she looked to see where his eyes had turned.

"No, my main competition is going to come from a man, an older male. Studies show that women have more stamina than men but lack the single-mindedness to maintain focus on one goal, and an older man is better suited than a younger man for this kind of endurance contest. So . . ."

Jess followed Tom's eyeline—past young Matt Brocklebank, the strongest and fittest, and the still waxy Jack of all Hearts in an otherwise scruffy pack of cards—toward the gray old wreck that was Walter Hayle. She lowered her voice further. "Walter? No way."

"These things are always won by older people. I researched it. Their bodies run slower, so last longer, run nearer to the death state, which is where the winner will have to get to by the end—close to stopping altogether. Old people can also manage their mind better when the other systems start to shut down, and that's because such shutdowns are familiar territory to them, part of their daily life already. You see? So the smart money, actually, is on him. Forget Boy Wonder over there, he's history. *Him*, the old guy, on a purely physical level, *he's* the big threat in the field."

Jess looked at Walter—bent-shouldered, mothbally, humbled already by his age and his own inner contests—he certainly looked like a man against whom this contest could have no sudden new effect. She turned back to look at Tom, disliking him profusely but seeing also that he might well be right. Grudgingly: "I see what you mean."

"But there are other factors that will come into play, apart from physical."

What a character, Jess thought. Did he ever stop talking?

"This contest is about what gives you more strength than your neighbor. What drive carries you the furthest? That's the question. Is it the will to win, to be the best, to conquer? Will such a person last longer than someone who's just desperate to save themselves financially? Everything else being equal, who's going to win between those two? Or perhaps someone who's doing this for a good cause—is this maybe the most empowering force? And as the pain increases, there are other questions. In what order will these drives cut out and quit? In what order do we start to say, 'It's not worth it. I don't love so-and-so *that* much,' or 'I'm not *that* hungry,' or 'I'm not so interested in conquest after all.' This contest will be interesting on that level too. Ought to provide a lot of interesting data, new empirical evidence. It's a lab experiment, if you like, where the animals in the cage are us."

Jess realized there was probably no end to the things this guy had a clear-cut opinion on, and that, if every issue had six sides, this man saw seven. "So why do *you* want to win, then? The money?"

"Sure, the money."

The last thing she wanted to do was offer this terrible man a compliment but could not prevent a small one. "You look like someone who can earn money pretty easily."

To this he did not reply, and when he turned his head away from her she was grateful not to pursue this any further.

PEOPLE HAD A right to go to the toilet. Again and again this point was made, and often loudly.

"I'm going to sort out this toilet thing," Matt Brocklebank told those near him. "It's a joke."

"Please. Someone's *got* to tell the organizers," agreed Betsy Richards from the left-hand side mirror.

Jess, with her internal discomfort plain to others now, looked imploringly at Matt across the front hood. "That'd be so fantastic."

"No trouble," he said. "The best person should win." He grinned his pedigreed smile and, as ever, a collective desire to know more about him arose quite naturally in those nearby.

The best person should win? Tom wanted to puke. Was this suddenly a popularity contest?

But Jess and Betsy couldn't conceal their hero worship. "Why are *you* doing it, if you don't mind me asking?" Jess asked.

"Me?" Matt became pensive and took some time composing his reply.

Why was he doing it? Tom could barely stand to hear the reply.

"I've been looking for something to do. I basically beg for money from my father when I need it. And I get it. But I don't have to *do* anything. We all need something to do, right? I mean, how else do you find out what you're really capable of if everything's done for you? So I need to stand on my own. Be my own man. Otherwise everything just goes on being *possible*." People around him nodded, seemed to get his drift. "Necessities, that's what I need. So I'm going to have a go at something. On my own. I want to test myself to the limit. And that's where this contest comes in. So when I saw this blimp floating up there, I thought, *Here's something. I can do* this! *I will do this.* It sounds pathetic, I'm sorry. I sound like a spoiled shit. I *know*. But I'm a bit messed up at the moment."

Tom showed the whites of his eyes. He turned away, too disgusted by what he'd heard to listen further. Of limited wit, barely capable of a *single* entendre, the kid was now pretending to *know* himself. An American trait. And one shared by all the young these days. Shallow self-diagnosis. Criticizing one's self before anyone else got the chance. Ha! Only a shallow form of self-protection. ~~Fake~~, Tom wanted to say, editing himself just in time. ~~Be silent, child, you're making a fool of yourself.~~

But Jess nodded her head in sympathy. For her part, she had never thought of it like this, never thought that money could present its own unique troubles. Abundant money came with a catch— how funny! And rather than despise him for this luxury problem, this Lexus dilemma, she found herself liking Matt Brocklebank all the more. Money didn't interest him, he was saying; it was real life he wanted to wrestle with. *Well, good for him,* she thought. As young as he was, he'd found out that there was no such thing as being alive and being worry-free. Where we lack *big* problems, small ones grow, take their place, exert the same power to bother.

"I wouldn't mind a few less necessities and a few more possibles," was all she offered of this welter of private reflections.

And then the whistle sounded. Two more hours had gone by. Just like that.

This time Jess was ready to be first to the toilets. She bolted, got to a Portaloo first and locked herself in. The lock snapped shut: OCCUPIED.

The girl, concluded the watching Tom, was learning.

"I JUST WANTED to talk to you. Only take a second. It's my blood pressure."

Hatch had no problem with this visit to his office, but reminded the old man of the time.

Walter Hayle sat in the chair where customers usually beat down prices or negotiated optional extras. Walter had a lame right leg. It had withered from childhood polio, he explained. The trouser on this side looked, to Hatch, almost vacated. The left leg suffered from restless leg syndrome and jittered constantly. The guy must be eighty, Hatch guessed. He had no business being here. The age-swollen hands, the broad, nicotine-stained thumbnails, yellow and curling. The pale face covered in a net of wrinkles.

"It was what you said in the rules about the blood test and so on before. 'Cos I been on some medication for blood pressure, see, which they tell me has some kinda steroid in it, I think, so I'm wondering."

"Walter? Your name's Walter? Look, you think there's any doubt about your health? Pull out. When did you last take a blood pressure pill?"

"Didn't take one today."

"The winner will be blood tested. Imagine you won. If steroids show up, you've wasted your time. These rules come down from the Guinness people."

"Oh, the Guinness people."

"This could go on a very long time. You're no spring chicken, Walter." And then Hatch said something he had never before said in his whole life. "It's just a car."

INSIDE THE TIGHT plastic toilet cubicle Jess released her urine. Sublime. She stared at the steel-plate floor with its raised chevrons for grip. The sound of her own water rose, amplified by the walls. Made her think of her dead husband. And she knew why too.

To be precise, she recalled how very different their toilet sounds had always been, his standing pee a full-throated, bestial outpouring that thudded into the bowl, sending up a sudsy wake, while hers, like all women's, had to force its way into the open, as when a thumb covers the end of a garden hose, producing constricted spray, the noise a *squeeeeeeee*, a soft hiss. Inside this tiny portable toilet, with the wastes of others not entirely ignorable below her, she tore off a double square of paper and dabbed herself in the same gentle way a bearded man in a restaurant will use a napkin after a meal, and thought of Maciek. He was always with her in her thoughts. Then she rose, pulling up her things, aware others were waiting in line outside, most of them waiting in vain. Smoothing her clothes and without looking back, she flicked a lever, flooding the bowl with chemicals before opening the narrow plastic door.

Twelve to fifteen faces stared at her, all of them in severe discomfort. And that's when she remembered more perfectly why she'd remembered her husband before.

It had been their honeymoon. She had just returned from the bathroom while he waited, naked under a sheet on the bed, spread out like some model on a dropcloth in an art class, and saying to her when she climbed back in beside him, "We're animals, babe, just animals in love."

She stepped down from the toilet and passed by her rivals with her head lowered. Back at the Discovery, Tom Shrift turned to her with a self-satisfied smile. Jess looked around her. Realized they'd both unconsciously gravitated back to their original starting positions, as had most people—how funny.

"Feeling better?" he asked.

TICK, TICK, TOCK.

"Go, girl!" and "You can do it!" and "Looking good, Ray!" and "Doing a great job there, Liz!" Such cries came regularly from the supporters' area. Part pep teams, part therapists, part medical support and mobile caterers, these backup units awaited the two-hourly return of their charges so that they could slap cheeks, massage shoulders, then fold out the aluminium deck chairs, put food in stomachs, raise the blood sugars and then send husband or wife, sister, brother or friend back into the fray, while shouting once more and even more vociferously: "Go get 'em, Freddy!" or "The car's yours already, Rachel!" or, if you were Lewis McLusky, whose wife Stella was the operational end of Team McLusky (as the blazon on the backs of their matching T-shirts pronounced), "This is our retirement, doll! This is how we put our feet up!"

Anyone who enjoyed such tireless support had to be put immediately on the list of favorites to win the car.

But there was one other thing these supporters did. As the first night descended they became vigilantes, telltales, informers: if for one split second a rival lifted a hand off the vehicle they would roar out the infringement and call for the marshals to eject the offender. By midway through the third session of this first day three more contestants had been eliminated by these means: a nose picker from Tooting Bec, an old lady with water-retentive legs and the transvestite (when the show glamor of the event wore off), all of whom had let their daydreams or inattention or fatigue or disenchantment lure them into one forgetful moment—so that thirty-three remained alive.

Tick, tick, tick, tick, tock.

Tom was feeling strong. Even if he lacked support he had prepared well. A book was providing company. His mind was engaged. And an engaged mind could take you far. Soon, a New Zealand novelist, two contestants along from him, became curious.

"What's the book?"

"Henry Kissinger's autobiography."

"What's he up to?"

"Bombing Cambodia."

"What are you reading that for?"

Tom gave the man a stern look. "So I can mind my own business."

Jess, once again next to Tom, could not believe her ears. To be so abrupt. How could you allow yourself to act this aggressively? And how unpleasant it must be, to invite such dislike.

Jess turned away. Overheard another conversation to her right. The self-confessing car thief was telling a man plagued, it sounded, by insomnia, "I'd say, in total, oh, sixty, seventy cars. Around that, yeah. Stolen about sixty cars. But this is my chance to go legit, in the words of Don Corleone."

Across the hood the nurse was telling the African, "Was up late last night too. Not the best way to start something like this. Delivered three babies. Boys, both of them."

"You said three. Three babies . . ."

"Oh, did I?"

At this point the beer-and-pizza man belched. He looked already to have adopted the wrong dietary strategy for victory.

Mrs. McLusky was staring at the Portaloos. "Very odd name for a toilet company."

The man from Zaire turned and looked over at the plastic green boxes. "Yes. 'The Third Company, Dublin.' I thought so too. Until you say it. With an Irish accent."

Mrs. McLusky tried it. She got it.

"WHAT HAPPENED TO Cambodia?" Jess asked Tom after a full hour of silence between them.

"Still bombing it." He looked at her closely again, as if weighing up whether she deserved to ask the next question. "Have you heard of the madman theory?"

"Madman theory? No. What is it?"

"Kissinger came up with it. Machiavelli updated. To get what you want you must make your enemy think you're crazier than they are, think you'll go all the way. When your enemy finally decides you'll never stop, that you're insane, their will collapses and they pull out. Kissinger was quite a genius."

A more distasteful idea Jess had never heard. "And this is how you make the world a better place?"

Tom shrugged. "'We live in a merciless world of random cruelty.' Charles Darwin."

"You really believe that?"

"I'd maybe add to that you get a lot of intentional cruelty as well."

She shook her head sadly. "You strike me as the kind of person who gets excited when a war breaks out. I bet you do."

"It's a hell of a way to make the world get a geography lesson."

The ex-soldier roared. Clapped Tom on the back. "That's a good one," he said. "Ha!" Brothers in arms.

But Jess was appalled. "Wow. My God. Oh my God. How did you fall so out of love with the world?"

"Out of love? What does that mean?" His eyes wandered left and then right, as if this accusation surprised him. She saw the flash of tiny veins in the whites of his eyes. "I say what I see. But I don't sit around discussing these things at decaf-latte coffee mornings and group hug-ins or by reading *Hello* magazine. I'm out there on the front lines. I say what I see."

"The front line? What are you? A cop?"

"No. I manufacture greeting cards."

She roared with laughter, couldn't help it. The unexpectedness of it. Greeting cards? This guy wrote greeting cards? What did they say when you opened them? "Fuck you?" But she only thought this. Would never say it. She just found it really, really funny—*greeting cards!*—and it was some time before she could even reply. "Do you really think you work on the front line?"

"Absolutely. You try and run a small business. So . . . what do *you* do anyway?"

It was Jess's turn to hesitate. "I, uh . . . work for the . . . the council."

He nodded, made what he liked of this, then asked, "So . . . that was your daughter before? In the wheelchair?"

"Car accident."

"She getting better?"

"No."

Had he been too rough on her? He took the edge off his voice and also off his questions. "You can take the back two seats out of a seven-seater like this. Get a wheelchair in there. If you win." He knew how to be helpful. Being helpful was all he was ever trying to be, actually.

Surprised, she turned to face him. How had this man guessed her master plan? "I know," she said.

"Me? When I win it, I'm selling it." With his free hand he stroked the paintwork that must soon be his.

"Why? Can't get enough birthday cards in there when you're out on the front line?"

So, he thought, *she* can *fight back*. Good for her. Maybe she stood a chance, after all.

A small smirk played on her face, and he noted a new smear of rouge or blusher on her cheekbones. Odd that he hadn't seen her apply it.

"No," he replied. "These vehicles are immoral, that's why. And besides, the councils make it impossible. All their cryptofascist parking wardens everywhere."

Her eyes widened.

"I'll tell you," he said, "after the apocalypse, three forms of life are going to survive: cockroaches, the green mold that grows in the grouting of your shower tiles and parking wardens. On second thoughts, the cockroaches and the green mold probably won't make it."

She stared at him, realization arriving like an elevator summoned, the doors of comprehension opening. Her face flushed. "Oh my God. It's you. You had sunglasses on. I thought I'd seen you before."

"What?"

"I know who you are. Oh my God. Where I saw you before, I mean. You—you're the guy who parked—at the side of the Odeon Mid City. You drive a yellow Fiat Punto."

"How—?"

"It's you. Parked illegally." She leaned closer and sniffed. Grey Flannel aftershave. "Oh my God. You're *awful*."

"That was . . . ? You're—"

"You're awful!"

"That was *you*?"

She nodded. "Yes. Satan's concubine."

"Oh my . . ." At this he laughed and shook his head. "Why? Why am I not surprised? Of course it was you. I'm so pleased to meet you again. Because I want to ask you a question I forgot to ask you at the time. How the hell can you do a job where you're abused like that from dawn till dusk? It escapes me. All the shit you take." He squinted his eyes in deep interest. "How do you stand the hatred?"

"I've got a really good idea. Let's not talk. Okay?"

"No, no, no. You charged me a hundred quid. How do you stand it? The hatred?"

A good question. She swallowed hard. Hatred indeed fell on her in vast daily amounts.

"How can you do it? A parking fine is the most grossly disproportionate stealth tax there is. First you don't provide enough parking spaces and then you charge a quarter of some people's weekly wage. You feel good about that?"

But true to her word, she didn't respond.

"Not talking? I bet you're not. Okay, fine. Silence is fine. A meter maid, Ha! 'I work for the council.' You sure do, honey"—under his breath—"sucking the council's dick."

Jess jumped. "Sorry?"

But Tom, sensing he'd once more gone too far, averted his face and reinserted his radio's earbuds. "Nothing. Silence. You got a deal."

NIGHT BEGAN TO fall and, dim through the gaseous layers, a full moon.

The contestant's high spirits of a few hours earlier dissipated with the light. The temperature dropped too and at the first opportunity hats and jackets were pulled on. A zephyr rose as the streets and sky equalized. With the yard's floodlights coming on, and with the cold biting and the night stretching out before the contestants, the last element that might have been called fun had gone.

At the first nighttime rest break, people demolished sandwiches in three bites, drank tea and coffee from Thermos flasks or filed for the toilets, most often returning unrelieved. It soon became clear that these breaks, so keenly awaited, were just too short to deliver rest, relief or refreshment to any worthwhile degree and in fact tended to be frenzied interruptions, compacted intervals of intense activity, none of which could *quite* be completed in time, so that each of the contestants was left feeling even more depleted and exhausted than before the whistle had sounded.

Vince, the relieving marshal while Dan took a nap, walked about taking a head count as the sixth session settled down. Thirty-three remained, and more than ten hours had gone by but, in the words of the man who had placed his faith in a diet of beer and pizza, it was still anybody's contest.

The man from Zaire still looked comfortable; Walter Hayle seemed no older than he did at first; the fat street kid, Tayshawn, not surprisingly, given that he was two days deeper into this than anybody else, had sleepy rings under his eyes but complained only of extreme hunger; while the stuttering insomniac from Billingsgate looked almost painfully alert. The Romanian must have been used to such nights, and kept suspicious eyes on everyone as if fearful a rival might alert immigration. The novelist looked to be deep in his mental search for that elusive something for which this event might serve as the metaphor; while the drummer and the convicted car thief, the ex-footballer, the midwife, the unemployed electrician, the jobless father of four, the Argentinean shepherd, the odd job man from Earl's Court, young Betsy Richards and beside her Jess Podorowski, and next to her Matt Brocklebank, that poor little rich boy, all of them—and Tom Shrift more than anyone—looked ready and determined to go on and on and on and on and on.

HATCH QUICKLY POPPED home. He needed a change of clothes. He found his wife in the kitchen, in a bathrobe, arms crossed under her breasts: the wrath of an unloved spouse.

"A loaded gun?" she asked right away. "A *loaded* gun?"

He went to the fridge to avoid her gaze and fumbled inside for a slice of ham, maybe a cheese slice. "It was the old man's. From his service days. I'm not gonna lie down for these vandals. Last Friday night three cars were—"

"And you left it loaded? Get rid of it now. You almost killed our son."

"I know. It's just—I don't have many of Dad's things." It sounded impossibly feeble, this answer.

"You have his *business*, remember? What's wrong with you? Now get rid of that gun!"

His fingers fumbled with the crepe-like plastic wrapping on the square of flimsy cheese. Somewhere hid the flap you pulled upon.

"The cheese is for the kids," his wife barked, telling him one more thing she felt he ought to know.

He stared at her, rage boiling up in him. The indignities! The daily indignities a man faced in married life. Was he a child? Then he too deserved cheese, didn't he? He put the cheese back nonetheless. Slammed the fridge.

"So what are you going to do now?" she asked as he quickly crossed the room.

"Gotta go back. I can't leave Dan and Vince in charge. I'm going to sleep in the office, if I sleep at all."

Angry, certain once more that he'd married a bitch, one of those women bachelors cite as the reason why they have remained bachelors, he took his coat. Left his house without saying another word. Drove hard. Drove straight over to see his mistress. And he felt not even a morsel of guilt in doing so. Knocked on her door. Pink fingernails curled around the door's edge.

"Hi," he said. "It's late. Sorry."

Pearl. She kissed so well. Maybe because her mouth looked continually so just-kissed, so pouty, moist, full. She was half Caribbean, with a tiny bridge to her nose upon which stylish rectangular frames sat, giving her a face you might see in a commercial: smart, executive, selling car insurance. When she was with Hatch she didn't wear the glasses. Her love life was conducted half blind.

Her mother was a maiden from Pumpkin Hill, Mooretown, Jamaica. Her old man a bill-nosed sailor from Padstow, Cornwall. In 1978, Kevin Sheers got Filomena Steady pregnant. Married by Easter. By Christmas the baby was in a carriage being pushed down the streets of Stoke Newington: in woolen whites this infant was Hatch's future lover. The Sheers thought of calling their daughter Majority. Didn't. Called her Pearl.

When Pearl was seven her parents divorced.

A beauty. Hatch couldn't resist her. Couldn't take his hands off her. And when she accepted he was married but not happily so, and was about to end it, was about to say the fatal words and walk away, telling Pearl this over and over, that his marriage was over and he was ready to break loose, she responded and let him sample her goods, allowed her own heat to rise. She fell in love too. She soon believed it when he said he was making ready to leave his family for her. She was prepared to wait. But for how long? Until he came through for her, he told her. Came through for them both. As he always said: they were each other's big last chances at true happiness.

They stopped kissing. Sat. Her modestly appointed flat was cluttered with secondhand furniture, but he liked even this. Nothing matched. Oaken colonial abutted Ikea birch, Chinese panels, garden furniture. Above the electric fire sat framed photos in which she was laughing. A happy woman. As Hatch sipped his favorite Châteauneuf-du-Pape, which she bought especially for him, he looked at these shots. All were only months old. On his mantelpiece at home Jen also kept photos of herself, taken at her best, when she was happy. But these were all a decade old.

Pearl: "So, do we have anything to celebrate?"

"I love you. How about that?"

"Anything else?"

"Pearl, listen. I couldn't. I'm sorry. But I will. Soon. Promise."

He wanted her touch. Not her questions. But she withdrew from him.

"Shit, Terry. I . . . actually, I think you should go."

"Look. I just couldn't. Not with what happened to Ronny and the gun, I couldn't."

"You promised. Once you got the contest started."

"The bullet just missed Oscar's head!"

"Don't do anything, then. Ever."

"It's hard for me. I keep thinking about . . . the boys. How my parents were with me. They would have died before telling me something like this. It's my background. I know, it's my problem."

Pearl: "I'm so sick of it, sick of . . ."

"Hearing about my kids, I know."

"How hard it is to tell them how your parents hated each other's guts but still stayed together for the kids. Well, my parents told me—and my dad walked out. Parents get divorced."

"I'll do it. I promise you. This week."

She stared at him and squinted, trying to bring an out-of-focus man back into focus.

ALEX LEE LERNER: *Of the top dream themes in a national survey, released today, celebrities appear in fifty-four percent of people's sexy dreams. Stars who come to you in the night include Sean Connery, George Clooney, Kylie, Rachel Stevens, Catherine Zeta-Jones, Jennifer Aniston, Orlando Bloom and Robbie Williams. As for our loved ones, the bad news is that they came in a very poor second to these stars. Only twenty-three percent of the total respondents say they have sexy dreams about someone they know. Of these, forty-seven percent dream of an ex-lover, and only eight percent dream about their current lover or spouse. In perhaps the only positive indicator of our character, only two percent of us dream sexily about a close relative. As for nightmares, however, a quite different picture emerges. These are all about people we know. Friends and loved ones dominate in our night terrors. . . .*

. . .

THE IDEA. THE very idea that a few Czechs in 1970 had held out for over five days already seemed impossible to Tom. How had they gone this long? Communism had brutalized them, clearly hardened them into machines. Pampered Westerners, though, they were not creditable rivals. Could barely contemplate such a feat. *Just look around*, he thought. This lot here hadn't been going for eighteen hours yet, and already most of them looked done in, wilting, yawning, regretting signing up for this in the first place and would, if they hadn't already invested so many hours in this, happily slip off home and slide into warm beds. And how was he doing? Not much better, it had to be said. But he'd be damned if he strengthened his adversaries by letting them see his own discomfort. He was doing great, his outward demeanor must tell others. Just fine. Eighteen hours? *Ha!* his body language had to proclaim. A *walk in the park!*

Tayshawn was telling Walter how he'd slept rough like this every other night when not down at the Salvation Army shelter, "so this here is no biggie." In reply Walter revealed that he'd been a security guard and so he too was no novice of the long night.

"Hey, what's with your left leg?" Tayshawn asked, noticing how Walter never stopped moving it.

"Restless leg syndrome."

"What causes that?"

"Not enough sleep. For one thing."

"Bummer."

The Romanian, in monosyllables, told Matt he was no stranger to this kind of thing either. He had lived many years in refugee camps in France back in the eighties, awaiting a sponsoring country. Three years, waiting for a single piece of paper, was a long time to wait.

The ex-soldier told Betsy Richards that there was little difference between this and sentry duty. When Tom asked him what guns he'd been supplied with out there, he even grew animated.

"All kinds of shit. You know guns, huh? Know what I found the best? In the end? A plain old shotgun."

"Really?"

"A plain old twenty-gauge with a wide spread of shot, maybe three feet around, best weapon you could have."

Tom nodded thoughtfully, said, "Is that so?" and "Who would have guessed that?" and "I've never heard of soldiers with shotguns before but makes sense. Interesting."

As for the insomniac, he was as bright and full of beans as an ordinary person would be at noon.

The remainder? Most of those whose conversations had petered out and whose feet began to sob with pain closed their eyes, if only to rest them, which forced their supporters, just to be on the safe side and maybe a bit worried for the first time, to chime in with "Atta boy!" or "Atta girl!" or the complete lie, "Not long now," until someone in the small crowd finally struck up a unifying chant that became the feature of the night: "You snooze, you lose. You snooze, you lose . . ."

By 3:00 a.m., this chant had segued into a dozy "Stand by Me."

An hour later, the singing died out altogether. All happy communion ceased and an irritable individuality descended. By 4:30 the supporters at the sidelines were as burned-out as the contestants and it became a grim vigil until dawn.

Tick, tick, tick, tick, tick. These hours claimed five more victims. With the support crews taking the chance to get some sleep it was up to Vince—and by 5:00 a.m., a refreshed Dan—to spot the offenders, quietly wake each one with a shake and send them on their way. Ejected in this way was the Romanian who fell asleep, pants down, on the toilet and had to be woken by rocking the cubicle itself; gone was the fourteen-year-old when her father angrily dragged her home; gone also the ex-semiprofessional footballer dreaming once too often of the big time; eliminated too the heavy metal drummer who perhaps lacked the necessary amphetamines and poppers he associated with this hour. As sunshine broke acutely over the horizon of roofs, warming again the twenty-eight who had fought through the night to remain, to survive, Tom and Jess and Betsy and Matt and Tayshawn and Walter all regarded one another across the hood of the Discovery rather like shipwrecked passengers clinging forlornly to a life raft after the liner had gone down and simply waiting now to see who'd be next to lose their grip and slide away into the depths of the frigid waters.

2

HATCH HAD HAD a bad night. On the heels of strenuous hanky-panky with a much younger woman between the hours of 1:00 and 2:30 a.m., well . . . five shitty hours of sleep on his office couch just didn't cut it. Hatch needed eight hours. Nine was even better. Nine, plus a siesta, he felt like a king.

So now, on his office couch, balled like dirty laundry, he felt badly beaten up. He rose stiffly, unfurled himself, went to the window, groaning, misshapen, then angled wide the venetians to see people, survivors, contestants. *My God,* he thought, with sudden awe and pity: *My God, the poor bastards, those poor miserable bastards.*

He went straight out for breakfast at an eatery down the road, reading all the newspapers, looking in vain for reports of the contest, and then, at ten to ten, he relieved Vince in the yard. "How'd it go?"

His employee looked burned-out too. "I don't know how they can do it. I'm knackered already. No way they can go on like this for five days."

"Get home and get some shut-eye. I'll take over till Dan gets here."

But Vince looked guilty. "He might not be coming in. We've been talking. Both of us are having, y'know, to reconsider our futures."

"*What* futures?" An insult. Perhaps intentional.

"Unless we get paid, we're leaving."

"Leaving! You can't leave! We've got a contest to run here."

"We can do another couple of days. But if it keeps going after that, we're out. Sorry. We've got families, same as you have."

Vince spun, walked away. Hatch was speechless.

He wandered among the bodies with his loud hailer, bereft now, doing his best to hide his dismay, a Napoleon at Waterloo, an Alexander before whatever battle had been his most ill-advised. He heard little chitchat now, little humor, no jokes, no laughter, no gestures of cooperation, none of the earlier esprit de corps. A torpor had settled.

But Hatch was not the only one moving between the cars and contestants.

A photographer. The man would raise his camera from time to time, only to decide against taking a shot—raising and resting the camera, raising and resting it—at least until he saw Jess Podorowski, at which point he spent an entire roll. As Hatch watched, the man recorded, at movie camera speeds, the woman's closed-eyes, head-fallen pose—*click, click, click, click*—before Jess opened her eyes, realizing she was being photographed and straightened her head self-consciously. By then, Hatch had also crept close to the cameraman and seen the image the photographer had liked: a woman, in her late thirties, a red tint to her sandy brown hair, exhausted, eyes closed, crouching, her head resting on her outstretched arm as if it belonged to a sleeping lover.

Hatch stepped toward the stranger. "You are? Can I help you?"

"*Daily Telegraph.* Sorry."

"Sorry? Yes, I'd apologize too if I worked for the *Daily Telegraph*. Ha! Good to see you. Excellent. Been waiting for you guys to show up. What kept you? So, where do you want me?" Hatch offered his hand. "Terry Back, the owner. People call me 'Hatch.' Hand on the car too—or what?"

The photographer agreeably took a picture of Hatch standing in front of the sign BACK-TO-BACK NEW CARS (OLYMPIA LTD.). A set of grinning teeth. Hands on hips. The scion of salesmen. Wind flipping his forelock the wrong way.

"Okay, I think I got something," the photographer declared as Hatch shook his hand again.

"Good. Well, come on down again and keep track of this. We'll be here for a few more days yet. World record in jeopardy, that sort of thing. If we break the world record you're gonna wanna cover that every step of the way. Amazing symbol of the human spirit, really."

"What is?"

"The contest. Every walk of life here. Pushing themselves to the limit, and beyond. Beyond. Going where no man has gone before. Sort of thing."

Feeling revived, eager again to rouse the sullen contestants to a renewed world record effort, Hatch lifted the megaphone and began another countdown as the 10:00 a.m. rest stop arrived. At zero he set them all free, and after that—as the marathoners drifted away from the cars to make quick repairs on themselves—declared in the shrill metallic voice of the loud hailer that twenty-eight people—"brave souls," he called them—had *officially* survived the first twenty-four hours.

ONE HAND ON the hood of the Discovery, young Matt Brockle-bank concocted a plan to break the monotony that, in its own way, was proving as corrosive as tiredness. The local burger bar was three hundred yards down the road. He was going to phone ahead to place his order—he had earlier taken down the manager's number—then sprint there, grab the stuff and get back in time. "No sweat. I'm hungry. The next break I'm going to do it. Anyone else want anything?"

Betsy was very keen. "Oh God, yes. A cheeseburger and a coffee. You're an angel."

Matt dialed the burger bar, began to place his order, then turned to Jess. "Want anything?"

"Me? I could . . . suppose . . . I could use a coffee but I don't want you to, y'know, get disqualified. Five minutes doesn't seem long to run all that way."

"It's fine. One coffee. I've actually got a track-and-field background."

Tom shook his head. A track-and-field background. He was going to be sick. He interjected. "Why don't you *want* him to get disqualified? Hey, I want *you all* to get disqualified. *All of you*—so I can go home."

Many faces turned angrily toward Tom. As obviously true as his comment might be, the verdict of the people was that this kind of statement was unhelpful.

Tayshawn chimed in, anxious not to miss yet another meal. With no supporters of his own, this kid had had to rely on the charity of others, the scraps from superior tables. "I wouldn't mind a Whopper."

Walter too: "Cup of tea. But are you sure? How you gonna run with all that?"

"Great," said Tom. "This I wanna see. Bacon-and-egg sandwich for me, then." He took a travel razor from his pocket and began to shave one-handed, trying to revive himself. The motor whined where the stubble was intense over the chin. The mesh of the head caught hairs, tugged at his face, helping to keep him alert.

One-handedly, Matt took off layers, got down to a white T-shirt. He looked in great shape. He was ready.

Three, two, one . . . and the whistle sounded.

Already in a standing starting posture, the young man sprinted off. Betsy shouted, "Go!" As did Jess. Five minutes suddenly seemed an awfully short period of time. A suicide mission. Most other contestants didn't know what was happening. As they heard about it, the consensus was that the guy was crazy. The burger bar would be farther than he thought. When Dan, the marshal, learned what was going on, he said the guy would really have to leg it.

Walter, however, was impressed. "The guy can really move. Look at him go."

Tom sighed, shook his head, then called out "one minute," then "one minute fifteen."

Jess stretched, took a bite of a cold cheese sandwich, sipped the last of the coffee grown cold, then from a makeup bag took out a homeopathic remedy and, using a pipette, squeezed five drops of Rescue Remedy onto the back of her tongue. By the one-minute-thirty mark Tom told people close to him that Matt would have to be paying for the burgers by now or he wasn't going to make it back in time. Tom used his own free time to open a bag of secret supplies and take out a bottle of vitamins, a fresh bottle of water and a clean shirt, which he began to change into right away.

"How long now?" Jess asked.

Walter glanced at his watch. "Two minutes."

Tom slowly took off his old, now odorized shirt and stood in a vest. Jess watched him out of the corner of her eye, stunned at the man's immunity to the tension that all the others were feeling intensely. What was the point of changing shirts in a contest like this? He caught her looking. She turned away quickly.

"Two minutes thirty," Walter announced.

"If he's not started back by now, he's history," Tom surmised. He turned to Jess, inserting his arms in fresh white cotton. "It's getting hot."

"Excuse me?" she asked, even though she had heard him very well. "Were you talking to me?"

How draining, Tom thought. How dull are these games between men and women. Such a waste of energy. He must try not to talk to her in the future. Cut her out completely. From now on he'd be less generous with his wisdom, more circumspect all round, conserving his strength by editing out of his conversations all the pearls and thought gifts whose value was almost instantly lost on these clowns. "It's getting hot," he repeated.

Jess (again!): "Are you talking to me?"

Eliminate, cut back, yes, strike out redundant comments, even phrases, words. Conserve. Conserve. At all costs save energy. ~~"What's the matter, are you deaf?"~~ "Gonna be a hot one." ~~"Forget about it, lady, you're not gonna win anyway."~~

Jess: "Mmmm."

She returned her eyes back to the road, looking expectantly into the distance.

~~"Go home. That's my advice to you. There must be some things you are good at but this isn't one of them."~~

Dan was also keeping time, looking at his wristwatch, holding the whistle close to his lips, ready to blow it and disqualify the young man if he didn't appear soon. As tension rose, as tick followed tick followed tick, and as all the other contestants began to return to their places on one of the two cars, Dan called, "Three minutes."

Jess felt that although she very much wanted to win, *needed* to win, for her whole family's sake, there were many others she wanted to see eliminated before Matt.

Betsy, for other reasons, was even more anxious. "Where is he? Oh shit."

Roy, the ex-soldier, wasn't quite ready to count Matt out. "Not over till the fat lady sings."

Even Tayshawn was riveted. "How long now?"

"Three minutes thirty," Dan said.

Tom slowly and calmly did up the buttons of his fresh white shirt, then tucked in his tails. He felt a lot better, restored by the crisp new fabric, which braced his skin like an astringent. Jess glanced back at him, at this big, heavy white shirt wearer. "How long now?"

"Who cares. Ask them."

Dan had it: "Closing in on four minutes."

"Something must have happened," the soldier concluded.

"There he is!" Matt was steaming back up the street. In his right hand swung a large brown paper bag. The legs were moving fast, the arms working too, as he grew and grew. Tom, the last to look up, watched the guy do it and do it easy. Matt Brocklebank could really move. Walter was right.

"He's fit," Tom conceded.

Matt fell onto the car, grinning his wide, good-looking, financially underwritten smile.

"Four minutes, three seconds," Dan pronounced.

Matt: "A whole minute to spare . . . ta-da . . . the burgers were . . . (breathless, but not greatly so) were ready. It was *great*. Now then . . ." He had recovered already and was now ready to dispense the food. Neat, warm, tissue-wrapped parcels for the burgers. Hot cardboard cups. "Okay. So. One, uh . . . Whopper for . . . the pretty lady? Yeah?"

Betsy shook her head. "Cheeseburger for me. And coffee. Thanks."

"Right, sorry, cheeseburger. There you go. No problem."

Betsy took the cup, bit the lid off and sipped eagerly. "I think we should get married," she told him. "That's if I'm not moving too fast for you."

Matt grinned even wider. "Not fast enough," he replied,

checking the next hot package. "One, looks like a Whopper, for . . ." He offered it to Jess, who shook her head, then to Walter, who also shook his head. "Okay, so this was for . . ."

"Yo," Tayshawn said.

"Sorry. Blood's in my feet."

Tom couldn't resist it: "Probably lives there."

"And we got one tea . . . for . . . ummm . . . oh, I've gone blank."

Walter: "I was tea."

Jess: "I was coffee."

"'Course. Something for everyone. Tea over here. Coffee there."

"Bacon-and-egg sandwich?" Tom inquired.

"Oh. I, um—sorry—bacon and egg? I, uh . . ."

"Don't tell me," Tom said septically.

"Sorry, it's umm . . . they must have forgotten to . . . sorry."

Tayshawn, meanwhile, in burger heaven, tore into the sandwiched meat. "I'll go down next time."

Tom's good spirits had evaporated. He owed it to the kid to terminate this particular delusion. "Lose fifty pounds, *then* go down. Before then, forget about it."

Tayshawn stopped eating and lowered his burger. A hurt look came into his rheumy eyes.

Several hostile faces trained themselves on Tom, forcing him to look away.

Defiantly, Tayshawn swallowed his mouthful and reiterated with even greater resolve, "I'll go down next time. Watch me."

HALFWAY THROUGH THE next stint, Jess looked up and saw her mother, a miracle vision. The woman was holding a Thermos flask. She had also come down with a rug and a raincoat and an instruction: "Come home."

Valeria Wisnewski believed in solutions reached behind closed doors, deplored public revelations of personal hardship. You didn't beg. You held your head high. This was the Wisnewski way. Her forebears had known nothing but hard times. And what Jess was doing, in Val's estimation, was tantamount to panhandling.

But Jess saw it differently. She believed in ruling nothing out in order to provide for Nat. Believed there to be little charity in the world. A widow on her wage couldn't afford to suffer in silence, or to take her chances. If the Lord was prepared to work in mysterious ways, then so would she. So Jess had to insist, raise her voice to be understood, which did not come naturally. Sometimes it wasn't enough to pray, to hope: not near enough. You needed to scrape, to maneuver, to compete and, yes, to be seen and heard if necessary, to raise your voice in the modern world in order to register above the roar. *There are those who get, and those who miss out.*

"No. I can't," Jess said during the next rest stop, sitting in an empty aluminium folding chair and stretching out her neck.

"The weather report said there might be some rain." Val shook her head. "Look at these people, they're desperate."

"Well, so am I."

"Examine your heart, Jessie. Then decide why you are doing this." Val coughed twice into her fist. Whenever unwell, Valeria had to cope with a bronchial cough, low blood pressure, fatigue headaches; at her very best, rheumatism and female disorders. "And then think of your daughter, whose mother will not have a job if I have to ring your work and cover for you one more time."

Val unscrewed the cup-cum-lid of the Thermos and filled it. Steam escaped. Jess put her lips to the rim. "Hot. Lovely. Thanks, Mumia. So who's looking after Nat?"

"I get Julia from upstairs to sit. Got to be going back in a few minutes. There are sandwiches in the Tupperware. Oh, and I bought you these. Take."

A set of rosary beads.

Jess smiled, and understood the significance of this gift. She remained a Catholic, and as such could never be counted out, for although the other contestants might have their ice coolers and windbreak screens and ad hoc support teams, Jess had—and would always have—Rome, the Virgin Mary, God, a Polish mother. Jess felt a tear come to her eye but quickly drew it back.

Val also wished to make light of the beads, and certainly of the tears, and looked around her instead, scrutinizing the competition that she faced in the form of rival support teams. Some of these had struck makeshift camps, were sitting on cooler bins, large bottles of water at the ready, offering strong shows of support. "Look at these people. So desperate. And you really think you can beat them?"

"No, but I'm still going to try."

Val shook her head in a manner that bespoke centuries of forbearance. "Look into your heart. And ask why. Look into your heart."

But at this moment Tom walked up to his knapsack, which was lying close by. While Jess made a display of ignoring him, Valeria took a keen interest. "I bring her the rosaries. She doesn't want the rosaries. She thinks she is not going to win."

Tom turned, surprised, and exchanged a glance with a red-faced Jess. "Supporter?" he asked.

Val was happy to accept this mantle and answered for her daughter. "Yes. I am her supporter."

"I wish I had support," he replied, surprised that this thought had escaped his editing process. "Support's, uh . . . important. Will probably decide who wins. Need, uh . . . people to keep you sane on something like this." *For Christ's sake,* he then quickly reminded himself, *be careful about what you give away!*

"But she doesn't think she can win."

He risked one more act of generosity. "That's where you come in, I suppose."

And Jess looked grateful for this remark. Val, however, looked merely puzzled. "Who can win such a thing?"

Tom shrugged. "Who knows. Maybe the one you least expect."

"The least? Then that's my daughter. Then that's her."

It was Jess's turn to shake her head. "Still jealous of my support now?" she asked Tom.

But instead of replying, Tom addressed her mother. Hell, he'd gone this far with his candor. "Your daughter has as good a chance as anybody. I've had the advantage of seeing her at work." A mischievous smile, a flashing glance askance at Jess.

No, not entirely unattractive at such moments, Jess reluctantly had to admit to herself.

"Well, I'd better be getting back. Nice to meet you. Ladies."

As he departed, Jess stared at him, surprised.

Val was also clearly impressed. "What's wrong with someone like this?"

"Stop it, Mumia!"

Val had said her piece, achieved her mission. She gave a terse good-bye, then walked away on her thick, meat eater's legs. But as tired as she looked, Jess knew that no one could count such a woman out. Given reason, her mother could cross continents on foot with that same plodding, arthritic, late-sixties step. In Poland as a young girl, Valeria had walked from Lodz to Gdansk in unmended shoes to escape the turmoil of two advancing armies. A journey of two hundred and twenty miles and a feat of tremendous endurance. Her will was immense. In fact, if Valeria were a contestant trying to win this car, Jess would bet everything she had on her.

'Bye, Mumia.

. . .

THE WHISTLE BLEW.

Tick, tick, tick, tick, tick, tick, tock.

Jess prayed. *Hail Mary, full of grace* . . . In her pocket her thumb and forefinger found, and held in secret, one bead after another. *Holy Mary, Mother of God* . . . Betting on these couplets to deliver salvation—one Hail Mary, one Holy Mary for each bead—she hoped for a quinella of peace and strength as she felt her way around the circle of fifty beads terminating in a small crucifix, the symbol of a crucified Christ, of mortal suffering.

After ten minutes she took the beads from her pocket to check how far she'd progressed, but she was only halfway around the circuit. This prayer lap was a long one.

"What are you doing?" Tom asked, once more standing beside her. He was watching her pull the beads from her pocket to examine them, while his own free hand was busy in a blind pocket searching of its own, seeking out the peanuts in a plastic bag full of nuts and raisins, kernels and other desiccated mysteries.

"You wouldn't understand," she replied, pocketing the prayer beads once more.

Tom raised his voice; as his molars crushed the nuts and finished her first page for her. "Hail Mary, full of grace, the Lord is with thee. Blessed art thou among women and blessed is the fruit of thy womb, Jesus." Half a dozen others around the car looked at Tom, then at Jess.

Surprised, she refused to show her pleasure, and after a short gawp turned her back again. She was learning that any delight in Tom Shrift was certain to be short-lived.

"Raised a Catholic," he continued, loudly enough for this to be public.

She turned back to him, her voice a whisper. "Do you mind?"

"Lapsed at age seven. The age of reason. Jesus and Santa walked out the door holding hands." He looked off into the distance. The direction of his vanished superstitions. "Your mother had an accent?"

She edged closer but only so that no one else could hear their exchanges. "Will you keep your voice down?" When he nodded, she asked the burning question: "What do you want?"

"Nothing. I just saw you were praying."

"And don't tell me, you don't believe in God."

"Of course not." He shrugged. Those big shoulders. "It's the giant fiction, isn't it?"

She turned away again, now with a sigh. *Hail Mary. Holy Mary.* But new thoughts at once invaded this recitation. On the beads, her right thumb and forefinger froze. *The big fiction?* What a thing to say! She had no time for people like this. Her own faith was strong, based on the official Catholic proof of God's existence, the time-tested "proof by subscription": namely, that God *had* to exist because it would be simply illogical for humanity to have worshiped *nothing* all this time. People wouldn't subscribe in their millions, age after age, to a fantasy, a delusion. A belief in God, in other words, was a vote for the good sense of ordinary people, and such an ancient proof was good enough for Jess Podorowski in modern-day London.

She wanted to tell Tom all this, and sharply too, but she didn't want to make a scene. Too many people around the Discovery were within earshot. So she kept it all to herself. Hoarding her thoughts, as ever. Anyway, it wasn't her job to save such a man. He was probably beyond saving. She'd kill for a cup of tea. Her back ached terribly. A cup of tea, milk, no sugar. *Dear Mary,* she prayed, *Mother of God, Mother of the Word Most Holy, how about a cuppa?*

Perceiving the protest in a woman's turned back, Tom tapped her on the shoulder until she faced him again. "Okay, I'm sorry. The cockroach thing was . . . you were just doing your job. Truce? The mold will outlive you. Okay? Truce?" He offered her his hand.

Jess very reluctantly shook it.

"So, your mother's Russian . . . or—"

"Polish."

"Polish. Okay. So. Big family, or—"

"Just me. Satan's concubine."

"Oh please, come on. I apologized for that already."

"Okay. Yes. I'm Polish. Sorry."

"Polish. Right. So, why wasn't Christ born in Poland?"

"Yeah, yeah." She sighed. "They couldn't find three wise men and a virgin. Very funny."

"Oh, you heard that one." He was smiling.

"Why are you . . . what do you . . . ? Why are you talking to me?"

"We're going to be here for a long time," he replied. "And . . . you're interesting."

"That's a lie. I wrote you a ticket. How does that make me interesting?"

"When you wrote me a ticket, I lost my temper. I unloaded, but all you said was, 'You're entitled to your opinion.' I remember exactly. You took it like a martyr. That interests me."

"We're not allowed to argue back."

"But how can a person with your personality do a job like that?"

"My personality?"

"Yeah."

"What's my personality? No, tell me."

"I'd say you were . . . a nice person."

"That's it? I'm disappointed."

"I suspect your self-esteem is all over the place, but you're a nice person."

"Okay." This almost amused her. "Anything else? While you're at it?"

"My guess is . . . you want to hear this?"

She hesitated, then nodded. "Yeah."

"Okay, well . . . one day you feel like a 'ten,' another a 'one.' But mostly you feel you're a 'one.' And ones can't afford *not* to be nice. Am I right?"

The look on Jess's face said that he wasn't far wrong. "Keep going."

"You're a people pleaser. You can't not smile, but you find it almost impossible to ask for what you want." At this, the smile on her face faded. "You feel you're making the world a pleasanter place but you're just letting people get away with murder. The world is actually worse off because of your niceness, and so are you. That's what you haven't realized yet. You expect other people to be as considerate as you are, so you think life isn't fair when this doesn't happen, which turns out to be most of the time. And as a result you live with an inner rage. While outside," he continued, "you keep a nice smile on your face. And it's a pretty nice smile. Your best feature. But what you've never grasped is that niceness is a crippling liability in a world where aggression is the most common mode of communication." He took a breath.

"I think you've said enough."

"Okay."

An inner rage? What a con man! How was he coming up with all this stuff? None of it was true or had any value. At the next break she'd go over to the other car. Surely he couldn't be so crass as to follow her across once she'd made it clear she wanted no more to do with him. "What makes you . . . God . . . what makes you think you . . . you know somebody . . . just because . . . ?" She looked him squarely in the eyes. "You don't know me."

"You asked for my impression. That's all I gave. And by the way, that job of yours. That's a killer for your type of personality— the intrapunitive type, never showing rage. My God, writing your little tickets, enforcing society's petty little rules, but you're actually writing yourself little tickets all the time, punishing yourself, and all the shit you get, people dumping on you, human excrement by the bucketful, and having to take it. You'll do yourself an injury."

Through gritted teeth: "Thanks for your concern."

"Read the latest oncology research findings. Seriously. Passivity is linked to cancer. Niceness is as self-destructive as smoking. Whereas a certain amount of aggression is cleansing, even curing. I'm not just talking here. Science has proved it. Take me, for example. I have this feud going with my neighbor. Started over my planning application to build a little balcony off my front room. He lives below me. He objected. I lost out. So I wrote him a letter. Got all my rage out in a healthy fashion."

"And what happened?"

"He put a dead rat through my mail slot. Which was fine. He got his rage out too. It was a healthy transaction."

"A dead rat?"

"A big one. The one they call *Rattus norvegicus*. He must have bought it at a pet shop—he's dedicated, you see. And so we have this little feud going on now. Actually, a few weeks ago he waited till I went out and he called the cops and said I'd collapsed in my flat. Told them bald-faced that he'd heard me call for help. So the cops smashed my front door down. I came home, found the cops everywhere, no front door. Now some people, some people, might give in to this kind of tyranny. But you know what I did? He loves his front lawn, this guy. You ought to see this front lawn. Mows it every second day—it's like the center court of Wimbledon. So I go out and buy some weed killer. And in the middle of the night I creep down and write a word on the grass. In poison. Go out in the dead of night and write a word right in the middle of his front lawn."

"You didn't!"

"This is my point."

"What word?"

"Doesn't matter. It wouldn't be nice to say. But the point is—"

"What word? What word did you write?"

"A four-letter word. Let's just say that."

"Four letters?"

"So it should be starting to show up right about now actually. And it serves him right."

"Oh my God." As shocked as she was by this action, she was also fascinated. Tom suddenly became fixed in her mind as the kind of person who lived in a world to which she had always forbidden herself admission—a rougher, more lethal world, but also a vivid and more unfettered one, where people did what they thought, acted on what they felt. "What word?" she asked. "What word did you write? Oh my God."

"The word? It doesn't matter. But believe me, he had it coming. I don't have a single regret. Not one."

But she couldn't contain herself. "Fuck?" She blurted this incautiously, perhaps too loudly. "Oh my God. You wrote *that*?"

"No. Actually no. But the point is I *acted*. I took *action*. I—"

She shook her head and dropped her voice low: "Not the . . . not the C word?"

He shrugged. Didn't deny it. "He deserved it."

"You wrote the *C word*? In poison? On his lawn? How . . . how could you . . . I mean—"

"He pushed me too far, that's how. I stood up to him, I called his bluff. Whereas you . . . what? You'd . . . what?"

But she was hardly listening. Was still shaking her head gravely from side to side, incredulous, hardly believing anyone could do to their neighbor what he had done.

To nail home his point, he continued, "Okay, tell me this. How much do they pay you? How much an hour do they pay? To be a meter maid."

"It's private."

"Let me guess. Minimum wage. Right? Five pounds, five pence, before tax? Unbelievable. You know who would accept that kind of dough? A nice person."

He turned away. Triumphant. The summit of his argument reached. And sensing that more words couldn't add further to this achievement, he planted his flag and fell silent.

"Everyone has to work," she told him feebly. But he couldn't hear her. He'd put in his earbuds and was listening once more to his portable radio.

AT THE NEXT rest stop Jess got to the toilet first, went inside and wept. Her body shook. She suppressed the sobs as best she could. Even clamped a hand over her mouth. But it wasn't easy. The emotions welled up again and again. Perhaps some sounds escaped but she did her best to suffocate them. And after three minutes or so she opened the door again and left that place, and nobody was any the wiser.

MATT BROCKLEBANK AND Betsy Richards laughed. Talked in conspiratorial whispers in the lengthening shadows before sunset. As Tom watched, the couple found excuses to touch, bump shoulders, graze downy forearms, look away, only to deliberately edge closer again so they could then look back at each other as if startled by the sudden proximity they'd magically achieved.

Spare me, Tom thought.

Under the applause of the flapping triangular flags that hung in a saw-toothed pattern from ropes marking out the yard, Tom turned his eyes away from this evolving sexcapade, taking peculiar comfort in the thought that Betsy might be beautiful now, plentifully rounded (he imagined an uninterrupted tan), but she was the type to be fat in a few short years—yes, she would soon lose her power to make a man such as himself look twice. She would become what she deserved to be, someone who wasn't worth looking at even once.

His eyes found Tayshawn and Walter Hayle instead. An even odder couple. They were also talking, forging a bond—here again, evidence of people helping each other! Was he the only one to see this as a war of attrition, a knockout contest? Walter had opened a greaseproof package and was handing the kid a sandwich. Unbelievable! What did the old codger think he was doing? Tom sighed. Tayshawn's big weakness was obviously his stomach, but what did Walter do? Go and feed his adversary, reestablish the boy's cellular advantage and by this fuel his own defeat. Why enter an endurance contest to assist your rivals? The sheer irrationality of it. Some people, thought Tom, needed no other enemies.

A noise distracted him. A metal clicking. A ring on a finger was idly tapping on the roof. Tom looked up. Roy, the former soldier.

"Hey. Please," Tom asked politely. "If you don't mind. Please."

"What?"

A constant song—along with other mental dissonances—was evidently playing in the serviceman's head, making him seem nutty, possibly clinically so. His humming and this rhythmic, semi-autistic tapping on the roof certainly gave the impression he wasn't entirely right upstairs. Tom imagined for the man a wifeless, childless home. Visits from a half sister, perhaps, and then only knocks at the door from reps from the Legion.

"You'll scratch it. Knock it off."

"Fuck you," the soldier barked.

"It may not matter to you but some of us actually have a chance of winning this car and we don't want it scratched. So stop it right now. Please. I asked you nicely."

But Roy only increased the tapping of his ring finger, in volume and tempo, until now it annoyed others.

"He's r-right," said the insomniac from Billingsgate. "Kn-kn-knock it off."

"You're going to scratch it. Stop," said the Zairian.

"If you win, then you can scratch it all you like," added the NHS nurse.

Finally, gentle Walter: "Come on. We *all* own this wagon. Give it a rest, pal. Let's talk. Tell me what unit you served with?"

An object lesson in how to deal with a loon. As a result, the soldier heeded Walter and stopped tapping the paintwork. The story came out, for all to hear.

Corporal Roy Sewell. Munitions expert with the Rifle Volunteers, a Territorial Army battalion. Had served in Kabul with the ISAF, the International Security Assistance Force. Saw action. Sent home because of chronic migraines. In civilian life, rewired by war, he must still hup-two, salute, obey the petty orders of everyday life: no parking, no entry, no smoking, start work on time, stand clear of the closing doors, et cetera, et cetera. Adjusting to these metropolitan battles wasn't easy. How to pay a bill. How to wait in traffic. How to woo a woman. No, it wasn't easy for Corporal Roy Sewell, not anywhere near easy, now that he was back.

"No hard feelings." Walter, looking admiring, offered his hand.

The soldier shook it. "No problem. No hard feelings."

Tom watched the exchange. Wanted to say something. But it wasn't the right time.

With the light of the day almost gone, the floodlights came on.

"And next there was light," Walter ventured from his repertoire of misquotations.

TWENTY-EIGHT, THOUGHT Hatch, watching from his office window. Twenty-eight miserable souls still standing. A world record? Were his chances of setting one still standing also? Yes, someone among the twenty-eight might do it. But just who among them looked like they could go all the way? Hatch looked out. Observed.

Beyond the glass, human beings. Inside those human beings, what?

THAT NIGHT. STAR-STUDDED. Under such stars a grim contest: Jess versus Tom versus Walter versus Tayshawn versus Betsy versus Betsy's blue-eyed boy versus twenty-two others versus the All-Governing Clock. Wills versus bodies. Motivations versus motivations. Hearts against hearts. In order for one to win, all others must lose; in order for one to triumph, this person must prove him or herself dominant: this is the algebra of survival, the real rules, Time picking off the weak, one after another, as the beads click on Nature's abacus . . . *tick, tick, tick, tick, tick.*

Eyes stung. Limbs ached already. Feet became numb. Pain rose up from the ankles into the knees and hips. Joints swelled and became problematic. Talk became less frequent. Tempers grew short. And to make matters worse, the temperature dropped. A sudden merciless dip. So much pain, so little good luck, at the same time.

Walter Hayle pressed his free palm to his eyes and complained that his restless leg syndrome was really troubling him. "Bloody thing's like a little electric shock going off. Feels like I've got a wet toe in a hot socket." He needed to walk it off but, unable to do this, he could only try to get through it. Tayshawn, perhaps in sympathy, took out a harmonica and began to play it mournfully, softly, poorly—he seemed to be hee-hawing for the old man's sake, charming the spastic leg into silence, but the formless tugging sound spread over the whole contest and actually lent the whole event the plaintive misery of a Somme calm between bombardments, the wounded infantryman's elegy to the dire news from HQ that no more reinforcements were on their way.

Twenty-eight people now; that was all. Hands on metal. Two cars, their grip on life. No one had been disqualified for some time, and it became crystal clear to all that the contest now comprised only diehards, each of whom was prepared to give it everything they had.

"My head feels like it's deep-fried in the Colonel's secret recipe," Tayshawn groaned.

Walter reached behind, grabbed his own buttocks. "It's my backside. Kill for a nice cushion to park my jacksie on."

"So how you holding up really?"

"I'm not. Haven't held up in ten years. But that's my edge. The way you're feeling now? A sneak preview of being old. I'm the only one used to this. That's why I'm gonna win."

"If this right here is old age, it's crap."

Betsy said: "I wanna die."

"You can't," Tom chimed in. "Against the rules."

Matt was massaging Betsy's neck. With murderous pain in her own lower back, Jess conceded that a human touch would feel priceless right now.

"Lucky for some, eh?" said Walter in a low voice.

AT THE NEXT break Tom approached Jess. She was sitting on someone else's deck chair. "You okay?"

She didn't want to talk. "Back. And a bit of a headache. Otherwise, so-so."

He moved away, found an area of the yard less light-drenched. Looked up. Beyond the floating blimp, bobbing up there like a barrage balloon during the London Blitz, he beheld the stars, dim through the radioactive murk of the city's glow. Standing on his own, stretching out his body and rotating his shoulders and squatting three times to move blood through the legs, he stood and arched his back, looking straight up, belly out, a friar in the Sistine Chapel. And these stars—each a nuclear reactor—the universe containing more of them than there had ever been human heartbeats going back to the dawn of humankind; a stunning statistic when he thought of one person's racing pulse rate after running on an ordinary treadmill—it was almost ridiculous. Tom could see only a hundred or so stars. The London sky was a joke. In Corfu last summer, where there was no city light pollution, the sky at midnight had been ablaze; and beneath those bright points Tom Shrift had felt infinitesimal—wonderfully so; and later he couldn't work out why such a feeling should have been so pleasant. In a quiet corner of this car dealership, now, he still couldn't figure it out.

He straightened out his body again. One thing was for sure, he was in no hurry to go back to his flat, resume the compartmental life that a big city imposed on you. The countryside allowed certain dignities—but London? Forget it. The masses lived like battery chickens, allocated only their few square feet; and right next to you, under you, above you, other fierce, dangerous creatures, ready to attack with piercing stabs at the carotid arteries. Every day you tried to find peace but all around you the appalling clucking of the poultry life. No, he'd had it up to here with his London flat, but where else was there to go, now that he'd been cleaned out?

He rested a hand on a new car that within still held the heat of the day. All these cars, these warm, gleaming contraptions, what did they actually betoken to the suckers who eventually bought them? What? They were a delusion. (His mind was accelerating once more.) So much cash was needed to own one, but within ten short years—if you held on to it for that long—you'd be describing it yourself as a piece of shit, as a worthless heap of junk. Well,

Tom could see behind the shining exteriors, see them as junk already. When Tom won his Discovery he'd sell it right away—no question whatsoever. Take the cash and run.

He heard noises. He moved into darkness around the back of Hatch's office. Grunts. Groans. Kissing. The smack of lips on skin. Love noises, coming from the shadows around the back, where old tires and hubcaps were stacked high.

And there, oblivious to Tom's soft step, a man and a woman. In limited motion. He could hardly believe his eyes. The woman, her back against the wall, blonde. A fair-haired man pinning her there, moving ever so slightly up and down. Were they . . . they were. The guy began to pant and grunt as the girl lifted her chin into the light, finally exposing her neck to kisses and her face to the light.

Betsy Richards.

Tom sighed. Unbelievable. Betsy bloody Richards! And so the guy had to be . . . yes. What the hell did these two clowns think they were up to? What complete idiots! What marathon could be won by stopping midway for the sex act? The two of them were literally screwing their chances of winning the car. Had opted for a love affair instead.

Holy Jesus. How did they get to this point so fast? Tom prepared to go back to the yard at hearing Betsy's small, eager yelps of pleasure, which forced Matt Brocklebank to try to quell them by slipping a hand over her mouth while he bent, carnivorous and maniacal, to her neck in a brand of lovemaking she clearly welcomed as she threw one calf around his legs, binding him to her. Modern life, what a mystery it was. Tom stood there unseen amid the sooty crankcases and discarded wheel hubs feeling something hard to classify that rooted him to the spot—a strange sense perhaps of being left out of something, not the sex per se, but comprehension of how sex this quick could possibly have come about. Then, after one last look—a young couple, imperceptibly joined,

Matt all ardor and industry, Betsy on one leg, a ballerina half lifted in an intense and willing pas de deux—Tom, strangely stirred up, withdrew. But in moving back he bumped a box. A tower of old hubcaps swayed, fell. Tom didn't turn to look back. He ran as the hubcap spun and described shallower and shallower circles toward a crescendo before it shuddered and stopped.

Back at the Land Rover, laying his right hand with relief on the cold steel, Tom remade his original oath: *I solemnly swear to escape the poultry life. Once and for all. For Christ's sake, let me never again be caged up with such people!*

And rather than look at the returning lovers who, when they finally reappeared, nestled and rubbed up against each other as they reattached themselves to the car, he chose to look up at the cold and cooling stars. And that's when he saw, at last, why it was so sweet to be infinitesimal: because as we become nothing, beneath the stars, so too do our troubles.

THE SECOND NIGHT—the second torment-magnified night—felt even more everlasting than the first. But for those who would eventually survive it, victory began to seem not only a possibility but tantalizingly close at hand.

And the contest was always changing its character. Talk became infrequent. And when it arose around both the contest cars it generally took the form of questions, mostly about the nature of sleep. On the Discovery, Tom was ready with answers. He had all the facts and figures for those who wanted to listen, and he'd decided it was of some advantage to dispense them. Total sleep deprivation in rats led to death in around twenty-eight days.

"Death?" Betsy gasped.

"In rats." His eyes turned to Matt Brocklebank at her side.

Betsy: "Oh my God."

The insomniac (within earshot): "So how l-long can the-the

body keep going without sleep? I mean, what's the r-record f-for just not sleeping?"

"The world record for staying awake? You'll never guess."

"S-six days? What? I don't know."

"Eleven. Eleven days."

"Eleven! No way."

"Some seventeen-year-old American. Played pinball most of the way, apparently. Went doolally toward the end but stayed awake. Randy Gardner, his name was."

"Out-out-out . . . that's-that's outstanding."

"But this was under ideal conditions, not out in all weathers like we are." Tom then warned his new audience, "As our deprivation becomes chronic, which ought to be around the end of day three, the biggest threat will come from *microsleeps*, mininaps that steal up on you. They might last for no more than three or four seconds but they can knock you out just long enough for your hand to slip off the car."

Betsy wanted to know even more. "What else? What else is coming? Tell us. How bad will it get? Like, I mean, what's it going to feel like after three days, four?" Her voice conveyed a vague panic now.

"Difficulty focusing, that's coming soon," Tom readily supplied. "Then we'll be recognizing objects only by touch. That'll be a lot of fun. Astereognosis, it's called. Then there's moodiness, of course, irritability, aggression, an uncooperative attitude, memory lapses as well. The worst of human nature. Politeness gets peeled away. Umm . . . what else? Difficulty concentrating, then difficulty talking. Talking will be harder and harder. Hallucinations. Did I say memory lapses?"

"Oh my God." Betsy quickly held Matt's shoulder for comfort at this news.

"It starts out physical but it ends up a mind game, all in the mind—mind against mind against mind—and that's where the winner will come from. It's mental, and where are you going to draw your inspiration from, when all else fails? That's the big question. What can you focus on that'll keep you saner than the next person, keep you going. What's going to inspire you and help you keep it all together?" Tom tapped his temple as he looked around him, saw that everyone was listening. "Oh, did I mention psychosis? Randy Gardner went mad at the end. At the four-day mark he confused a street sign with a person. So. Lots to look forward to."

Matt had heard enough. "He's just trying to freak us out. No way is it going to get that bad. No way. We'll either fall asleep or we won't. That's the end of it."

But the general silence that followed seemed to suggest otherwise, especially as Tom's list suggested symptoms over and above their already swollen ankles and knees, inflamed spinal discs, calcified necks, stinging eyes, stress headaches.

But Jess discovered that there was one thing—perhaps the only thing—that helped you to redress this steady buildup of purgatories.

The failure of others.

Amazing the lift this gave you. What a surprise to discover the exhilaration she felt when someone else collapsed, staggered away or failed to return to the car. As guilty as she felt, it made no difference. After midnight, when the Norfolk fishmonger simply bent at the knees and folded like a car jack to his haunches, she felt terrific. Sincere condolences were offered as the man tearfully broke down, then shuffled away, but Jess couldn't deny that for a while afterward the going was a lot easier, an entirely lighter proposition even—and not only for her. A party vibe sparked up after every default. The failure of others lifted you higher, simple as that. And as the night wore on these lifesaving rebirths—each at the cost of someone else's misery—came thicker and faster, and were more and more welcome.

At two, just as everyone was beginning to feel flat again, the NHS nurse came to everyone's rescue when she was found asleep on the Portaloo during a rest stop and the marshals had to bang on the door to revive her. She had made herself extremely popular by tendering medical advice to anyone who sought it, and there was a great deal of lip service about how much she'd be missed, but right after she'd been noisily waved off someone started singing and the singing caught on and was taken up until laughter was unmistakable around both cars. Buoyant talk returned. Jokes. The prize drew closer to each outstretched hand—you could even hear in people's voices the restoration of patience, the rediscovery of goodwill. Jess wasn't used to taking comfort in the misfortune of others but slowly, slowly the contest was teaching her how to surrender to this.

In the early hours of dawn—"a tough period biorhythmically," as Tom forewarned—Beer-and-Pizza-Only Man simply didn't make it back to the car from his tower of beer cans, staggering and tripping on a hose pipe and coming down wincingly hard on the concrete. This personal disaster from such a boisterous threat provided such a two-hour uplift that dawn suddenly seemed easily reachable now that their total number had finally sunk to just twenty-five, and then, at 4:30, to a mere twenty-four, when the Zairian also succumbed, his hand sliding from the car into his lap and witnessed by Tom, who duly reported him. How could Jess possibly withdraw now, when one by one, fewer and fewer people stood between her and a life-changing victory?

Tick, tick, tick, tick, tock.

AT HIS OWN personal lowest ebb, about 5:30 a.m., Tom—who, for a change of atmosphere, had switched to the Subaru—decided it might help to talk to someone new, so asked Walter, who had switched as well, just what the tattered piece of paper was that he'd just been showing to Jess, the third migrant.

"Oh this? Just—well, here. Have a look."

The old man revealed a diagram.

"WHAT? WHAT IS it?"

"Know what this is? This is the image. The image that's on the plaque on board a space probe, right now, that's just now passing out of our solar system. It's gone farther from this earth than any other man-made thing. That's the image of the human race that the scientists put on board. It's our message to another civilization. It's us, in a nutshell."

Tom was quickly ahead of the old man. *"Pioneer 10."*

"You're onto it. NASA sent it up in—"

"Seventy-three."

"Close. You're good. Seventy-two. Amazing. They thought it had run out of power years ago, but they've just heard from it again. Amazing thing. A very weak signal. It's still alive, even though it's powered by a battery about the strength of a child's night-light. A weak signal, all the way from the edge of our solar system—imagine! Anyway, this picture, can you work it out? Lemme show ya. A man. His right hand raised. Why? In greeting? Nope. *To show the opposable thumb.* Our biggest achievement, apparently. A hand that has a thumb. Beside him a woman. Look at her. Bored almost, weight resting on one leg, not smiling, standing in front of . . . a what? A *spacecraft*—that's *Pioneer 10,* see. They were going to highlight her uterus. Didn't. Anyway. At the top left, that's the symbol for hydrogen, the most common thing in our universe. Below it, see, these spokes, they show the relative position of our sun to the nearest galaxies. That's our *address,* basically. Our galactic post code—how we can be found."

Tom glanced with puzzlement at Walter. Who would have thought it—a security guard, one past his retirement age, carrying around something like this? A penchant for weighty matters like the destiny of the human race. Sometimes people surprised you. Usually in a bad way but occasionally for the good.

"...And...see?...at the bottom, a diagram of the solar system with *Pioneer*'s path marked. You see? Here's man. Here's where we live. Come and find us. Great, isn't it? Keep it in my wallet. It's our SOS, see. Do you see? The SOS from a worn-out species is what it is. It's our message in a bottle, a distress signal. 'Help.' I reckon the scientists have kept this a secret from us. How bad our situation is. Unless we get help, we're finished."

Tom was impressed—the idea of a secret SOS was paranoid, sure, but at least the old man was *thinking*—and in terms of civilization, a worn-out species, messages in bottles. "We're finished? You may be right. I'm impressed. I've followed *Pioneer 10*'s progress as well."

"Oh yeah?"

"But did you hear? NASA has just recently given up on it. The last signal was some time ago actually. Just before it entered the heliosphere."

"Come again?"

"The heliosphere, that's the bubble defined by the sun's magnetic pull, the last boundary of what they call the empire of the sun, the region where the solar force fades to equal the radiation of the surrounding stars."

Walter nodded, in admiration at Tom's command of the facts, the raw data, all the scientific jargon. "You don't say. I didn't know, uh . . . that, about the empire of the sun 'n everything."

"And from there the lonely scrap of junk will go on beyond. In space nothing corrodes, so in about thirty thousand years, that diagram you have right there will pretty much be passing through the constellation Taurus. And in the next one million years it'll pass at least ten more stars. Suns." Walter's mouth fell open. "And five billion years from now, that little vessel carrying the original of that diagram you have there will still be speeding through the Milky Way when our sun becomes a red giant and burns up the planet that launched it. Think about it."

Silence. Walter staring, speechless. Infinities revealed.

3

"**G**O!" THEY ALL shouted. "Go!"

And Matt could run. There was no denying it. As the young man rounded the corner heading back to the yard and becoming visible again, it looked to Tom as though he would record an even quicker time than yesterday, and by quite a few seconds. How? Something wasn't right. Drugs, Tom concluded. The guy was bound to fail the drugs test when the time came to give blood. Only drugs could explain it. How else could a person look so fresh as they began their third day without sleep? It wasn't natural.

"He's amazing," Jess said.

And Betsy nodded, agreeing. Early love was growing in the pink-cheeked pleasure she took in watching this athletic stud run. Such pleasure makes a girl's skin shine and her hair bounce, even after lost sleep. Happiness hormones at play. In the morning light, she looked as if she were on some kind of upper too. The two were helping each other, even on a chemical level, Tom decided, and it wasn't fair.

BUT JESS WAS pleased for the girl. With her free hand she squeezed Betsy's arm—a silent message that said "good luck."

The two of them, Jess and Betsy, had talked during the night, and Betsy had shared her story.

She had been unlucky, it seemed. For all her lovely looks she had consistently failed to find a trustworthy life partner—at any rate, one whom she truly loved and who truly loved her back. "I've seen more rats, honestly, than the Pied Piper. I swear to God," she'd told Jess. "I'm not kidding. You should see them follow me home!"

Stung by serial disappointments, Betsy had tried lowering her standards. Didn't work. Raising her standards? Same deal. She was now hell-bent on finding someone who was "remotely ball-park okay." Entering her fifth year of wanting to settle down, of yearning to be somebody's missus, soon thereafter somebody's mum, she ached to be able to phone her girlfriends and discuss the problems she was having with her au pair, her architect. Yearned for blue water in the bowl of her toilet. Wanted just once to pluck from the back floor of her new four-by-four a piece of used chewing gum pricelessly indented by the milk teeth of her own child. Yes, Betsy Richards had great big, third-trimester, one-carat, loft-converted, silver anniversary daydreams, but they were turning sour fast.

At least until Wonder Boy had shown up. And how timely his arrival. Not a second too late to get back to the Discovery and not a second too late for Betsy either, both the official stopwatch and her own fast-ticking heart announcing that Matt Brocklebank had beaten both clocks.

Tick, tick, tick, tick, tock.

Barely panting—"Unnatural!" Tom protested, but only mentally—Matt laid out his fast-food orders on the roof of the Discovery, rich booty for all to share.

Lucky girl, thought Jess to herself. If it all worked out, very lucky girl.

Matt passed out food and beverage. Betsy Richards beamed

as she took her coffee. Hood-eyed now, clearly weakening, this girl was being kept going by Matt in more ways than one. She had done well to survive the night, one in which two more fit-looking and capable young men had dropped out, both letting their hands leave the metal as they'd nodded off. Dan had sent both packing around 7:30 a.m., reducing the total number to twenty-two.

From forty to just twenty-two. And of the twenty-two, who still looked dangerous? Tom took a survey. Betsy, for all Matt's help, couldn't last too much longer. Matt was on drugs, clearly, so forget about him. Walter was still a threat, with his iguana metabolism. The insomniac, yes, he still looked durable, as did the car thief. The weirdo soldier too, he was a wild card that couldn't be written off. The McLuskys, with their bad (nigh appalling) dentistry, still looked united in purpose. A few more on the other car looked strong enough to perhaps surprise, but you could already form a picture of who would still be standing in twenty-four hours' time.

Tom turned to check on Jess Podorowski, who looked quite lively as she unwrapped the surprise gift of food. But she presented only a minor threat. If truth were told, she should take a reality pill—take two—and go home now. All she had going for her, as far as Tom could see, was her sex, her genetic advantage over men, but this edge was negated by her victim character: she was the self-annihilating type, expecting herself to lose, in the end. As he watched her hungrily chomp her cheeseburger and tell Matt with a smile that it was delicious, he saw only a victim entertaining another delusion.

Tom monitored all these cooperative relationships springing up around him in silence. How idiotic. Did no one know their economics, their game theory? He shook his head. Wanted to lecture them all, and loudly, that individual success lay in your neighbor's misery, not in their salvation. Look at these dummies, how they took care of each other—insane. The zero-sum game taught that for one to win, another person must lose, balance at zero. (*Hey, Dr. Kissinger, as with persons, so with peoples, states, nations, right?—you knew this well.*)

"I'm gonna do it, at the next break," Tayshawn said.

Walter shook his head, lifted tired eyes. "Don't do it. Don't even think about it."

Matt: "If he wants to go . . . as long as you don't stop. And get your order in fast. You'll be fine."

Tayshawn: "No sweat. I'm going. Next break. No probs. It's not far."

Walter: "Then, here, take this. Here." He loosened his wristwatch, gave it to the kid.

"~~Suicide,~~" Tom almost said, before saying it anyway.

THREE, TWO, ONE. The whistle.

Tayshawn sprinted off—or at least, gave his best impression of a sprint. More of a hyperactive waddle. The clock was the only thing truly running fast here.

Betsy shouted, "Go!" Jess too. The news spread that Tayshawn was going to get a burger.

Matt began to laugh as he watched Tayshawn run. "Look at him go. Ha! Ha! Ha! It's brilliant."

Tom shook his head. "Having fun?"

"He's gonna be fine," Matt replied. "Trust me."

"Hasn't got a hope in hell."

Jess, her hands cupped around her mouth, was shouting her loudest encouragements, but at the same time she was worried. Matt explained to everyone near him that Tom didn't know what he was talking about and that Tayshawn could make it quite easily—it wasn't that far—just so long as he didn't hang around buying too much stuff. This was the only worry. The guy had better not get greedy. He had to grab what was ready to go, then slip away fast.

Tom checked his watch. "We'll know whether he can soon enough. In about six or seven minutes actually."

"He'll do it easily," Matt confirmed.

"We'll just see, shall we?" Tom countered.

Jess bit the nail on her index finger. Said nothing. When Dan then came over and found out what was going on, he commented blithely, "The kid'll need a cab."

IT WAS GOING to be tough. But he wanted to try to do it.

Before dropping by the newsagents to check the morning papers for coverage of the competition, Hatch called by the car recyclers.

A little errand: the small matter of getting rid of the gun.

Rufus—ring name "Dr. Death," ex–pro wrestler, the sort paid primarily to be pinned down and groan in agony—was on the phone when Hatch walked into the office. He nodded for Hatch to go ahead and do whatever they'd earlier agreed to do. Jerked a thumb in the direction of the crusher.

Hatch headed over. Quite some place, this. The deformed hulks of wrecked cars were stacked in two-story-high corridors and Hatch moved down these rusting avenues, the only living soul in the graveyard.

The crusher was huge. Took only seconds to turn a car into a pallet no thicker than a mattress. Merely watching this collapsing in of metal gave Hatch spinal shivers. Here, everything that he traded in, made a living from, to some extent valued his personal worth by, was pulverized to a pulp. And while Smash Palace was making huge bucks from recycled junk metals, Back-to-Back Cars, with its virgin autos, was dying, crushed out of existence by the hydraulics of commerce, tax regimes, falling buyer demand, fucking eco-concerns and his own inexperience. Hatch gave a don't-mind-me wave to one of the boys operating the gantry crane.

Going up to the next car due for demolition, he reached into his coat pocket, took out the gun. All he had to do was toss it in the front seat of this Ford Capri. *Should throw myself in here while I'm at it.*

Two years after his old man had passed away he'd found the gun when going aloft to fix a ball cock in the water tank of his mother's house. Wrapped in an oilcloth, tied up with string, there it lay: an Enfield Number 2 Commando, a World War II officer's special. So Hatch had taken it. Had prized it. Decided it was kind of like having his dad at his side once more.

The crusher fell, mashed another car. The sound went right through him. Associations of carnage, lost lives. You half expected police to show up, ask if anyone had seen what had happened.

But then, Hatch thought, two years later the gun had gone off. *Almost killed my son.* So it must be destroyed. Because of what it had nearly done. So why hesitate now?

It bounced once on the seat after he tossed it in. Settled. Re-cycled, it might come back as a motor-mower blade, as a Japanese Ginsu steak knife.

"All done?" one of the lads was calling, ready to hook up the Capri to the gantry.

Hatch nodded, waved again, but then indecision rose. His trademark doubt. And when he didn't shut the car door or step away from the Capri, the lad called out again, "You sure?"

It was a question that Hatch could no longer answer.

BY HIS WATCH Tom called the one-minute mark, then the one fifteen. Tayshawn had diminished into a point, and from then on, after he'd become lost around the bend, his brave efforts had to be imagined.

Quite far down the street, but not as far as he should have run by then, Tayshawn caught his first blessed sight of the burger bar, the promised land, oscillating in his field of vision.

He wasn't built for speed, that much was certain. He was built for game consoles, for staying put and for finding optimum ways to put his feet up. All ballast and flab. And underneath this a small frame, fragile, unmuscled. The weight hung off him like an ill-fitting suit. A school doctor had once dubbed him "morbidly obese." To Tayshawn, this sounded like a death sentence: like it should mean Dead Fat Person. In actual fact, so he later learned, it meant anyone who was forty percent over ideal weight. No way was he that. Carrying thirty percent of surplus weight, tops, suffering his fate as an ugly and even unlovable person, he grew excited as he bore down on his destination. . . .

BACK AT THE yard, Jess took a bite of a cheese sandwich, sipped the last of the coffee now grown cold. From a makeup bag she took out the medicine bottle and pipette and squeezed five more drips of Rescue Remedy onto the back of her tongue. Tom announced, with a head shake, that the two-minute mark had gone by. Tayshawn had to be there by now if he was going to make it.

"Two minutes fifteen."

IN THE BURGER bar, gasping, poor Tayshawn could hardly get the words out.

"Sausageandchipsandtwo . . . sausageand . . . andchipstwice and . . ."

The burger bar boy: "Come again, mate? Slow it down, sunshine."

"Sausage . . . and chips . . . twice! Quick! I've gotta go!"

"Two sausage and chips, yeah?"

"I've. I've. I've . . . here! I can't . . ."

"Bit out of breath, mate, in't ya?"

"Quick. Here. Here. How much?"

Tayshawn fumbled and unfurled a filthy fiver on the counter as the burger boy bagged the sausage and scooped flaccid chips onto open sheets of paper, which steamed on the counter like the opened entrails of an animal.

"Salt and vinegar wi' that?"

"Here, here . . . just . . . *give it!*"

Tayshawn reached over, grabbed the sweaty package, balled the meal into a bundle and tucked it under one arm the way a rugby player carries a passed ball. Once in the street he accelerated back to his full speed and, thanks to the adrenaline now pumping through his clotted arteries, he felt himself to be running faster than he'd ever run before.

VAL WISNEWSKI ARRIVED to find her daughter, and nearly all the other competitors, crowded at the edge of the forecourt, looking down the road in high excitement and shouting to no one. "What are all these goings-on?"

Jess barely acknowledged her mother and instead nervously asked Tom, "How long now?"

"Four minutes . . . one minute left."

Val could see nothing down the road. Who was meant to appear?

"No sign of him," the ex-soldier said. "No sign. He's blown it. Blown it."

"Not f-fast . . . fast enough," stammered the insomniac.

Tom: "You've got to blame the people who encouraged him."

Matt looked less certain of himself now. "He can still do it."

Even Betsy had been revived by the tension of the attempt and she was the first to see Tayshawn appear a hundred yards away. "It's him! Is that him?" It was. "There he is! Come on!" She cupped her mouth. "Come on, Tayshawn!"

He was indeed visible. Apart from Tom and a superanxious Walter Hayle and a confused Valeria, almost everyone on the yard joined in and began to shout "Go!" and "Come on, Tayshawn!" to this galloping kid from off the streets, a teenager with age on his side but also an obscene agglomeration of short- and long-chain fatty acids. The athlete hiding somewhere within was handicapped by eighty pounds of extra matter and his straight-line path had begun to acquire a wobble that grew in amplitude the closer he got. By then, not even Walter could contain his nervous tension.

"G'won, big man! You can do this! Come on!" He was misty-eyed. Tom, watching, realized that it really did mean something for the old boy if the kid could make it back. And Jess too began to grin and laugh, to get misty-eyed too; she screamed and clapped as success began to look possible.

But then, to everyone's dismay, as continuously as Tayshawn's legs and arms pumped and drove hard, his progress toward them strangely slowed until his running was a kind of ineffectual loping motion of ever more limited effect. How could a person run so hard and make so little progress? But it was a fact. As Tayshawn ran out of gas his form fell apart, and the greater the effort the less the gain, so that when Dan informed the crowds that only fifteen seconds remained before the contest would be restarted, the jubilant shouts for young Tayshawn to "Go!" and to "Run!" also fell away into a stunned silence, and the countdown, when it reached ten, then five, then zero, and finally the whistle sounded and Tayshawn was still quite far off, a number of people had even turned their backs, unable to watch anymore.

So it was that Tayshawn's final limping, wheezing, half-wounded but still hopeful arrival back at the yard was quite uncelebrated and near silent. No one wanted to tell the guy what he could surely see for himself. And yet, he continued his last few jogging steps, his cheeks shaking with the impact of each foot-fall, until he slapped a hand on blue steel and leaned heavily on the hood.

Home.

Walter, old Walter, looking almost set to cry now, was the only one with any prepared words. "Fantastic. You're a champion. How about that? That was amazing."

Tayshawn was bent over double, clutching one knee. "Did I—did I—make it?"

It was ghastly. And no one had the heart to tell him, not even Dan, who lowered his head.

"Good effort," Tom felt obliged to say, when what he really wished to say was "Bloody daft idea."

Walter again: "You did great!"

And that's when Tayshawn looked up and read the truth in all the faces looking back at him. "Shit. I didn't make it, did I?" And when he got no reply, and when Dan still couldn't even look him in the eye, he took his hand off the car. "Fuck it. Ah well. I'm out." With a flip the hood came back over the head, preventing anyone from seeing how he was really feeling, and he was once again a shadowy figure, one who, when you passed him in the street, made you want to check again which pocket your wallet was in.

"You did great," Walter repeated.

But Tayshawn was already walking away, not wishing to be comforted, heading back to obscurity, stopping only when he remembered the watch on his wrist. He came back, handed it to Walter, who took it, but then thought again and pushed it back into the kid's pudgy fist, saying, "Keep it. It's yours. You won it, lad."

Tayshawn stared at this thing in his palm as if it was alive, anxious only that he'd be able to keep it that way. And he managed "Thanks" as he put the hefty watch back on, buckling it around the spongy wrist, then tightened his hoodie, shrugged and wended his disconsolate way through the cars.

Empty minutes followed. And instead of the inner rejoicing that had followed previous dropouts, all that settled around the cars this time was a shared sense of guilt. Tom, uncomfortably touched by this weird exit, turned to Matt, surprised by his own anger.

"See what you did? Had your bit of fun? Watch the fat kid run?"

"Oh come on. He wanted to do it. He wanted—"

"He didn't have a chance."

"That's rubbish. He—"

But for once Jess interjected, and on Tom's behalf. "No. We should've stopped him. Tom's right."

Tom, a longtime stranger to support, was almost taken aback as everyone turned and faced him. He found it necessary to speak again: "Hey, I don't want to stop anyone from dropping out. I'm glad the kid's gone. In fact, I think you should all take a little run down there at the next break. All of you."

But Jess was determined to praise him. "You were right."

Three more unexpected words Tom couldn't have imagined receiving in this world. "Stick around," he managed. "I usually am."

ON HIS DRIVE back to the dealership, and still in possession of the gun, Hatch picked up all the major newspapers, though his hopes for a sales boost from the press coverage lay mainly with the *Telegraph*.

At his office desk he turned the pages. Finally, there it was. A picture. But not of him, not of his smiling face, hands on Backian hips under his great sign pronouncing his world record effort, the blimp jiving overhead. Not that. Only a shot of one of his contestants: Jess Whatever-her-name-was—the shot he'd observed being taken the day before. His initial disappointment passed as he realized that it was publicity nonetheless, and the picture had an accompanying article, one focusing on the efforts of Jess, a likeable woman who was doing this for a disabled daughter. Heart strings were being strummed. The beneficiary of such music? Himself.

When Vince came in he stood and allowed his employee to read the piece.

"That's great," Vince said.

"Now, you watch—you watch sales take off. We're gonna be fine now. Trust me. You and Dan aren't going anywhere. We're a family."

AFTER TAYSHAWN'S DEPARTURE everyone was a little cooler toward Matt, and he lost something of his irresistible gloss, most people finding him guilty of a small deception, and in response the rich boy showed a new irritability that didn't square with the cheerful person who, for the last seventy-four hours, had seduced so many of the contestants. When Betsy tried to cozy up to him now, tried to draw strength from him, he moved away from even her, and looked at her as if she'd mistaken him for someone else. *Their first tiff,* thought Tom, with no small amount of pleasure. *Doesn't take long.* From zero, to fucking each other, then back to zero in a day. Love in the new millennium.

Noon passed without another elimination.

And then, shortly after 2:00 p.m. . . . the ants.

Many dozens of them moved around the feet of the contestants as if deeming them carrion already, ripe to be carried away by the insect world. Some even climbed up shoes and socks and nipped the skin.

"Oh God," Betsy yelped.

"Where did they come from?" Jess wanted to know.

"Fucking things," barked the car thief, stamping furiously and visibly distressed by their numbers. Five, ten, fifteen hands were raised in complaint, calling for something to be done.

Vince soon came over. "Yeah. I'll take care of it. They're from the alley. The bins don't get picked up." He returned with some fly spray. Coated the ground. Used two cans. The smell of the poison was noxious. Many people coughed. He repeated the process an hour later, killing hundreds, possibly thousands. The tiny bodies shriveled, halved in size, to be blown away by the wind.

Only the car thief continued to complain. Two hours after this he said the ants were back, but no one else could see any. From then on his claims of still being bitten around the ankles were considered merely indicative of an eroded state of mind.

UNDER A SKY the color of slate roof tiles, Valeria waited two hours to talk with her daughter. She didn't approach, not while Jess was competing, and she took no notice of Jess's hand signals for her to go home. She just sat where she was, waiting on a low wall in the shade of a car marked MANAGER'S SPECIAL, her crumpled felt hat tight on her head, her face anxious, set for business, the weak line of her eyebrows redrawn to make them serious and strong. Finally, Jess joined her.

"What?"

"Two hours, waiting, you talk to me like that? And don't thank me for phoning your boss. Telling him you are sick. Lying for you. He did not believe it, by the way. He knows something is going on."

"Mumia, everyone else is getting support—"

"Don't thank me for that."

"Look at the support they're getting! Why can't you just support me?"

"It kills me to watch you. You know that? You are out to kill yourself. But you are killing me. You are not like these others, Jessie. You are not a messed-up person."

"Aren't I?"

"Why? Why do you want more? What is this always wanting more? You have *five times* more than I had." Valeria held up her hand, spread her fingers. "Five times. And ten times more than your grandmother had."

"I'm doing this for all of us, actually. I'm trying to hold us together."

"Natalie. Whose birthday it is tomorrow, and where will you be?"

"If I'm not there . . . Nat will understand."

"Then listen to this. If you are not there, no more support from me."

"Mumia!"

"No more."

"It's only a party. This is more important right now. Natalie knows."

Valeria was already walking away, returning home. Clouds were gathering.

THEN IT RAINED. Heavily. Rain ricocheted off roofs and car hoods, drove low the heads of contestants who scrambled about for something to hold over them—lids of ice boxes, coats, groundsheets, everyone improvising awnings against the sudden weather. And the shower did not pass. It deepened. Set in. The clouds remained open, and with the rain the daytime temperature dropped to a new nighttime low. Lightning fissured the sky, thunderheads boomed. In a mere few minutes Olympia wintered. It slid back six months, impersonating mid-January. And all around the Discovery the contestants, faces contorted, eyes squinting through the

densely stinging downpour, hoped for a respite that simply refused to come.

Pressing together for protection like field animals, they waited.
And waited. And as the storm lengthened into half an hour, and
then an hour, and then two hours and more, spanning the next
break and continuing unabated into the next session, and as hands
grew cold and as water penetrated clothes to run down spines,
backs of legs, pool in shoes, numbing feet and their collectivized
will to go on, as all these miseries accumulated and pooled and
became unbearable when added to all the older complaints, then
the first new resignations came.

A Scottish butcher's apprentice withdrew angrily, as if the
weather were some evil trick. "This is bullshit. This shouldn'a be
allowed." He lifted his hand, just gave in, his knees so swollen
from standing all this time that he had to be supported to the dry-
ness of the showroom, still shouting, "You can'na expect people to
stand out here unprotected like this!"

Agreement spread. The management was to blame: Back-to-
Back New Cars was denying them shelter in order to end this
contest quickly, but if they joined together, acted collectively, then
maybe they could bring about changes (an awning at least). And
with the intoxicating idea taking hold that solidarity could resolve
their individual problems, one brickie from Penzance, one made
delirious by this rhetoric, lifted his hand and in a fit of socialism
proposed that everyone else do the same. Instead, he found himself in a sober minority of one, isolated and disqualified.

They were down to nineteen.

Rain. Godforsaken rain. It drove down. The survivors bur-
rowed under coats and plastic sheets and makeshift bivouacs, one
hand always exposed to the weather, keeping up contact with the
car until, slowly, one by one, three and then four and then five and
then six more people allowed the rain, the wind, the chill, their
sneezes, their sudden misery to get to them, finally deciding it

wasn't worth it, and so lifted a hand and released that anchoring grip. The contest was suddenly down to just thirteen. So many had fallen.

At this rate, thought Jess, there'd more than likely be a winner within the next twenty-four hours.

Even with her eyes stinging, her body in anguish, her L2 almost spasmic, her right foot and ankle numb, and her mind starting to perform minidelusions, she did her best to think of the rain as the best thing that could have happened. At least her rivals were being knocked out quickly now.

But at the same time, if it got any colder, it would finish her off as well. She didn't have a lot of strength or will left and the foot numbness worried her. She pondered asking Tom Shrift about it—was a numb foot dangerous?—but decided against it. One more night, then if the winning post wasn't in sight she too would pack it in and just go home: to sleep. Oh dear Lord, what a thought! Sleep, the most luxurious freedom of all. Sleep, yes, her top priority now, and after that, to decorate her daughter's cake, dress for the birthday party and resume a normal life.

Even most of the support groups withdrew from the yard, most retiring to cars parked in the streets or to their homes, unwilling to be weather-punished alongside their friends. The lucky/luckless thirteen were essentially left alone in the rain.

Jess found a place beside Matt Brocklebank. With the storm came the need to be with cooperative types. Soon, over the din, the young man was explaining his private dilemma further, and she found herself offering support instead. "I just feel that this kind of thing we're doing here, pushing ourselves to the brink, that this sort of experience has got to happen to me before I can get anywhere. I need to get beaten down, crushed. I honestly feel that. That's the only way I'm going to learn anything about what it really takes. That's the only way I'll really be able to understand."

"Understand what?"

"How everything operates. History. All of that. The Long March. I'm reading history at university, you see. Hannibal's army. Or Shackleton, like on that icy sea in that two-man lifeboat sailing eight hundred miles . . . I read these things, and I'm stunned all the time. Dunkirk. What people can actually do, I mean. The life of a Welsh coal miner. Fuck me. Alexander's crossing of the Persian deserts. Y'know? I don't know *anything,* not in the *slightest,* about what anything takes. Ease, that's all I've ever known. I've been drugged by it. I have no idea whatsoever about my limits."

TOM, HUDDLED BESIDE the ex-car thief, was also listening to another's life story, albeit one punctuated from time to time by slaps to the ankles where unseen ants lurked.

"And that's when I retired. Stealing cars for a living. Bad excuse for a life. I got out."

"You retired?"

"Yeah, well, I got caught. A forced retirement."

"You got caught?"

"Oh yeah. Everyone does sooner or later. But took the cops three years to work out our scam. Three. Had a beautiful operation. Poetry. Cops couldn't suss it out."

"What kind of scam?"

"Rental cars." His eyes gleamed. The memories of grand escapades. "We'd hire a car for a month, see, then take it straight to a lockup, change the plates, see, knock up some fake ownership papers for the new plates, then sell the car through *Exchange and Mart.*"

"Hang on." This didn't sound too smart to Tom. "The rental car company would have had your name. The police could trace you. I don't get it."

"No. That was only half of the scam. I've just told you the bit any moron coulda come up with. We woulda got nicked in three months flat if that was all. No, the poetry was the next bit. This was my touch." He tapped his temple, inside it a devilish mechanism. "What we used to do then was . . . we'd leave it a couple of weeks, see, then we'd go around, nick back the *exact same car* off the geezer we just sold it to, 'cos we'd always make sure we knew where he lived, yeah? So then we'd take this same car back to the lockup again, put the original plates *back on it,* and then drop it back to the rental car company on the exact date it was due back for return. We'd say *grazie, grazie,* fanksverymuch to Mr. Hertz or Mr. Avis and how's ya father! Rental car people happy. Us, delirious. The stolen car is sitting right where the cops would never look for it—on the forecourt of Hertz or Avis! Cops looking everywhere for all these stolen cars, scratching their heads. Fucking *gorgeous*!"

Tom had to admit it. A genius-class larceny. Shrewd, cynical, fully up on the workings of human nature. No wonder some of the best minds of every generation went into either crime or big business. Both types liked to test the system. Act on hunches. This man had seen the exploitable holes in the system, just like a Bill Gates or a Rupert Murdoch. Tom wondered what holes such a man had seen in a contest like this, what ways to cheat?

"But you got caught, you said?"

"Not for three years, we didn't. And only then 'cos one of us got nicked for something else and spilled the beans. And the cops, they had to admit to us it was the best scam they'd ever come across. Respect, see. They knew. It's all a game. Rob Peter to pay Paul. Law and order is just a game."

"You did time?"

"Three years—same as it took to find us. Who said God hasn't got a sense of humor."

"And what was that like?" Tom was curious. "Three years in prison? What was that like?"

"Like three years." The thief looked away then, slapping the side of his neck. Had a fly landed? Tom could see none.

And then Tom's phone vibrated. He looked at the LCD screen. His mother; his aged, love-incapable mother, trying to reach him once more, now that *she* was in need. But he chose not to answer it and turned off the phone. He recalled, instantly, standing at the school gates, standing there for what seemed hours, the straight-A student who ought to be celebrated, to be picked up by a limousine and by a glamorous mother, waiting there instead until the sky drew dark. The principal had to drive him home instead. She'd forgotten about him once again. The cheap, lousy cow had been shopping. Or seeing a boyfriend. Now, decades later, she sat in a wicker chair in a public day room, silver-spun hair, collapsed features, unvisited. Like most people, her mental efforts were devoted to justifying herself to herself. Just last month her nurses sent him the SOS that she was dying. Churned up with complex reactions, he rushed to her bedside, but with her untimely survival he returned to West London. The calls from her had resumed as before.

He put the phone back in his pocket and looked around him at the competition he still faced.

AT THE NEXT rest stop Vince blew a whistle, told them all to place their hands on just the Land Rover Discovery in future. The Subaru had done its job and could be cut loose. Thirteen people could comfortably convene around just one car. And so, after a disheveled parade of people filed in and out of the Portaloos, fumbling with belt buckles and flies, all decorum abandoned, thirteen hands resettled on the Discovery alone.

"You snooze, you lose," Walter Hayle reminded everyone above the noisy rain.

But the warning was soon forgotten by Corporal Roy Sewell, the ex-soldier. Tom was the first to see his eyes close. He nudged Jess, so that she looked and saw the soldier's head drop, his hand slide, fall off the car for a few seconds, before he sleepily reinstated it. A microsleep.

"Okay?" he asked.

"Okay what?"

"You saw that?" Tom raised his free hand to report the offense.

"Leave me out of it," she replied.

"I know you saw it."

"Leave me out."

Watching events from the office window, with the rain falling just past the end of his nose like a curtain, Hatch told Vince, "Tell them we need it right now."

Vince was on the phone. Had a marquee rental place on the line. "We need it right now," he relayed. "That's right. How long? How long till you can put one up?"

Hatch looked back out the window. Saw Tom's wave. He put down his coffee mug, sighed, pulled on his wet-weather jacket and went out to see what was up.

And what a shock it was to be outside. The downpour almost hurt, hammering thunderously on the hoods and roofs of the waxed fleet, close to doing damage. Walking half-bent over as if avoiding a helicopter's rotors, he got to the Discovery.

"What's going on?" He visored his eyes with a hand.

"This guy. He took his hand off," Tom reported, standing up, too wet to care anymore.

"Who? This guy, who?"

Tom pointed out the soldier, who straightened from a crouched pose, aware that everybody was now looking at him.

"Anyone else see it?" Hatch shouted above the din of rain.

"Yeah. She did."

Hatch turned to Jess, his new media starlet. "You saw?"

She was slow to confirm it at first, but in the end nodded. "Yeah." Unhappily. "I saw."

"Two people saw it, then." Hatch faced the soldier. "You're out. That's it." He wanted to get back inside ASAP.

But even with the testimony of two people against him, Roy refused to surrender. Wanted to fight on. Shook his head with mad intensity so that Hatch finally had to try physically removing the man's hand from the car. When the soldier resisted, and started to rave, exhibiting for the first time something more than just angry protest, Hatch stepped back, unprepared for such a violent response as the rain beat down on them all. And for several seconds they seemed lost in a stalemate until Dan, burly Dan the junior salesman, appeared through the gloom.

Dan, in his own words, gently but forcefully retold the soldier that it was all over, only to absorb his own barrage of hysterical ranting and rocking back and forth, but the young man was far more decisive than Hatch had been. When the soldier began to beat on the hood of the Discovery in angry defiance, so that the other contestants started shouting that the soldier should give it up now and "just let it go, let it go," Roy, finally deranged by the seeming injustice of it all, threw a surprise haymaker at Dan's head. Bad idea. After Dan had caught the blow on his muscle-knotted forearm, he responded instinctively with a rabbit punch of superlative economy, which dropped the soldier to one knee in a pose almost prayerful. Blood appeared at the side of the serviceman's nose, on Dan's fist and also in vivid crimson drops on the forecourt, to be quickly washed away by the driving rain.

When the soldier stood back up, he faced Tom, whose eagle eye had started it all. "I'm coming back for you, arsehole."

"Oh yeah? What with? A shotgun?"

The soldier's withdrawal from the scene was at the sluggish pace of a mightily disorientated man.

There's a contest going on. You may not have heard about it. And up till now I've kinda tried to ignore it. For those of you who have missed my previous denunciations of this event, let me describe it. It's a contest to win a car by seeing who can keep their hand on it the longest . . . apparently the contestants are getting near the end of their third day without sleep. Now I've been trying to ignore this thing, but this morning I picked up a newspaper and there it was, toward the back of the paper. A story. With a lovely big picture. So I read it. And it seems that people from all walks of life are down there right now, standing out in the driving rain at this minute. And many of them have been interviewed and you get all the usual stories you'd expect— there's someone who's down on their luck, another one needs a second car, Harvey Bingham from Dorset wants to impress his girlfriend, good on you, Harvey, on and on go the reasons. And then I came to the story of the woman featured in the photo. Jess. Jess Podorowski her name is, a traffic warden no less. "Boooo," I hear you say. Hissss. But before you all start slagging her off, or phoning in with all your favourite traffic warden jokes, I have to say . . . her story has really touched me. Really touched me. She says that she's trying to win this four-wheel drive so she can fit a wheelchair in the back, the wheelchair of her young, disabled daughter. Now, if that doesn't make you want to root for her, then nothing will. I've been thinking about this all morning. And I have a question I'd like to open up the lines about. If you were going to put twenty quid on this, how would you pick the winner? How? How would a bookie work out the odds? What would they have to consider? If you've got any ideas, I'll take your calls: Oh-eight-seven, double oh, triple nine, triple nine. What factors decide these things? Let me know your thoughts. Will youth conquer all? Will the fittest person win? Will a man prove stronger than a woman, or vice versa? What do you think? Give me a call. And how about deeper impulses. Self-belief? Does that come into it? Or do nice guys finish first? Or last? Is supremacy compatible with decency? What really gives a person staying power? Do the reasons a person is doing it for matter? Oh-eight-seven, double oh, triple nine, triple nine. Let me know if, like me, you'd take a punt on motherly love . . . this is the Alex Lee Lerner Show. It's a business doing pleasure with you.

Hatch watched through the streaming, tear-stained glass as the cuffs of his shirt and trousers dried in the radiator's warmth. As "All You Need Is Love" started to play, he turned off the set. What was going on? Was the DJ taking the mickey? Still, at least they had some radio coverage, and if, just like the papers, the station wanted to latch on to the Jess Podorowski angle, then hey, it was hunky-dory with him that they ignore his world record attempt and try to turn this whole sodding thing into a soap opera about a widow with a heart. Their loss. *You can lead a horse to water but you can't make it think.* That'd be his rebuttal, if he were the type to phone a talk show.

He steepened the venetians. Didn't want to be seen too obviously gazing out the picture window. Though no racist—no way, José—he hoped vaguely that a Brit would win the Disco, someone like himself, born and bred here, with a family tree that one branch earlier didn't start in the Ukraine or Addis Ababa—though what difference this would make escaped him. It'd just be nice, he thought, like seeing your own child win the egg-and-spoon race. He thought then about Pearl. Had a notion to phone her up, ask her what she was wearing, what color panties. He overrode this urge. How wonderful though to want to call a woman and talk like a sex fiend! Yes, he was alive again, and he had Pearl to thank— Pearl, who was a decade his junior. Twice weekly for two years now his middle-aged heart had been able to pump depleted blood into their capillarious affair and have it come back refreshed. Youth, laughter, fun were transfused into him.

Where had he found such a woman? On the Internet. He'd used a nom de plume: ferrariV12. She'd been pearlof-yourdreams. He clicked. She clicked. Love. That was how he'd dived and delved and found his Pearl. Where his family didn't like him very much, Pearl loved him, adored him. Where they drained him, Pearl restored. Where his family demanded, Pearl gave. Where Pearl made him feel young, happy, hopeful, his family made him feel like his own father had been: old, grumpy, stern, a joyless provider.

But if she had given him such a boost, what had he given her in return? Two years of waiting, with too many broken promises, and with perhaps only some fraction of the fun he derived from her. A rotten deal. But this would change. He was ready to devote himself to her happiness. She deserved nothing less, given her unhappy past, which she'd only told him the half of. What a servant she'd find in him from now on. Once this contest was over with he'd break the news to his family: he was going.

So he needed the contest to keep going, to take off in a big way and push up sales sharply enough to save the family dealership, but at the same time he also needed the contest to end, and end as soon as possible, so that he could escape with Pearl.

His future was consequently no longer in his own hands, but rather in the hands of twelve strangers out there on the forecourt, suffering like beasts in the rain.

Dan came in with a question. But Hatch cut him off, telling him he wanted to talk privately to Jess Podorowski at the next rest stop.

· · ·

HATCH HELD OUT a coffee mug to her. "You want some?"

Jess took it suspiciously. "Thanks." Her face was tight from accumulated strains.

"I've got an umbrella for you too until we get the canopy up. They say tonight. Hopefully tonight." He smiled. "Here, take this. Thanks for your time. And you can use the staff toilets on the way out if you like. Anything we can do."

Half gaga, she was not so far gone that confusion didn't still register on her face as she tapped the tip of the umbrella on the floor experimentally. "Thanks."

"Your story, y'see. It's touched me." He placed his hand flat on a newspaper opened out on the desk. "Really . . . uh . . . touched me. Your daughter's plight, I mean." He tilted a small desk picture her way. "Four kids of my own, you see. So. If there's anything we can do."

"Okay . . ."

She moved to the desk. He spun the newspaper for her. She read. Put down her coffee cup. Went even more pale. "I'd . . . I'd better be getting back," she finally said.

He opened the door for her. "A lot of people are hoping you're not gonna let them down." He grinned, then winked.

Jess stared at this gesture, dubious enough in its way to be worthy of, well, a car salesman. She felt vaguely frightened.

THE COMPLIMENTARY UMBRELLA was big enough to shelter two. And Tom was standing there, right next to her once more, so what could she do—leave him out there to soak? Deciding that it wasn't right that she should have an unfair advantage over others, she gave Tom cover too.

He looked at her, his face reflective with water, his hair plastered flat on his head. "Thanks."

In close new proximity, he was the first to speak again. "Want me to hold it for a while?"

She shook her head. "It's fine."

An uncomfortable intimacy. Well within range to make either emotional progress or inflict serious damage. Nerve endings on yellow alert.

Tom was the first to take a risk. Studying her hand holding the umbrella handle, he observed cautiously, "No wedding ring?"

"Oh please."

More silence. "Divorced?" He received no reply. "Divorced, okay." He nodded, jokily, then paused. "So . . . some guy poisoned the well and now you're the bitter, antimen type? Am I close?"

Immediately he saw that she was appalled. The joke had gone south, *far* south—Patagonia. But from the bottom one could only bounce back: so long as you remained alive, disaster was a trampoline, not a marble slab—and even as she leaned away from him, moving the umbrella with her, forcing one of his shoulders back out into the driving rain, he tried again. "Did you hear the one about the Polish surgeon?"

"If you must know, my husband died." Her eyes blazed wintry and green. "You don't even realize you do it, do you?"

"What? We're just talking here."

"No. I talk. You *insult*."

"I mean well."

And he did. Why did nobody see it?

But she shook her head, inspecting him from inches away and then, as if dismissing him for all time, leaned back toward him, renewing his asylum for now under the rainbow-striped umbrella, but only because he no longer mattered.

"Okay, I'm sorry," he offered, as penitential as he had ever been. Perhaps *more* than he had ever been. "So how . . . umm . . . so how, uh . . . so how did he die?"

"What do you care?"

But then this nice girl thought better of being so tough on him. Tom could see that, from somewhere, she found the will to give him a second chance. "Car accident," she said.

"Car? Okay. I see. Because your—uh—your daughter—you said she was also—"

"Same car. Same night."

Tom nodded his head, was touched by this, even stopped talking for a while. "I'm . . . I'm sorry to hear that."

"I sent my husband out in bad weather to pick up a prescription for me. Our daughter wanted to go along for the ride. He never came back. And my daughter never walked again after the accident."

"I'm sorry."

She wiped her cheeks of rainwater while Tom thought: *We're talking. This is fine. And I didn't even put my foot in it.*

But Jess, for her part, was worried already. Her face became fretful. This man made her very tense. "It was all my fault. And I try to put it behind me, I do, but . . ." Emotion caught her, struck her suddenly. "But after two years . . . it's not gotten any easier for me." Tears, suddenly. And as her eyes became watery he, for his part, seemed to respect this and take her sadness on board. And so it was with great and sudden insight that he replied, "So that's why you're a traffic warden."

"What?" Her head swung right. What had he just said? Her tears had hardly begun to fall. "What's that got to do with anything?"

"I mean . . . I just mean . . ." He was in deep water once more. "Forget it."

"No. What are you saying? What's what I told you got to do with being a traffic warden?"

He took a deep breath. Knew he was on the verge of deeply insulting her but decided that what he had to say next might just be of vital use. He liked her too much to deprive her of it. His head, capable of conceiving gems, had just done so again, so why not try to assist?

"You just said it yourself. You blame yourself for what happened. And so maybe you put yourself in awful situations where you'll be punished in order to absolve yourself. It's classic. Beating yourself up for something that happened in the past that actually wasn't your fault at all." This situation was so crystal clear to him, it begged full expression. "But hey, being a Catholic, no surprise you've taken it all on board, since guilt is basically infused into the baptismal water, right? I mean, even being here, in this contest, this all fits into your overall effort to self-flagellate, right? If what you really needed was a car, why not just ask for government help for your transport needs? No. You're a type of person, that's all. It's very common. It happens. And it explains a lot, that's all."

Her mouth fell open. But Tom was used to seeing shock in reaction to his purest thoughts. He lived with such reactions. Had learned to tolerate them. He had simply, but valuably, gone too far once again, and now it was time to change tack. He saw this; he was not a barbarian. The deepest home truths had to be administered by pipette, not by the ladle. And, after all, *both* of them were weak and tired.

"It should—uh—should stop raining soon. The weather report said it was just a squall."

"Wow. You . . . my God . . . wow." Her head was shaking from side to side. "Oh my God. You can just sit there and . . . and just spout this stuff?"

"What? We don't have to talk. It's your umbrella. I'm your guest."

Jess paused. Before she told him that she never wanted to speak to him again—not ever!—should she possibly make sure there wasn't a single grain of truth in his words? No. There was no way this guy, a stranger—and such an unpleasant one—could know more about her than she knew herself. But try as hard as she could, she felt thrown, angry, churned up by his words. Why should they affect her so much, if untrue? And how should she reply to them? Should she protect herself and deny it? And even if Tom was right, even if for a second she allowed this possibility— that her life was an attempt to set something right that was beyond the setting—who asked this guy to tell her such things? Even if he was right, even if *entirely* right (and it was quite possible that she *was* a self-flagellator, a self-punisher), who asked him to throw a hand grenade into the most private places of someone else's life, and then talk about the weather while the wreckage burned? Two words erupted inside her. *Fuck you!* Yes, as unused to swearing as she was, the words reached her tongue and she was grateful for them.

"Fuck you!"

What a defiance she felt! She could be outrageous too. And she knew what to say to him next as well. "You're scared I'm going to win."

"Interesting angle."

"That's your trouble. Ha! I can see that now. That's why you're making all this effort to get under my skin, undermine my confidence. You're scared of me. That's why you've targeted me."

"I . . . actually . . . targeted? Actually, I don't need to undermine anyone's confidence in order to win this contest."

"Want to know what *your* trouble is? You think you're special."

"That's only a problem if it's not true."

Clever. As always he was clever. "Better than other people. That's what you think. And you think this gives you the right to say what you like. So you're really smart, really special? Then what the hell are you doing down here? Tell me. How does such a special person get so desperate that they have to come down here and get their hands dirty like the rest of us? You know what I think? You're pretending to be something you're not. And that's *your* problem. We're all just ordinary people around this car, and you're no different. You're as ordinary as everyone else but you're even worse off. You're not even nice. You're horrible."

He took some time to defend himself. "You don't know anything."

She took less time to apply the coup de grâce. "And you don't know *everything*!"

With the rain pelting down on their low hood, he was silenced at last.

Triumphant. That's how she felt. For perhaps the first time ever, Jess felt the powerful pleasure of telling a person what she really thought of them. And she suddenly saw the huge appeal of living an entire life this way, expressing exactly what you felt, when you felt it. How great it would be to not carry around all the things you shouldn't say, weren't meant to say, let alone *think*, just spitting things out instead, giving as good as you got, first thought, best thought, a clarity in how you did everything, a clarity from not having a head stuffed with murdered thoughts. But then, you'd also have to be really, really tough to suffer the consequences of indulging in nothing but straight talk. People would hate you for it. Really hate you. You'd have to be able to handle that hatred. You'd have to be even tougher than a meter maid.

Even now, her own spasm of triumph was going, going completely, as he pulled away from her and moved back out into the rain, away from the umbrella's protection, visibly offended, taking the full force of the weather on his head in preference to standing close to her any longer.

Her guilt returned—the guilt that kept her a nice person. As always, it was just too hard for someone like Jess Podorowski to upset someone else, then convince herself she'd done them a favor.

. . .

EVENTUALLY, A CANOPY was erected over the Discovery: a rented, sideless, toothpaste-striped awning pitched to protect the remaining twelve contestants from the rain, if not the chill wind. And as this wind rose and as night began to fall around them, Tayshawn returned, coming through the watery night with a red cushion for Walter.

"Here, I dunno, for your restless leg whatever."

A crimson cushion, a velvet seat for a crown: Walter looked touched and lost for words as his fingers dug into its softness. "Will you look at that? Just what I needed. How about that? Isn't that something?" He turned to the others close to him, his face shining again. Held up the gift. "How good is this cushion, huh? Fantastic." He then made a show of pretending that the kid's present gave him some kind of contest-winning advantage. "The rest of you haven't got a chance now."

And who was to say this wouldn't be the case?

Tom looked at the velvet cushion with its brocaded edges and thought: *He stole it from a hotel lobby.* He opened his mouth to say so—"That's a five-star hotel cushion, you little criminal"—but bit his tongue at the last second. At the same time he ached to lie down on something himself, if not a bed, then a cool patch of grass—how nice that would be! To lie down! He thought suddenly of his neighbor. How was his neighbor handling the slow death of his lawn?

Tayshawn looked chuffed as the others nearby nodded and smiled and said, "Could be," and "Might as well give up now."

"See how scared of me they all are now? See? Look at their faces. Terrified."

Tayshawn nodded, pulled back his wet hoodie. Grinned. Lamplight showed his teeth, surprisingly, to be perfect.

Half an hour later, after Tayshawn had slunk back into the night, Walter leaned over to Tom Shrift.

"'Theirs is not to do or die . . .' how's it go again? 'The Charge of the . . .' y'know . . . 'Light Brigade.' 'Theirs is not . . .' Buggered if I can remember it. 'Valley of death.' How's it go?"

From his sullen stupor Tom came to, and tried to remember the first verse for the old boy's sake. But it was no use. Something was haywire. He'd gone completely blank. A poem he'd known since childhood was suddenly strange to him. And the more desperately he pushed, the more elusive it became: "It goes . . . I've got it. Ummm . . . 'Theirs . . . not to do and die. Theirs not to . . .' Rhymes with die." He tried again. Even visualized the regiment on horseback. How many troops? Six hundred, or nine? And what were their orders? *So this is what Alzheimer's is like.* Deeply irritated, he turned away from the old man as the first light rose in the sky. "I'm not in the mood. Sorry. Ask someone else."

Only twelve remained as morning came—theirs not to reason why, theirs but to do and die—twelve. Just twelve survived.

Sixty-three hours now. Into the valley of death rode the . . . rode the . . . into the valley. Rode the brave. Rode the. Rode . . .

JENNIFER BACK GLANCED up from her magazine as her husband came into the living room.

"Still up?" he asked. "It's nearly two." He closed the door behind him. No reply from her. She'd gone back to her magazine, moving through it as if each page: Contained. Only. One. Word. Of. Interest.

"We're down to twelve now," he said. "Something for nothing, it's incredible. You should see these people."

Flap. Flap. Flap. Flap. She turned the pages angrily, a victim in a waiting game of her own.

"The cops might close us down. Weather's ruining it. I have to go back there. Only came for some clean clothes and to drop off some dirty shirts."

There was only silence in this place that he must soon cease to call home. He was about to resign, to surrender the role of husband and father. And then Ronny appeared, in his pajamas, his round, pale face and suddenly infant voice making him seem impossibly fragile, much younger than he was: "I wet my bed."

"I'll do it," Hatch told his wife, going to his son, kissing the boy's crown before taking his chubby, adhesive hand, leading him into the dark hall, fighting back emotions he couldn't share with anyone in this house, while the sound, the wave-like cresting sound of pages being turned, continued unabated behind him.

Only when he had gone did Jen rise and take her husband's dirty shirts to the laundry room where, checking the pockets as she had done for well over two decades, she froze. Two earrings. Silver. Chandelier-style. Not hers.

Her heart exploded.

Upstairs, careful not to wake the other three sleeping children, Hatch quietly dressed his son in new flannelette pajamas, then put him back into bed, soothed him, stroked his back. The shoulder blades stuck out like little wings. His angel. "Bit of a bad dream, was it?"

The boy didn't reply. Hatch struggled to find a very good thing to say next. What do you say to your children to make them feel better about a near-fatal gun blast that was echoing on in their dreams? "At least no one was killed?" No. Such words might soothe an adult—they had soothed Hatch himself—but a child needed to forget the trauma-inducing sound of the gun, the smell of cordite, the jolting recoil, the explosion of woodwork at the side of their sibling's head, the sheer, thunderous death-delivering power of the killing object in their hands, and all this wasn't so easily erased by a single phrase—not, at least, when you were six.

"It was all my fault, champ." Hatch settled on a guilty plea. "Nothing to do with you. Not at all. I should have put it under lock and key. But I was trying to be clever. But you know what I'm going to do now? Know what?"

"What?

"The gun's gone. It's history. You'll never see it again. I don't want it around anymore. This has taught me a big lesson, champ. It was all my fault. Daddy made a big mistake keeping Grandpa's gun, but sometimes daddies do that. Sleep now."

Ronny put his arms around Hatch's neck and squeezed with boyish might. "Good night, Daddy."

"I'll stay with you a minute, okay?"

The boy didn't reply and pretended to be asleep. Hatch pulled up the covers, hid those wings (not quite big enough to carry him away) and kissed the boy's apple-shampoo-smelling hair. He felt suddenly like sleeping here with his son, the whole night long, and his body couldn't resist this call. So, on an impulse, he lay down behind him, sharing half the sweat-damp pillow and adopting the same posture, the same question mark curl of the legs. Side by side, father and son lay in the half-light leaking from the hall, the son's pose figuratively asking of the father, Do you love me? Will you always?, while Hatch's body duplicated these questions, but on twice the scale: Do you? Will you?

Hatch fell asleep.

Then awoke. How long? One minute? Five? He sat up. And his eyes focused on a bedside photo of Grandpa, his own father. Hatch picked up the frame, studied Burt Back, part of a foursome playing golf in the seventies, glancing up handsomely before taking a putt, a putt he would have made. From the rough or sand trap on the back nine, Burt could be relied upon. They called him

Mr. Consistent. And just as his golf partners had benefited, so too had his customers and his kids, the latter in more ways than could ever be tallied on a scorecard. So what did Hatch's own scorecard currently read? Since the old man had passed away, leaving the dealership in his sole care, what kind of golfer had he turned into? He took a guess: midway through his life he was carding about eighteen over after nine—the score of a rank amateur, a Sunday fluffer. One double bogie after another, that was the sorry truth.

He rose, went downstairs. Miserable. Grief broke over him as he decided to stay—in this house, and under this roof. But then this idea so frightened him all over again that he decided just as powerfully to go. And right away. Yes, leave before it was too late. He stood there, breathing heavily, as the impossibility of leaving slowly returned. On the hallway landing, another photo. His eyes settled on the family shot. A wife. A husband. Four children. So many lives, and all of them *his*. His to hold. To protect and serve. He could maybe walk out on two kids, or even three. But four? Four against one. The scales were tipped heavily against him. But in a panic to save himself he realized he had yet to place his own unhappiness on his side of the scale. What weight to give it? If he gave it inflated weight then maybe it would level everything up, allow him to go—didn't he also have a duty to himself? But did his own happiness truly weigh more than each of theirs? How, how could you determine such things?!

His wife was in the bathroom: he could hear a tap running. He took his coat and knocked lightly on the bathroom door and, half hoping she wouldn't hear him, called good-bye, then went out the front door with no decision made, heading back to the dealership and returning to the contest.

4

THE PLACE HAD only just opened for morning cus-
tom, the signs just been put out, when the door burst
open in a manner to which the management of the burger bar was
slowly becoming accustomed.

As on three other mornings, the young man ran in, panting
hard, greeted the three-person staff, said he'd come to pick up the
order he'd just phoned through, then darted into the toilets.

What the staff were less used to, however, was a second visitor
arriving very shortly after and in pretty much the same state. "A,
uh . . . whatever you have . . . a Whopper, I dunno, with a . . . with
a . . . gimmeanything! Whopper meal! Two of them. And coffee!
Come on, come on, come on!"

When Matt returned from the toilets, in a whisker under a
minute, drying his hands on his trousers and frustrated to see that
his order wasn't quite ready yet, he was shocked to be tapped on
the shoulder and turn to see Tom Shrift.

Tom stood there, beetroot-faced, wheezing, somewhat triumphant, filmed in a sweat so shiny that Matt barely recognized him.
"Jesus! It's you. How did you . . . ?"

"What?" Tom gasped. "Easy."

"You . . . you managed it?"

"Not too bad. Not as hard as I— *gasp*. Still got two minutes up my . . . sleeve. So *pant, pant* . . . screw you, fuckface. A foot race back?"

"You're kidding."

Tom barked at the burger boy, waving a ten-pound note. "Come on! Let's go, let's go!"

UP THE ROAD they ran, side by side. And if this gallop was Matt's top speed, then Tom could match it, at least for now.

In truth, Tom hadn't actually wanted the burger, the fries or the coffee he carried, but he felt that the daily adulation lavished on Matt every time he sprinted up and down the road needed to be put into perspective. Everyone, especially Jess, treated this kid's jog as a daily miracle, but Tom knew all the time that any relatively fit specimen, of which he was one (and Tayshawn patently wasn't), should be able to do it. So, risking a great deal, he'd undertaken it.

And there was another reason. One less easy to admit. Jess had impugned his character. Was he ordinary? How dare she. He'd had setbacks, of course this was true, but he'd bounce back. This was what she couldn't see. Few—perhaps no one except himself—knew in what abundance he possessed this elastic capacity! So this morning, right after the whistle blew at first light, he'd let Matt shoot off to great fanfare, and then, quietly, unceremoniously, while everyone else was cooing about the kid's prowess, he walked to the edge of the forecourt and set off himself.

Dan had seen him go. "Don't be daft! What are you doing?"

Tom knew the answer. He intended to show this young stud—plus his coterie of fans (the meter maid in particular)—just who was boss here; he'd prove that stamina came with age, with experience and, most importantly, from the knowledge hard won (and not simply gifted by Daddy!) that when the body said, "Stop, no more, not another step," in actual fact this was a false message, a mental hoax. The best of you was yet to be tapped into, dredged up and put into service. But you didn't learn such things about yourself at twenty. At thirty, you still barely guessed your deeper capabilities and often collapsed at the first obstacle. At forty, the first inklings of your true stickability came, allowing you to take initial soundings and fathom just how *un*fathomed you really were.

Tom had always been precocious in the development area, ahead of the pack ever since his shoulders had broadened at thirteen, leaving him, at forty-two, a veteran of such insights about himself. Great depths lay unseen beneath his unpopular surface. If he didn't yet know the full shape and scope of these emergency reserves, he knew they existed.

I know, he thought as he ran, his arms and legs pumping.

I know. I know . . . Side by side with a twenty-year-old, his feet more or less in unison, Tom drove himself on, thinking, *When push comes to shove, when no one else is left standing, the real Thomas H. Shrift will emerge. This I know, I know, I know . . .*

ON THE FORECOURT, meanwhile, Jess—the contest's overnight superstar—was amazed to look down the street in the first murky rays of dawn to see two men round the corner together and steam toward her at a healthy clip. She hardly believed Tom Shrift capable of this run, having assumed when he'd shot off down the street, with his bulky piston strides, that she'd seen the last of him, that this dash was perhaps his way of resigning.

It wasn't impossible that he might choose such a face-saving method of doing so. Overnight she'd seen that he was really weakening, even as he tried to hide it, with his dry shaves and his clean shirts. This guy, whom she'd always assumed would win, so fiery was his determination, was now fading fast. She had watched an awesome struggle take place in the small hours of dawn, one equal to her own. After telling him he wasn't special, she'd kept a guilty eye on him. And while she had also struggled to keep her own eyes open, withstanding her back pain and bladder ache, and while two then three and then four other people much stronger physically than her had one by one succumbed and fallen asleep or collapsed and dropped out—the minicab driver who had gone through hell in order to own a new working vehicle; the jobless father of four who must now tell his kids he wasn't Superman after all; a triathlete who said he had never done anything so grueling as this; a hippie type from Earl's Court whose meditations and centeredness and knowledge of the Eightfold Path had, in the end, offered no advantage at all—during this night of regular and spectacular collapses, she'd seen Tom actually nod off three times and fight his way back to consciousness without his hand ever quite slipping off the car's body. It had been riveting to watch and had helped to keep her awake, increasing her own heart rate . . . his head drooping and falling, his body swaying and often keeping contact with the car by no more than a single fingertip before a small seizure of panic, maybe his dread of defeat, of coming up short, shuddered him awake, saving him every time.

What was the nature of his panic? She should not have told him he wasn't special. He was a proud man. It was a rotten thing to do. Sure, he'd asked for it, but in truth she'd only been taking a guess at his true character. For he remained a mystery. For instance, what was his secret strategy for winning? And why was his need to win so strong? A single man with no children, no wife, and living in central London, he had no great need of a car. And there must be a million other, far easier ways for him to make money. And yet, when his chin would snap upright again after sleep had carried it down, forcing his eyes to open, blinking, angry at himself, afraid even, anxious to see if anyone had seen this near failure, he looked as though his life—his life!—depended on winning this car. And look at him run now, resurrected, pounding alongside a much younger man, clearly in agony, but somehow running nonetheless. Look how he tried and tried and tried. There was something impressive, surely, something worthwhile in that.

She had to smile. Yes, she thought, making a belated mental reply to his accusation about her, she might be an expert in suffering, a turbine of unexpressed rage, even someone who punished herself over and over; yes, he might be right about all of these things, but— and she had just now seen this—it took one to know one.

THE TWO MEN arrived back at the car at more or less the same instant, Matt looking barely the worse for wear, Tom, his chest heaving, looking as though he'd just made the biggest mistake of his life.

"Well done," Jess told Tom when he collapsed on the car beside her, red in the face, a whistling sound rising from his bellows chest.

"No big. Deal. Fine."

"You don't stop, do you?"

"You stop when you're . . ." but he couldn't pull the air in fast enough ". . . when you're . . . dead." He gripped his knees. His heavy head hung low, as if he was performing some kind of devotion. When he stood up again, he turned to her: "If the thread on the nut holds, you have to tighten it."

Then, astonishingly, from the brown paper bag at his feet he took out two burgers and offered her one.

She shook her head. "No thanks." She was too thrown to accept.

"Take it."

She declined again, then changed her mind. She needed the fuel, and he'd risked losing a new car for this burger. Plus, he was making a rare effort to be nice. This should be rewarded.

As she ate she turned away. Didn't want to let him see her relish. The sunlight just cresting the terraced houses made her squint, but she let the light blind her. The delicious juices filled her mouth, ran down her chin.

Physically, her biggest problem after three days lay with the eyes. To go without sleep this long was like having something in them always—soap suds, an eyelash, dust or, at its worst, iron filings. Such a sting didn't go away either, not even when you closed the lids, rested them. No, this only made the sting worse, forcing you to open your eyes again. In addition, your joints ached continually. Even the hinges of your fingers! In the end you had to do something—and that's when she'd resolved to stop taking her painkillers. They had a sedative effect and she couldn't afford that now. She would pass up relief in favor of sleep-preventing agony. When her eyes now became lead weighted—she thought of a doll whose eyes close when you lay it down—she would shift her weight onto the other leg and the back pain would twinge like magic. She would be good for another ten minutes. Microsleeps had been close by all night but the pain technique had worked. All the same, she felt the next twelve hours would prove decisive. And not just for her. Everyone was hitting some kind of wall and very few would pass through.

"Quit."

Opening her eyes, she saw Tom looking at her. "Quit," he repeated as he took from his pocket a small electric razor, flicking it on.

"No. You quit."

"Quit. Go home."

"No."

He set the razor against his cheek, but the battery was low and the engine whined on the first stubble, puttering to a stop. "You can't win. Don't do this to yourself." He knocked the razor three times against his leg but failed to coax much more life out of it. "Go and do whatever it is you do well. This isn't going to help."

As he turned the razor off and accepted a certain look of dishevelment from now on, she turned away and found, to her dismay, that Dan the marshal was videotaping them all.

AT NOON, A mixed blessing. The heat rose. England, Tom observed, was turning into Spain. At first welcome, allowing one outer layer of clothing to be shed, the temperature passed into the mid eighties: a six-month switch in seasons, breaking a new record for September, just as last September had broken the previous record. America's tailpipes, two thousand tons of toxic gas a day (Tom was still able to quote exact numbers), were to blame for this, drifting at altitude to Britain on the jet stream. The gagging, greenhouse oven that resulted felt like a crime to those on the forecourt. And the person affected first was the insomniac.

He insisted that the car be hosed down, cooled, that it was too hot to touch. Dan came over, tested the hardtop for himself and said it was fine, totally fine, and that the man was imagining it. And this was not impossible.

At the 1:00 p.m. rest stop Tom stepped away from the car. His windpipe carried a tickle that bouts of coughing could no longer clear. He moved stiffly, numbly, through air thickened by others' pain, focusing on his own. He felt oddly light, a little dizzy as he swayed like a man on the deck of a ship. He leaned out, steadied himself against a purple car. He tried to focus on its chrome name . . . Volvo S40 FlexiFuel. He closed his eyes. Behind his eyelids now a strange green glow. He didn't seek to identify it but only added it to the other dysfunctions of his body.

Regaining his balance, he made for the toilets, climbed the steps, went in and closed the plastic door on himself, engaging the half-broken lock. In the cramped space he undid his buckle, feeling vulnerable. The stink had worsened in the heat. A sprung flap in the bottom of the bowl, meant to separate you from the soil of others, hung open, the spring broken. The latrine stench rose. Too late he held his breath.

His lungs harbored the swampy odors, and he thought of Kierkegaard. To hell with Kierkegaard too, believing that the freedom given to mankind leaves the human in a constant fear of failing its responsibilities to God. *Not me, it's my responsibilities to myself that worry me. Look where I am!* He turned, sat and the reek rose between his legs. He exhaled and took a third breath that he held inside as he forced a bowel effort. But he was too seized up inside. Nothing came. And yet he badly wanted to clear his system. He persevered, pushed hard in the way doctors warn against in their hemorrhoid brochures. In the end he managed only a pathetic fraction of what he needed to produce, a walnut instead of a good cord of wood. *A further thought on Jess's idea that I'm scared of being ordinary. A central question. Invisibility in the modern world. The dread of not mattering.* If he was afflicted by this, so then were billions of others. *Just look at all the barbarities committed by people who feared they didn't matter . . . striking out in a violent declaration of "I exist, I exist . . ."* Tom cleaned himself quickly with the shiny tissues, then rose, drew up his trousers, sure he could escape without needing to breathe again. But the door lock gave him trouble, wouldn't shift. He had to open his lungs, draw deeply and he almost gagged, dizzy as he fought with the lock that delayed his exit by several excruciating seconds.

Outside, he gulped fresh air, or at least air as fresh as America would let it be. Even here he was breathing in the muck of others. One thing was for sure: he'd never go into those portable toilets again. He'd rather copy a Mumbai urchin—lower your dhoti and just do it in the street.

He took his bearings. His vision was going. Where the hell was the car? Much was out of focus, and his swollen eyes stung with iron tiredness. He rested against a Volvo, the rear door of which was open—and a wonderful idea came to him. To lie down in the backseat—the luxury of even the thought itself! Spongy leather springing up against his back. . . . He moved closer, and was startled to see that somebody else was already doing just this.

Jess Podorowski.

Lying there on the backseat, her eyes were closed. Was she asleep? Had she collapsed? Tom couldn't tell. And then Dan called out, "Thirty seconds!" Jess didn't stir or show any sign of being awake.

What should he do? Wake her? If he didn't, she might miss the countdown. She would be out of the contest.

He looked at Dan, then back at Jess; Dan pacing, counting, consulting his watch; Jess, not moving, eyes shut. A stark choice. *Long ago we lived in villages,* he thought to himself, *amid extended families. And this is where altruism was born, and where it had a brief reign, in prehistoric times, when if you helped someone else they helped you back. But then big cities arose. Now, we no longer live among family or kin or people who will ever reciprocate our good deeds. Altruism no longer has any point. Helping other people is a prehistoric reflex. End of story.*

And so he decided. He left her there in the backseat, asleep.

Crossing the yard, navigating the cars and feeling woozy, more unshaven than he'd been in years, his heart beating heavily, he lost his balance and fell. The ground loomed. His shoulder and hip bore the brunt. His head escaped a big blow on the ground. After lost seconds he found himself being lifted back to his feet by Dan and being asked if he was okay. He nodded. Yes, he was perfectly fine. "Must have . . . have tripped on . . . on something."

Returning to the car, he steadied himself against it, resetting his hand on the blue metal. Along with the others, and with his back to the yard and to the Volvo in particular. How his shoulder throbbed.

Dan counted down. "Fifteen, fourteen, thirteen, twelve . . ." A terrible time to trip up. Tom regretted showing people this weakness. "Eleven, ten, nine." And as for Jess, it was the right call not to wake her. She couldn't win . . ." Should be home with her child. He was doing her a favor. "Eight, seven, six, five . . ." And a big one too. She ought to thank him, actually. No, he'd never regret not waking her, he thought, as his heart pounded.

But then her hand touched the car just in time. He looked down at her hand, a mirage: narrow, untanned. He looked up at her. She was sleepy. She'd come to, and just in . . .

"Time!" Dan called.

And what did Tom feel? Disappointment, or relief?

JESS RESTED HER head on the side of the car but Dan stepped forward right away and tapped her on the shoulder. Not allowed. Her last warning. She nodded. She wouldn't do it again, she promised. It had been a mistake to lie down in the back of that car: now all the tiredness in the universe was passing through her. She was done in, had nothing left, had been running on empty for two days now. A verse from Job repeated in her head: *And now my life ebbs away; days of suffering grip me. Night pierces my bones; my gnawing pains never rest . . .*

Half in and half out of sleep, in the grip of such pains, she felt a man's hand reach over the blue hood and cover her own.

She felt its human warmth. Matt? Was it Matt's hand? She was slow to look up. Or Tom's, perhaps? No. Neither of them. It was Maciek's hand. He'd come back to her. She looked up. His hair, whitened by a long summer's sun, just as she remembered it from on their last holiday together in Crete, his face tanned, the eyes exaggeratedly blue against the blue of the car, the way the blue walls of a pool make water look extraswimmable. Her first man, her last man: the first ever to undo her bra strap, doing so in a cinema by pinching through the cloth—*snap!*—she was released; the last to kiss her on the mouth. And since then? Paralysis of a kind. Never such a kiss again. She imagined being hugged so tightly that all the bones in her back would click back into alignment.

She withdrew her hand, slid it out from under his. Her husband's smile faded. He even looked stunned, rejected. It used to be the other way around, him who would always pull away into some twilight, but now she turned the tables and withdrew first. And with this withdrawal a tradition was broken between them.

She forced herself awake.

Saw that Tom was looking at her.

"Microsleep. Watch out. Just go home."

"No. You go home."

"Go home."

"You go home."

Jess, Tom, the insomniac, the ex-car thief, Walter, Mrs. McLusky, Betsy, and Matt were going nowhere.

AND THEN THE ants returned, at first just one ant, zigzagging across the hood of the car, perhaps a random scout, but the car thief, methadone-eyed over the last day and talking about the "ants, ants," and saying "the ants are biting me" until it was clear that these tiny creatures had taken up some kind of residency in his mind—he tracked it all the way across the hood, his eyes never shifting from this loner until he spied a second ant arriving, so that suddenly there were two ants, both of them heading in his general direction. And then a third. And then a fourth. This was beyond suspicious. Two ants might be a coincidence, three explicable, but four, and all four of them heading more or less toward him? No, this was a pestilence, an outbreak and suggested a level of mass organization, a counterattack, the one he'd been awaiting for more than two days.

Soon the hood held fifty ants, then not long afterward a hundred, with yet more coming every second, swarming up over the tire and wheel guard so that the thief, a bona fide carjacker who wasn't easily intimidated, started to sweat through his shirt, to lose any vestige of poise and control, overwhelmed by what he was seeing: hundreds, literally hundreds, of ants taking over the car from bumper to bumper as if the entire global empire of antdom were rallying to revenge the genocide of the previous day, a vast summoning of ant tribes to decide once and for all just who—man or ant—had principal claim to the earth.

"God! God!" he shouted.

The first army ant had risen up from the ground to reach the man's collar, stepping onto his neck.

The other contestants turned to see him slapping at his arms, body, neck, even his cheeks. The poor man. There was nothing anyone could see that needed slapping. No cause for alarm.

The thief jumped up and down—"God! God!"—so that everyone within earshot realized that one of their number had broken down, and broken down badly.

"He's gone," Tom decided, raising his free arm, calling for attention, while watching the man rave and beat himself up for no visible reason. "I told you he wasn't right."

"Get them off me! Get them off me!" The thief batted at his face with one hand but, unable to save himself that way, clearly felt he had no choice but to remove his second hand from the car.

And with that he was out.

Yes, another one gone.

Dan was quickly at the scene. He grabbed the hallucinating man, hugged him, stilled the flailing arms in his lifeguard's embrace until, with the peak of hysteria fading, the thief slowly began to regain enough of his senses to realize that the terrifying creatures of his nightmare—if not entirely phantom—were at last withdrawing, and that he was safe, albeit out of the contest.

"Starts out physical. Ends up a mind game," Tom repeated.

"YOU'RE MAKING A mistake," Hatch argued. "You're not gonna get an offer like this anywhere else. Look, Ed, let me show you something else. You don't want the Toyota? Fine. Forget it. Never existed. I'll show you something else. Before you go. I'm going to do a *very* special deal for you. It's your lucky day."

But the buyer, his mind hermetically sealed against any more sales talk, was shaking his head already and saying, "Sorry," and "I wish I could," and "I'm sorry" and "I've really, really got to go now, Mr. Back."

"Five minutes. Stay. Ed. Ed. Ed. Sit down. Listen." But they were wasted words, and Hatch knew it, but it didn't stop a salesman trying—call it the ritual humiliations of his profession. "Give me five minutes. What's five minutes? In a day? In a life? I want to show you something. Ed, please. Okay? Ed, wait till you see what I've got to show you, please."

"I've got to go. I'll see you. I'll see you."

With that, the prospective buyer was gone, gone out of Hatch's reach, the only person to come remotely close to buying a car from the yard during the entire contest.

Failure. The enormity of it, despite Hatch's facility with figures, could not be calculated.

He kicked his desk, then went to glare at the picture of his father hanging on the wall. *What? What?* What did a person have to do? Beyond trying as hard as you could, what else? But the picture delivered no paternal fiat, no healing answer.

He turned back to the view on the yard. Look at those crowds! More and more people had come just to watch, swelling the ranks of the supporters, doubling their size—but none seemed interested in his cars, none.

Vince and Dan appeared in the doorway. "Hatch? We've got something to tell you. We're leaving."

Hatch turned. "Leaving?"

"Dan and me."

"Leaving? Who? Who? What do you mean? Come on." Hatch looked genuinely disorientated, lost.

"We'll finish today, help you out today, but that's it."

"That's . . . what?"

"Hatch. We're leaving. Quitting. It's over."

Hatch finally found his tongue. "Come in, Vince. Sit down. Dan, take a seat. I need to talk to you about something. Please."

"We don't want to talk about this."

"Sit down." He raised his voice; his temper was going. "Please!" Then dropped his voice. "There's a reason I haven't paid you. Shut the door. I haven't told you everything. Shut the door. Please."

Vince finally relented and shut the door. Hatch sat soberly in his chair and rested one palm facedown on the leather-inlaid desktop, as if offering some sort of testimony, taking some oath. "My back's against the wall, guys. I've kept something from you till now. But now you deserve to know. I'm in six feet of shit and I'm five foot eleven, understand? I've told no one. Not even my wife. The business is going under. I've been standing on tiptoes for two years. I'm bankrupt. I'm finished unless this contest makes a difference—and I can't run it without you."

"Bankrupt? Are you serious?"

"I'm in your hands. Your hands." He pointed to Dan first, and then Vince. "I should have told you. That's why I haven't paid you. I'm sorry. But give me two more months. Don't you know I would have paid you if I could? You thought I was keeping all the money back for myself? There's nothing for myself. But let's all three of us turn this around. Together. Let's use all this great publicity that we've generated and turn this around."

The boys stared at Hatch. Dan replied unsteadily, "We got our own families—"

But before this argument could sway even the speaker, Hatch retaliated, employing twice the passion of the two younger men combined. "I need you. So help me to help you. I'm asking you, I'm begging you even. Let's work this out together. We're family. Let's not give up on each other—not now, not after all this time. You showed loyalty to my father"—pointing to the glassed-in picture of the man who had given both young men their start—"now show it to me."

Vince and Dan had expected resistance, but had little armor against words like *please* and *beg,* against surprising words like *bankrupt* and *sorry,* or rending words like *family* and *loyalty:* these cut through their defenses and left them stranded, unable suddenly to reject outright this request, even though two minutes earlier they'd been certain there was no way Hatch could talk them around.

But before they could even speak, the door opened behind them.

The male half of Team McLusky—pale, panting, saying, "Come now!"

WALTER.

There was something very wrong with Walter. No one could rouse him. The facts were sketchy. He hadn't spoken during the last two-hour stretch, then he'd gone missing. Halfway through this rest stop he'd been found sleeping, sitting on the ground, his back against the Land Rover, his chin on his chest, the red cushion in his lap.

Hatch was summoned. He pushed through the crowd, found Walter sitting just like that, his color very bad. In fact, there *was* no color. The guy was giving no life signs. Tom Shrift was already attending him, shouting for an ambulance as word about Walter started circulating.

At first Hatch didn't know what to do any more than anyone else did. Wasn't prepped for this. The rising noise level made it hard for him even to think straight. The color, the old man's hue— a yellowy marzipan white—looked bad.

"What is it? What's the matter with him?"

Tom said exactly what he thought. "I think he's gone."

"Gone?"

"I can't feel . . . no, nothing," Tom said. "No pulse. Nothing. I think he's . . ."

Many gasped. Turned away. The word *gone* and the color and the stillness seemed to close the case. Some reached out to whoever stood close by, felt the need to just touch someone else and be touched back.

"There must be a pulse," Hatch barked. "Check again. Keep checking. Keep . . . just keep . . . Jesus Christ! What's the matter with him?"

Tom looked up, red in the face, preparing already to give mouth to mouth. "I told you. Get an ambulance!"

Jess put her hand over her mouth. Matt and Betsy stood by, staring down, and Matt held Betsy tightly. The insomniac, and the remaining supporters and onlookers, all watched in silence.

Tom was the only one who knew what to do. While on his own forehead four raised veins fanned upward and out, anxiety lines that hadn't been there till now, he laid Walter down, tipped back the old man's head, extended the neck and then, with a forefinger, probed into the wet mouth, extracted the dentures with two fingers. These, warm and filmy, he handed to Hatch, who held them, cupped them, in his joined palms.

Dan, late arriving, unzipped his jacket. "I'll take over. I'll do it. Stand back." The lifeguard's big moment had come.

Vince meanwhile looked at his watch. And remembered something. "Oh. Twenty seconds, everyone else! Till the contest starts again."

"To hell with the contest," Matt muttered, pale at last.

"Oh God," said Betsy, biting a thumbnail as Matt's arms failed to stop her trembling.

"I'll take over," Dan repeated. "Let me in. I'll do it now. I'm a trained lifeguard. Let me in. Let me do it now."

But Tom refused to give way and had already begun CPR, applying his mouth to the gaping bristle-encircled lips, Walter's chest rising and falling between breaths.

"Please. I'll do this now. I'll take over now," Dan insisted, but again Tom ignored him and began to drive the heel of his hand into Walter's chest, counting aloud as he pumped hard.

Vince was marshaling the other contestants. "You others, back on the car. Back on the car. We can handle this. Back on the car." He looked anxiously at his watch again, then turned to Hatch. "We're gonna blow it."

This finally gave Hatch something to do. "Okay. You heard. Everyone else! Back on the car! Come on! Contestants, back on the car!"

Vince crouched then at Tom's side, put a hand on his shoulder. "Tom, you too. The ambulance is on its way. Dan, you take over." But slow-witted Dan still didn't force Tom aside and merely nodded, eager, compliant, so that Vince had to bark at his colleague. "Now! And Tom? No sense in this. Ten seconds, Tom. Put your hand back on the car. Seven. Dan? Get going! Tom? Five. Four. *Tom!* Three . . ."

And as Dan finally pushed in, Tom gave over the CPR and put his one hand back on the Discovery.

And just like that, with Dan now beginning to hammer the old man's chest so strongly that onlookers winced (obliging Tom to inform them that it had to be like that, and that when you did it right you should crack a rib), and with Betsy crying on Matt's shoulder, and with Walter lying there, and with Dan trying to save his life, the contest resumed.

WALTER WAS ALIVE. A pulse had been detected. The paramedics from the ambulance divulged as much before they stretchered Walter, awfully gaunt and with his eyes still closed, back to the waiting ambulance. This piece of hopeful information circulated quickly. Walter was going to be fine. The old boy had just given everybody a real scare. There was nothing to worry about. What a relief!

But Hatch was taking nothing for granted. He went indoors and made calls to the hospital. He was a relation, a cousin, he told the nurses, and could they call him back when they knew anything?

A half hour later, St. Mary's called back. News.

Walter had died.

Fuck. A powerful gut wrench. A dizziness. Blood moving in the wrong directions. Systems backing up. Balled fists. Hatch was all alone in his office with no one to see him. No one there to tell. Outside six people labored on in a contest that had been all his idea. Fuck. What was happening? What had he done?

He thanked the nurse, then put down the phone. Called in Vince and managed to say, "He's gone. Walter. He passed." Hatch told all he knew—that by the time the medics had got the old man to A&E the heart had stopped. Couldn't be revived. Cause of death not yet available. He told Vince to go get Dan, then waited. Looked at the phone thinking, *Dead.* And then, *Did I kill him?* No, he refused to think this. Oh Walter. Jesus, it was terrible. Terrible.

"Holy Jesus," Dan said when he heard. Vince added, with a slow release of chest air, "I know." And then the phone rang again. An inquiry about a Renault Laguna. Hatch cut the call, asked the buyer to ring back tomorrow.

"We gotta call it off," Dan decided. "The contest. Don't we?"

Hatch nodded, then shrugged. "I don't know. But we have to handle this somehow."

"Poor bastard," offered Vince. "It's so weird. One minute you're here . . ."

The way it looked to Hatch right now, the contest had to be over, but at the same time, the contestants were owed a car. Vince and Dan agreed—it wasn't a clear-cut thing—then bowed their heads spontaneously. Dan even folded his hands. "God rest his soul."

"What the hell do we do?" Hatch asked, looking more toward the picture of his father than at the two junior salesmen.

Vince lifted his eyes. "Uh-oh."

Out the window he'd seen a police car pull into the forecourt.

TWO OFFICERS. THEY'D been notified about Walter, and they stood now in Hatch's office, their faces stony, obdurate, set against him.

"In the light of what's happened here, permission to stage this event has been withdrawn," the more senior officer said, one officious thumb tucked into a belt buckle heavy with appended weaponry and anticriminal technology. Hatch glimpsed a sidearm, a small, holstered snub-nosed gun, buttoned down. The contest had clearly passed into a new category—it was unsafe. "Do you have anything to say?"

Hatch, humbled, shook his head. "I'm willing to fully assume my share of responsibility." Had they even come to make an arrest?

"You've got till five p.m., then."

"To—"

"Clear the yard, sir. Just clear the yard."

HATCH'S WHOLE BODY was invisibly aquiver as he switched on the loud hailer. When it squawked, he switched it off for good and with his natural voice asked everyone to step into the showroom.

On the whistle they filed inside. Hot coffee was set into six cold hands. Hatch addressed them all. The worst imaginable thing had happened, he began.

Jess gave a little gasp, clamped her left hand over her mouth, anticipating the rest.

"Walter. I'm sorry. Walter's gone."

Betsy let go a squeal and cried. Matt comforted her, lifting back strands of blonde hair from her face. Tom turned toward Jess to try to do something similar, but she was hugging the red cushion. As for the insomniac and Mrs. McLusky, these two could only stare at Hatch and nod mutely.

Matt was the first to speak. "You can't do this."

Insomniac: "No way."

Matt: "I'm not leaving. Not after all this."

Mrs. McLusky shook her head. Exhausted anyway, and on her last legs, this was perhaps the mental excuse she needed. "That's it, then. You cheated us. You're a cheat."

"I'm sorry. I really am."

And with this, Mrs. McLusky made her way out the showroom door. The others watched through the glass double doors her return to her faithful husband, who had been supporting her on the yard since day one. They fell into a tearful embrace.

Tom was the first to speak again. "I'm not going anywhere until I get a brand-new car. I don't know about anyone else."

Jess also: "I have to have a new car."

"Well," answered Hatch, "I'd love to give you *all* a new car, I really would, but this contest is now illegal."

The insomniac, disgusted, but resigned, worn-out entirely and therefore more disposed to adopt Mrs. McLusky's line: "So that's it, then? You got everything you w-w-wanted, didn't you? Publicity. And you get to k-keep the car as well."

Matt spoke defiantly: "We're not leaving. No way. Not without compensation."

Tom too: "You'd better sort this out."

But Hatch opened his balled hands, showed his white palms. "How? Tell me how? I feel terrible. I want to continue. For me personally, I want to go on. But . . ." He raised one hand, then set it on his chest ". . . but the police have left me no choice. I can't break the law. And they'd close us down anyway."

Jess, silent, lowered her chin onto Walter's cushion, held tightly in her hands.

Matt shook his head. "To hell with it. We're not going anywhere. I'm not going anywhere. Not unless someone gives me a new car."

And on this point, Matt and Jess and Tom—and to a lesser extent, the insomniac and Betsy, who both looked to have accepted the inevitable—stood firm. They stared down the car dealer with determined faces. Gridlock. Tom framed the salesman's difficulties perfectly. "Looks to me like you've got a problem on your hands." Glancing at the time, he added, "And by my watch, the five of us have all got about . . . thirty seconds to get a hand back on that car."

. . .

IN ADDITION TO her other complaints (all-over body pain, memory loss, coordination problems, difficulty focusing), Jess found that her speech patterns had begun to break down also. Her head, already functioning badly, left a tired mouth destitute. She had to struggle to make her point. "He was on meds. On medication. For his. His. Heart. But he stopped. Taking the pills while he was. He told me that. I mean. He . . . that he . . ." She sighed—too weary for tears—then clasped Walter's red pillow tightly with one arm, resting her head on its velvety softness. "He told me that."

Tom looked at his watch. The police must soon appear.

Betsy then whispered something to Matt, who reacted with less surprise than might have been expected. "Are you sure?"

Betsy nodded, before looking up and addressing the others. "I can't do this anymore. I don't think this is right. There's no point anyway. I don't want to go on."

Taking a deep breath she turned back to Matt and smiled. "I won you instead." Laying her head on his chest, closing her eyes peacefully she told anyone who wanted to listen: "I won him instead." And with her eyes still closed, she finally lifted her hand off the car.

Just like that.

It was done.

Her hand rose above the blue metal and hovered there.

Betsy was out.

"Free. Free at last," she said.

The others stared at her, speechless, as if so radical a course of action had never once occurred to them. Even the gusting wind fell away to nothing.

She'd performed her own magic act. She'd liberated herself. Done the unthinkable. Had taken her hand off *intentionally*. And with her suffering abruptly at an end she lifted her hands higher, covered her face entirely and groaned, "Oh God!" Was she about to cry? "How does that *feel*!? Oh my God!" But when her hands slid away they revealed a rapturously smiling face. "That feels . . . *sooo* good." In that moment, as the others watched, Betsy became the perfect advertisement of what a mass with-drawal from this contest would feel like. With their dead eyes trained on her arms raised to the sky and on that delirious, sad, ecstatic grin, they saw their own dreamed-out vision of victory dissolve around them.

Matt kissed her forehead. "Go home. Get some sleep," he said softly. "I'll see you back here when you're ready."

Betsy nodded, smiled at their lovers' pact, then stepped away from the car and walked with slow, dragging footsteps toward the supporters, who rose to give her a solid round of applause.

As the contest teetered on the brink of collapse after that, with the four remaining survivors toying seriously with the idea of following Betsy's lead, and with all keenly aware that their endurance feat of four days standing would be all over by 5:00 p.m. with no reward for any of them, few now spoke more than a word.

Fittingly, perhaps, it was the insomniac who broke the silence. Proposed a solution. Expressionless, slurring, his eyes reptilian red, and his stutter weirdly half cured as if it were only the most recent bodily function to quit on him, he outlined a plan. He lifted his head and opened his eyes.

"Okay. I don't even want to suggest this because I was going to beat you bastards, but . . . the cops are on their way. It's over. Unless we do something."

Matt, Jess and Tom slowly raised their eyes.

"We end this now. Before the . . . before the cops do. Four. F-four of us. Okay? We all take our hands off the car, share the prize. Split it. Four ways."

Tom stared at him. The insomniac looked a complete mess. The threadbare mustache matched the exhausted verdure of the scalp. The facial skin had become eczematous. The man breathed now through an open mouth. Crazed-looking, the extruded eyes were unblinking. He was clearly finished anyway. Was he asthmatic as well? Tom imagined a bedside ashtray full of butts. In horrible shape internally too. This was what really lay behind this appeal, Tom conjectured. Not some grand impulse to share. No, this was the idea of a beaten man. The single eye in Tom's profile blinked slowly. "The moment you suggested that, you just lost."

"We're gonna come out of this with nothing! Unless we do this together. Three, two, one, we all take our hands off. I'm gonna do it. Join me."

Tom was already shaking his head. "What are you, a Communist? I need the whole thing."

Jess sleepily agreed: "Me too."

"But that's not gonna happen. So be smart, okay? Be *smart!*" The insomniac's eyes blazed with the sudden excitement of a man promoting an idea too irresistible to be rejected. "By fighting each other we all lose. So let's beat these bastards. So here we go. On the count of three I'm lifting my hand. If you do too, we all win. If you don't we lose. *We lose.* The cops break this up and we get nothing. So here we go." Those wild eyes, content to accept a much-reduced share, looked to confirm in the eyes of his rivals that they would join him. "I'm doing it. So here we go . . ."

But Tom cut him off: "The moment you suggested that, you just quit."

Matt shook his head also. "Count me out. But you go ahead."

The insomniac hissed, "See sense!"

But Tom was emphatic. "If you want to take your hand off, you're on your own."

On his own? The insomniac stared in disbelief at this refusal to accept his perfect solution. "Losers," he hissed, with no choice now but to go on contesting a car none of them could any longer win. "Go on, then, fine. Keep going till the cops show up. Have your full share of zero. To hell with you all. I'm-I'm-I'm ashamed to have even been part of this." But instead of making a powerful final statement of disgust by walking away from the event at this point, the man remained where he was, along with the others, making a complete mockery of the great nineteenth-century, European-born non-zero-sum solution he'd so passionately championed just a second before.

Silence on the forecourt.

Until Dan came up to the car. Under his arm was a framed picture of Walter he'd hastily mocked up using his computer. It showed Walter, smiling, with a hand on the car—a shot from day one. With deep Christian respect, the part-time lifeguard set the frame on the roof of the Discovery. Everyone nearby said this was lovely. And from then on, with the roof of the car firmly established as a repository for flowers and cards in memory of Walter, the four survivors more and more resembled pallbearers with one hand on a flower-decked coffin.

THAT WAS WHEN the soldier, like some plague in the Book of Exodus, walked back onto the yard.

Great, thought Tom. *All we need.*

And something was amiss with Corporal Roy Sewell. His semisanity of the first couple of days must have been a triumph of medications, because now he looked scary. Free of whatever personality inhibitors he had been on, the man was now dressed in camouflage gear and high-laced jackboots, bizarrely battle ready, his eyes blazing with some kind of combat readiness.

He walked straight up to the Discovery. And in a machine-gun burst of speech announced that they all had ten seconds to take their hands off the vehicle or someone would get hurt.

Hurt?

"You heard me! *Hands off!*"

Hands off?

Tom appeared to be the only one who could work out what was going on. "Terry Back's behind this," he said. "It's a stunt. Hey, Rambo! Good to see ya. So where's your shotgun? You forgot your shotgun."

"Ten, nine, eight . . ." The soldier's voice was raised to parade-ground levels. "Seven, six, five, four, three, two, one . . . time's up."

And then he walked straight up to the Discovery and dumped a nylon knapsack on the roof, right next to the photograph of Walter.

"IN THAT KNAPSACK IS A BOMB. DO NOT ATTEMPT TO TOUCH THE KNAPSACK. YOU NOW HAVE TWO MIN-UTES TO RETIRE FROM THE VEHICLE BEFORE I ACTIVATE THE EXPLOSIVE MATERIAL INSIDE . . . TWO MINUTES . . . STARTING NOW." He stared intently at the large sports watch on his wrist.

What had he said? Did anyone else hear this? A bomb?

"What's going on?" asked the insomniac, as if all this had to be some kind of joke.

"He said he's got a bomb in this bag!" Jess said. "He said he's put a bomb in this bag! He said it. He said he's going to activate it. That's what he said."

"This must be the dealership trying to get us to walk away," Matt concluded.

"IN THAT KNAPSACK IS A BOMB. DO NOT ATTEMPT TO TOUCH THE KNAPSACK. YOU NOW HAVE ONLY A MINUTE AND A HALF TO RETIRE FROM THE VEHICLE BEFORE I ACTIVATE THE EXPLOSIVE MATERIAL IN-SIDE . . . TWO MINUTES . . . STARTING NOW. DO IT! DO IT NOW!"

The contestants all stared at the soldier, and when an onlooker stepped toward him, Roy raised high a mobile phone and told him sharply, "STAND BACK OR I WILL ACTIVATE THE EXPLO-

SIVE MATERIAL." Then came the first scream from the crowd. It gave chilling credence to the man's threat. The unhinged look in his eyes finally told the contestants that the man wasn't kidding around. They were all standing beside a car that had a bomb in a knapsack on its roof. All four contestants swung and stared at it, black, nylon, zippered, sitting there right beside the picture of Walter, beside Walter's flowers.

But while panic grew in the onlookers and they began to run about, Tom and Jess and Matt and the insomniac didn't move a muscle. The soldier grew tired of this. "I WON'T WARN YOU AGAIN. DO AS CORPORAL SEWELL SAYS." The voice was almost electronically simulated, so monotonically droning was it. "THAT'S AN ORDER. ONE MINUTE THIRTY LEFT. STEP AWAY FROM THE CAR, OR I *WILL* ACTIVATE THIS DEVICE."

A bomb threat in a car dealership in Olympia. Suddenly the contest was the epicenter of a nightmare, one of global significance. A soldier, lost in some interior battle scenario, was saying he was prepared to take lives. Cold, clinical, who could doubt him?

"WHEN I PUSH THE CALL BUTTON ON THIS PHONE . . . IT WILL RING THREE TIMES AND THEN THE KNAPSACK WILL EXPLODE. IS THAT CLEAR? I DON'T WANT TO HURT ANYONE. I REPEAT, I DO NOT WISH TO HURT ANYONE, BUT I *WILL* PUSH THE CALL BUTTON ON THIS PHONE. SO DO AS I SAY AND TAKE YOUR HANDS OFF THE CAR AND MOVE AWAY."

A young woman with a child in her arms screamed, "Bomb!" Confusing in its implications, but crystal clear in its power to generate public panic, this word—coming from her mouth—activated the crowd and drove them back. Many turned and ran full tilt down the street. Memories of Liverpool Street. The Oxford Street bus bomber. The IRA campaigns of the seventies. Urban terror-

ism in its latest manifestation. Recent atrocities made new luna-
cies seem almost to be expected. *Of course* there was a bomb in
the knapsack, ready to be detonated with a cruelly simple phone
call. Why wouldn't there be a bomb? This was London, twenty-
first-century London. And so they ran.

But Matt and Jess and Tom and the insomniac remained right
where they were. So surreal was the moment, so out of the blue
and so unfathomable to people so sleep-deprived and struggle-
weakened, that they didn't move a muscle, but looked at one another questioningly, speechless, confounded, confirming by quick
looks and inaction that this threat was . . . well, it was simply more
than they could cope with right now, and unless they heard more
than just random talk of a bomb, or at least *feared* the word *bomb*
more than they feared the consequences of taking their hands off
the car, then they'd just stay where they were.

It was a standoff.

A great insubordination.

And the soldier, holding his mobile phone aloft, stunned
to find his wishes not respected, stared at the four who stared
right back at him, equally stunned and unmoving, and his voice
became shrill.

And then Dan arrived. It took this lieutenant several valuable seconds to get up to speed with what was going on. Quickly
briefed—"A bomb! He has a bomb!"—he nervously prepared
himself to do as he'd once been trained to do. Save lives.

"Okay, everybody leave the yard! *Now!*" His voice sought
authority. "Everybody back! Everybody back! Back! Everybody
back!"

The machine-like soldier looked at his watch, then at the four
contestants who refused to heed him. "FORTY-FIVE SEC-
ONDS." He'd gone to a great deal of trouble to be taken seriously.
"I'M NOT KIDDING AROUND HERE. I'M EX-MUNITIONS.
UNDERSTAND?" At this, he held up his mobile phone and men-

acingly backtracked fifteen paces, allowing everyone a vivid spatial sense of the carnage he intended to wreak. The uniform, the camouflage colors, the army history, made it unthinkable that he didn't have the means to make a bomb. Who could doubt that such a guy, rewired by war, very damaged looking, had the will to press the call button on his mobile phone?

Insomniac: "We . . . we gotta get outta here. We gotta d-do as he s-says."

Jess: "Should we do?" Uncertain, she looked to Tom for an answer, but received none in reply.

Matt was growing in panic too. "We've got to do as he says. We can't just . . . we can't just . . ."

"What should we do?" Jess asked Tom urgently, but again drew only a deep sigh from him.

"Look, it's a con," he finally offered, looking as if he was revealing a secret. "He's just trying to . . . to ruin the whole thing. But hey, you guys take off. Fine. I'll wait here."

For Matt and Jess, at least, this statement altered the complexion of the threat, downgraded it two levels. Tom seemed to know something, and suddenly the bomb seemed more like his own work, designed to test who had the stronger nerve within a massively compressed time frame.

"THIRTY SECONDS."

Ignoring Tom, the insomniac preferred to take the word of a soldier in battle dress. "It's a bomb. He s-s-said. In that bag, there. We . . . we . . . we gotta do as he says."

But Tom, with a shrug: "Then take your hand off the car."

Yes, it was almost as if Tom had organized this diversion himself, and resentment and anger showed in the faces of Matt and the insomniac.

"No. We all do it. Together," Matt insisted. "We take our hands off together. If we do it, we do it together. Or else . . ."

Jess looked at the knapsack sitting only a few inches away

from her hand. The cheap nylon black zip-up with ADIDAS written on the side looked so harmless, but she dared not touch it. "How? How do we . . . do it together?" she asked.

Matt: "Are we agreed?"

"TWENTY SECONDS!"

The insomniac's eyes had grown livid. The shakes had set in big time. Only twenty seconds to live. The man looked as if the taste of cordite was already on his tongue, as if he sensed the shrapnel lodged already in his pancreas, in the back of his brainpan, shredding his legs, arms, his scrotum. "Twenty seconds," he said! "Twenty seconds." By the time he'd said this, only sixteen seconds to live.

Matt, his eyes wide: "On the count of three, then. Okay? Everybody? *One!*"

The four looked at one another. Eyes sought eyes, wishing to bind one another to their shaky agreement. And while Jess looked at Tom for direction, Matt looked to find consensus in all three faces before he deigned to speak the next number.

"FIFTEEN!" the soldier said, getting in first.

Matt, more importantly: *"Two!"*

Matt's too-slow process of counting, drawn out by fears of last-second betrayals, was unacceptable to the insomniac, who was poised to explode in his own right. "Let's go! C-come on, c-c-come on! Let's take our hands off." He was taut and ready and saw hope return to his plan of sharing the car. "We split it four ways! Come on!" Too many numbers. Far too many counting people and ticking threats. Death. Death was coming. "Hurry up!" he shouted.

And then Matt finally said it. *"Three!"*

But who lifted their hand off? Not even Matt himself. Even then they found themselves incapable of fusing their personal plans into one grand scheme.

"Do it!" Matt screamed.

"*You* do it," Tom replied with an eerie calm.

"Oh shit!" Jess wailed, trapped, realizing at last that she was in some kind of prison of her own making.

So there they stayed, unable to let go, programmed to do nothing more than keep a hand on a car, no matter what—to struggle toward a finishing line grown entirely hallucinogenic.

Corporal Sewell called, "FIVE!" even more brutally, keeping at least three seconds between every beat—not a precise, chromatic countdown now but rather one calibrated to allow for maximum tension and changes of heart. He really did seem to want to give these people a chance.

And with this, the insomniac lost it. Pallid and spooked, he too vividly saw his life and his career and even the atoms of his body flashing before his eyes. Everything in him quit. He hadn't lost all rationality, not yet, so lifted his hand, lifted it—it was only a car after all. And then he turned, and on the count of "FOUR!" and then "THREE!" he ran, determined to save himself, and so he was ten, then twenty, then forty, fifty feet away from the Land Rover by the time the soldier hailed: "TWO!"

On the car, and feeling that Jess would be next to break, Tom reached out with his free hand, placed it on her car-bound one. "The guy's full of shit," he whispered urgently. "Stay where you are. Listen to me. Nothing's gonna happen." He set his mouth close to her ear so Matt could not hear. "There's no bomb. It's a hoax. Understand?"

Jess stared back at him, her brows ridged, then said, too loudly for Tom's liking: "How? How do you know it's a hoax?"

Tom shook his head, dismayed, and turned to see that these words were all the livid-eyed Matt needed to help him stick with this contest for the last remaining seconds.

"How do you know it's a hoax?" she repeated.

"ONE. *ONE!* Last chance!" shrieked the soldier in his loudest voice yet.

"Trust me." Just that, from Tom. A whispered "trust me."

And with Tom's spare hand keeping Jess's vital one in place, she didn't retreat. She did what she was told, and in by far the longest second of her life she stared only into Tom's face, placing her trust in this near stranger, this weirdo whose sleep-extruded eyes told her she had nothing to worry about.

And what came next? A bloody holocaust? The jolting dissection of bodies? No. Only silence. A blessed silence. Was this what eternity felt like, Jess wondered. This breathless waiting?

No, no one died. No blast tore them to pieces. Only the entirely lovely silence, the ecstatic stillness.

Jess and Tom didn't take their eyes off each other, not until the soldier came close and said, "You people are crazy."

He was standing close to the contestants now, still holding aloft his terrible phone but apparently no longer astonished to find that he was being entirely ignored. An almost admiring tone marked his departing words: "I hope it's worth it, you crazy bastards."

With this he grabbed the nylon knapsack off the car roof, then turned and ran, throwing his phone into the crowd at the yard's edge, where it fell at the feet of Vince, holding the breathless public at bay, just as Hatch ran out to see what was going on with his dealership, his contest, his life.

The panting insomniac, standing at a safe distance, watched as the soldier, looking not dangerous now but afraid, brushed past him. Seeing him at close range, he realized he'd been fooled.

Vince stooped and picked up the mobile phone, now smashed. Its insides were exposed as being molded plastic.

"A toy," he declared. "It's a toy." He raised his voice further so all could hear. "It's only a toy!"

BACK IN HIS office again, shaken by so much chaos, Hatch began to count the cost. With Vince, he stared at the window at the three still refusing to walk away from the car he'd offered as a prize. How ridiculous the contest suddenly seemed. "I gave it my best shot."

"You did." Vince consoled his boss. "You did."

"I really *tried.*"

"You couldn't have done more."

"And if this thing out there hadn't happened, and the cops hadn't . . . hadn't imposed this . . . we could have . . . who knows."

"I know. No one's blaming you. No one."

Hatch looked at his employee with deep gratitude. In a grasping world, one in which he'd hardly done the right thing by this man, Hatch was being repaid with loyalty. An unforeseen rebate. "Thanks, Vince."

The salesman and Vince were staring forlornly out the office window into the yard when Tom walked in on them. He had an idea.

Hatch: "What idea?"

Tom cleared his head. "I realize you've probably got your own solutions by now but I'd like to offer a suggestion." The two men stared back at him. "We take the show, the contest, on the road."

"What do you mean, *on the road*?"

"We get the four-by-four up on a flatbed, you drive us around. We get to keep a hand on the car, you've cleared the yard. We go mobile, take to the road."

He waited for a reaction. Hatch and Vince exchanged looks, and then Vince at least showed symptoms of interest.

"Could work. Why not? Hey, why not. That's not a bad idea, Hatch."

Hatch was already foreseeing the problems. "We'd have to . . . we'd have to run it by the Guinness people."

Tom: "THEN I SUGGEST YOU RUN IT BY THE FUCK-ING GUINNESS PEOPLE!"

So three remain. So my spies tell me. Despite a bomb scare—yes, a bomb scare—despite a hoax intended to

*deter them, three brave and near-demented souls are now
into their fourth day without a wink of sleep. That's one
hundred and fifteen hours, I'm told. And I have chosen my
heroine. How are you feeling, Jess Podorowski? My money's on you, sweetheart. And I'm not alone. Our lines are
jammed with people wanting you to show us that a selfless
love will conquer all. Now you may say I'm a dreamer . . .*

When the police arrived back at the yard at twenty to five, Hatch was
for a minute unsure about whether they'd come about the bomb
scare, or simply as promised. Nonetheless, he was ready for them.

"Let's get a move on," he told Vince and Dan. "Clear the yard.
But don't tell anybody the reason yet."

Vince and Dan moved toward the crowd, started ordering
people to leave. Loud questions arose but no explanations were
offered. Two just-arrived members of the press, sensing a head-
line, sniffed tabloid gold in this unexpected twist. What were the
police doing here? They stepped forward, crowded Hatch. What
was going on? Was the contest in jeopardy?

Hatch revealed nothing. Instead, he returned to the police,
asked if the three remaining contestants could be allowed to reach
the next official rest period before leaving the yard permanently.
"That's just ten minutes away. All I'm asking."

The coppers consulted, looked at their watches, then agreed
to the request. "Ten minutes."

Hatch joined Dan and Vince in drawing down the blimp. No
sooner had they loosened the fastening cleats, however, than they
were taken by surprise by the strength of the wind and by the
blimp's helium pull. In a second they lost grip of it. The cable shot
through their fingers.

Up the blimp rose. Majestic, fast-fleeing, the text on its side,
WIN A NEW CAR, soon an eyesight test for those on the ground,
harder and harder to discern until clouds swallowed the balloon

entirely. The contestants, not to mention Hatch and Dan and Vince, turned to look at the police for their reaction.

Hatch was the first to speak. "It'll pop when it gets high enough. It's sorted. We were told that, if this happened, they implode at ten thousand feet. I've got all the guff on it inside, I can show you."

As the police phoned their base to clarify the matter of a feral blimp, and the two reporters waited, Hatch and Dan and Vince locked down the yard, sealed doors, drew chains over the drive-in, fastened padlocks on the garage, untied the yellow WIN A NEW CAR banner and began to wrap it around a trailer with high-sided cage walls.

Tom pulled out his earbuds. His vision was wonky. He felt drugged and in danger of collapse. His knees had swollen badly. Someone in the crowd vocalized unexpected support . . . but not for him, of course.

"Go, Jess!"

No, never for him. He turned, and noticed that Jess was staring at him.

"So—you just proved me wrong about you," she said. "That was special."

Tom shrugged. "Obvious. The army don't issue shotguns to their troops. Everyone knows that. The guy was a total nutter. Never been in the army. I spotted right off that he was a fake."

"Not just that," she added. "Coming up with this idea. Of taking the contest, on the . . . on the . . . of, um . . ."

"Road. Obvious again."

"Go, Jess! Go, Jessie! All the way, girl!" shouted two rouged and hennaed elderly women standing with a couple of schoolgirls and a teenage boy, all smiling and waving their support now as Dan blew the whistle for the next rest stop and as Vince tried to herd everybody off the forecourt.

"You're quite smart, then, aren't you?" Jess asked him.

"Some have said so." Tom couldn't resist a half smile before his eye flicked to the crowd, his vision slowly focusing on two female protesters holding placards that read STOP THE CONTEST and PEOPLE ARE VALUABLE TOO. Were they here to defend him? Then why were they singling him out for their angry looks? Wasn't he valuable too?

Jess was studying him anew. He'd stopped shaving. The fresh shirts had also ceased and his current one looked grimy. Somehow, she preferred him like this. "And you were right about me, by the way."

He shrugged. "Forget about it."

But for her the moment had come, and the words gushed out: "People say I should move on. I know they're right. I would if I could. But I don't know how to." She spoke with cracked, dry lips, but it felt good to have these words pass over them. "I *am* a mess," she confessed. "I know it."

"Okay. It's none of my business. But actually you're fine. You're totally—you're great."

"You—you? You know what you want. And settle for nothing less. I admire that. To go for what you want." She had so much she suddenly wanted to say, a backlog of the unsaid. "I can't beat that." She looked closely into his reddened, shadow-rimmed eyes and saw that he was indeed a man who, when he looked at you, really looked at you. *I must look awful,* she thought self-consciously. *I must look like death.*

"Jess is the best!" came a cry across the forecourt.

Tom nodded in their direction. "They've picked their favorite."

She couldn't help but smile. "Have—have you got two heads? 'Cos I'm seeing you with two heads."

He smiled back. "Yeah. I've got two heads. You're fine."

"I don't think I can go any further," she confessed, watching Matt, looking relatively fresh, walk away to sit down and take refreshments. "I'm finished. I can't win."

"Really? Well, I'm not sure *they'd* agree with you."

Tom was looking over her shoulder, and so she turned and saw her mother pushing her daughter onto the yard. On Nat's knee a large cake tin. A birthday party on wheels.

THE CANDLES, NO sooner blown out, reignited. The flames wavered again, clung on for dear life, and on the next blow—the same thing, the flames returned to cling on once more.

"In the newspapers they saw your picture," Val reported while Nat cut the cake. "Your lovely picture. So they call me. They fire you." Valeria held out a paper plate. On it was placed a spongy wedge. "You lost your job. So. Now you are famous. Some famous person. Without a job in this world."

"Go, Jess!" sounded from the crowd, which perhaps made Val spit the word again so loudly, "Famous!"

Jess turned away. "I can't take this anymore. I'm going mad. I'm going to quit."

"Well, you can't. Not now. You have to keep going. There is nothing left to lose."

"Two minutes," bellowed Dan through the distorting megaphone.

Jess slipped to her knees, gripped Nat's wheelchair by both armrests and kissed her daughter again. "I'm going to keep going, then. Shall I? I'm going to try, then."

The young girl's pale, oval face—everywhere the Polish genes of the grandmother. "I really don't mind living at that school. It's free, so . . . I might as well live there full-time. And you won't need a car to drive me, then."

Jess felt tears driving their way upward. "So, you . . . you don't want to live with me anymore?"

"If—if—no, I just mean . . . no, I don't mean—"

"If that's how you feel, that's okay too. If you'd rather live away from home, if you'd rather be away from me . . ." Jess rose, badly shaken, straightening her aching back and hiding her face from her daughter.

But Nat needed to say more. She reached out with one hand. "I didn't say that. I just . . ." But there wasn't enough time. Dan was already calling the one-minute alert and by then Jess was already saying, "It's okay. You go home, sweetie."

Tom limped by, returning to the car. "You'd better get back," he said. "If you're coming."

"We're going on the road. With the contest—" Jess said to Nat.

"On the road?"

"She lost her job," Val interjected, touching Tom's arm, adding, "Jessie. She lost her job, because of this contest, so if she doesn't win the car she has nothing to show. Nothing."

What could Tom reply to that? "I'm ah—I'm—" He turned to Jess for explanation or instruction but saw only a look of mortification on her face. He looked then at the fresh-faced daughter, and then back again at the antique matriarch with her yellowed eyes, precancers on her temples—essentially these were three generations of the same face; and what exactly was this aged version of Jess trying to tell him now? That he was—what?—a monster to deny Jess the car? He decided to shake this old lady's hand quickly then take his leave. "I'm sorry. That's really tough. Tom Shrift. How do you do? Nice to meet you." He then offered the daughter his hand as well.

"Don't beat Mum," the girl told him, right to his face.

"Sorry?"

The girl repeated it. "Don't beat Mum."

"Nat!" Jess barked. But the damage was done. Tom was horrified. But Jess was horrified too. "Natalie!"

Had the girl *really* said this to him? *Don't beat Mum?* Tom withdrew his unshaken hand and looked rapidly at all three Jesses.

"I'll . . . ~~What the . . . ? What the hell kind of question is that?~~ . . .
I'll . . . ~~Is this a setup?~~ . . . I'll . . ." he stammered. "~~You get me
over here, ambush me, then get a mad old lady to pluck the heart-
strings and then get the young girl to say . . . *that?*~~" But finding
nothing appropriate to say, nothing that could survive even the
most gentle censorship, he turned and walked away.

"EVERYONE IN THE cab of the flatbed truck, please. Now."

Jess and Tom and Matt narcotically obeyed orders, moving
as best they could toward the superlarge vehicle that had been
backed onto the forecourt. Dan had attached two metal ramps
to the back of the low deck and Vince was just then gingerly
steering the Discovery up these and, with a sudden burst of
gas, onto its new home. Under the watchful and suspicious eye of
the police, Dan then passed the megaphone to Hatch, who addressed the crowds now confined to the footpaths hemming
the yard.

"Ladies and gentlemen. We have a little announcement to
make. We've been denied permission to stage this event on private property by the police. I wish to thank you all for taking your
leave of this car yard in such an orderly fashion. You'll understand
the reasons for this in due course. Thank you." Lowering the
megaphone, he then went up to the police. "Okay?"

The policemen nodded. "Okay," the more senior officer
replied.

And with that Hatch moved to the elevated Land Rover, got
into the driver's seat and closed the luxury door, while Vince, at
the wheel of the immense flatbed, revved the belching diesel en-
gines and, to the dismay of the uninformed crowd, appeared to
drive off and away with the remains of the contest.

. . .

ONE BLOCK AWAY, and watched by the surprised burger bar boy standing in his shop's doorway, and with the precious seconds of the current rest stop ticking away, Jess and Tom and Matt were helped down from the cab of the truck and assisted into position on the flatbed, where they were asked to place and keep one hand on the glass of the Discovery's rear window.

Vince blew his whistle. The contest was back on.

"That's it. Keep a hand right there at all times, yeah?" Vince patted each person on the back. "One hand on the glass of the rear window so we can keep a good close check on you from inside the Disco as we go. Yeah? Way to go, guys. You guys are legendary. And don't worry, we'll be taking it real slow, until we find somewhere permanent to park, yeah? You're completely safe."

When Vince stepped off the back of the truck, he ran into Hatch, coming back to take a look at the setup. The two men embraced. They had never embraced before. Might never again.

FROM TRAFFIC-MIRED Olympia, the four-by-four and its trailer made for Hammersmith, while Hatch on his mobile phone inside the Disco kept the radio station and its audience updated on exactly where they were and where they were heading.

Behind them, a ragtag convoy was able to form. Turning to look behind him, and with the wind flipping his hair over his eyes, Tom was able to list some of them. Besides a press car—the two journalists had wasted no time joining in—supporters trailed in their own vehicles. Maybe eight to ten cars in all, some blasting horns occasionally, forming a slow parade that soon passed into residential streets of terrace houses, wending its way by sooty warehouse districts, by metamarkets, a prison, budget hotels with flags of the world, by flyover off-ramps to complexes not yet built, past Victorian sweatshops adapted now to health centers where Tom knew you paid seven hundred pounds a year to sweat your arse off, by shopfronts surmounted by flats with filthy lace curtains permanently drawn, hiding ghastly lives, then by new glass-and-steel office blocks—vast greenhouses—where workers in suits *tock-tock-tock*ed on computer terminals in full view of the passing traffic, with Tom and his last two rivals all the while moronically pressing their hands to cold glass and being treated to a kind of open-air tour of the very city that held them captive.

Tom's hooded eyes took it all in. Overcooked London, what a city!—with its railways and airports and buses pouring in their hourly contributions from every corner of the kingdom and of Europe too; no longer a capital but a country in its own right, the business of nearly fifteen million human beings exporting its hard-boiled ways antithetical to the gentile island that ringed it and had to tolerate it. What had Samuel Johnson once said?—yes, he could retrieve at least this quote—"When a man is tired of London, he is tired of life." *Well*, thought Tom now, on his diesel barge, *screw Johnson. I'm bored with it, terminally. So what does that tell you? Yes, I've had it up to here with the roar of the henhouse!*

Shaken from their own troubles by the honking of horns, pedestrians stopped and stared at the creeping, crawling Disco, perhaps wondering what new flash-in-the-pan celebrities were being created by this particular little stunt. Was it all part of one of those new reality TV shows? Looking about for faces they might recognize, they saw none.

Hatch—up front, inside the Disco and occasionally filming the three hands on the glass from the inside for his official records—was enjoying every aspect of this. Not only had he bested the police, but the Guinness people had also cleared his strategy, keeping the contest alive. A world record remained a clear possibility, and he was driving toward it without recourse to the A–Z.

"Amazing," he said to himself, shaking his head as he lowered his Digicam and marveling at this insane demonstration of staying power. "You people. Amazing."

Retuning the car radio, he found a better signal for "London Live," stopped on Lee Lerner's familiar voice: *As Yeats said. As Yeats said, the best lack all conviction. But what did he know? For those of you in the High Street area . . . watch out for a navy blue Land Rover Discovery. . . .* The thrill this gave him! Hatch turned down the volume and angled the rearview mirror to take in the three stars that were Jess and Tom and Matt's hands. How was the popular favorite doing? Yes, Jess's hand was stuck to the glass just as pluckily as the others. Still fighting. He loved all three of these people now. What guts. They blew out of the water his own conception of what a person could truly handle.

"Amazing," he said to no one at all. "All of you."

BLEARILY, JESS TOOK in the teeming masses from her position in the middle of the two men—the gorgeous, the unlucky looking, the young and old, all of them effortful, with intent looks on their faces, determined, in a hurry. From her church prayer group she remembered what Bishop Fulton Sheen had written about religious experience: *"We are each drinking from—"* Now, what was it? Not a glass, no, a cup. . . . *"The teacup of finite satisfactions. . . ."* That was it . . . people were drinking from the teacup of finite satisfactions *". . . when what the soul actually craves is to drink from the ocean of Infinite Love."* On her slow-moving platform, in a death-approximating state, this ex-meter maid drifted through West Kensington thinking suddenly of the soul's oceanic needs.

At her wit's end, she wondered again, *Can I still win?* But she lacked the energy even to pursue this question. Her head ached. Her knees and feet throbbed. Her back pain, untreated, drove knives through to her solar plexus. Her balled-up stomach muscles would take weeks to relax, so that each ten-second parcel of time now amounted to a minicrisis. How long? Lord, how much longer?

She moaned in silent conversation with herself: *Mary, Mother of God . . . Mother of the Word Incarnate . . . whose only begotten son suffered on the Cross, died and was buried. . . .* As a child she had had no staying power. At six her mother had tied her to a chair to stop her from leaving the table at mealtimes. Actually roped her down. Lodz tactics. But what ropes bound her now? What bonds kept her here?

She couldn't decide. Remembered only that she carried in her pocket a mobile phone she hadn't used yet. As the convoy stopped at the next set of lights, she pulled it out. How did you operate one of these things again? She stared at it. Why had she brought it even? To connect her with her family, that was it. And she needed her family right now. As a dying person knows, you want your family close by at the end. So she speed-dialed. The receiver chirped, then clicked. A voice. And whose voice? Her own. Metallic, thin, it greeted the caller, gave instructions. Jess didn't like the whiny sound of this other woman on the line. Disgusted, she hung up. If only it were this easy to cut her off for good.

She put the phone away. Her mother and daughter were out of reach. Perhaps Val even meant to create problems now, argue that Jess was no longer a fit mother—because of this contest. It could happen. Her mother could be spiteful. And the contest *was* insane. Did Nat love her grandmother more than her mother? The intimacy lines were certainly more open between them. Valeria had dealt with Nat's first period before Jess even knew about it. Nat's boy talk had also skipped a generation, leaving Jess out. And who did Nat imitate when she wanted to sound like an adult? *Bubshia says I need to take responsibility now . . . Bubshia says I can stay up later now . . . Bubshia says I can have a TV in my room . . . Bubshia says I've done enough homework for tonight.* Jess was an eyewitness on her daughter's life. All this she suddenly saw, from the back of a flatbed with her hand stuck on the latest-model Land Rover.

. . .

HER FACE—HOW would her face look beside him in a bed, with the blood of passion pinking her skin? He blinked this image away, struck out the thought: the strain of thinking on so many levels at once was draining . . .

But Tom's mind still wouldn't behave. His fast-blinking eyes brought new half-broken reflections. What would Jess be like to live with? He allowed this thought. He'd never lived with a woman, not for more than a few weeks anyway. Her medicine cabinet would contain antifungal creams. (Too much walking in sweaty shoes.) Many painkillers too—half a dozen brands. Why had he just thought of this? About her medicine cabinet? He was going crazy. The rational half of his brain—no, this wasn't even right, the rational *half* of *one-tenth* of his brain (what was the undeployed part up to, awaiting what tasks?)—told him, *I have never known true love.* The hard facts? *The most I have ever felt is deep rapport.* Was this true? Only deep rapport? What a joke. His thoughts raced. He canceled this line of inquiry. With one hand he reached down and changed stations on his palm radio, just in time to hear a journalist say: *The missiles were fired from helicopters, striking the religious school that allies claimed was a refuge for militants. Villagers rallied. And while wailing laments, they laid out the eighty dead in the town square. Among the corpses were twenty-five small children. The military today claimed that the strike was "necessary" and a significant blow to their enemy. . . .* He turned the radio off. He thought of his downstairs neighbor. Where was motor-mower man now? Weeping over his dead lawn? Had Tom's strike really been necessary? No—too much to think about. His mind flipped back to the earlier question of deep rapport. Jess was right about that much. He *was* a failure, a dunce at least in the romantic arena. To have known nothing more than rapport—what a flop! But he'd never prioritized love, so what could you expect?

A new detail sprang to mind; a statistical finding from the Zogby pollsters: *People who strive for popularity and material wealth report a lower quality of life than those who go for self-acceptance and personal growth.* He smiled, nodded. This was obvious. In other words: don't expect new goods to heal an old pain.

But he'd never heeded such truisms. As a man equipped to do great things, he'd gone after money in the bank, a buoyant career. In the end, Tom, typical of many, he liked to think, opted for grief and tensions, deadlines and overextension by choice. And only when he had escaped the poultry life could he afford to focus on "quality of life." For now—went such life logic—discomfort must be felt. The words of Jess Podorowski's daughter came back: *Don't beat Mum.* The nerve of it! What a thing to lay on a stranger fighting for his own survival. The kid was way out of order, wheelchair or no wheelchair. ~~"Hey, a wheelchair doesn't give you license to say anything you like."~~ And why hadn't Jess stepped in and reprimanded her right away? And the grandmother, why had she been so smarmy, offering him help when he was the enemy standing in the way of her daughter's success? Only one answer made sense. All three were in cahoots—yes, all three of these Jesses, past, present and future, were trying to break him down with kindness, were applying the heavy guilts, wanting him to elevate their plight over his own.

In the back beside Jess, he turned and took in the profile of this avowed handmaiden of the Lord who had just lost her job, and who, if she didn't win this car, would reportedly be in dire straits. But instead of pity he felt the stirrings of attraction and the same thought: how would she look on the pillow beside him? Just looking at her brought heat to his face, a quickening of his pulse. A prickling tension. He had feelings for her. And he respected her in a funny way too, even if she was a connoisseur of losing. She was no ordinary woman underneath all that. She was a toiler, a singular person when it came to stickability, one whose capacity to hold on was enormous. A worker, she actually made society tick in needed ways. A bizarre image came to him just then: *she was the grouting that allowed bright tiles like Tom Shrift to stand in place!* No. This was disgraceful. She was so much more, more than grouting, and he—wrestling with a behind-schedule life, who was he kidding—he was hardly a bright tile any longer. So why be so harsh on people? What a blighted person he'd become. The *real* loser here. While Jess—hey, she was a person he could learn serious things from. Yes, really learn. She represented the possibility of personal growth. Perhaps this was why he was attracted to her. Perhaps this was even why anybody chases after love in the first place, not because it's a system of pleasure, but because it's a campaign of betterment. *Bombs fell.* Sure. *But the villagers rallied. Laid out the dead. Lamented.* This was the truth at the center of that news report, the timeless subtext of the daily news. And it was this tender collection of bodies, so far away, cared for by loved ones, which gave Tom, here and now and light-years away, an impulse to touch Jess's face. To place a hand on her knee.

She was a far better person than he. And why? Because she was *necessary.* How utterly necessary was he? Who would suffer if he ceased to be? Who would grieve, lay him out? His father? No, he was probably in the grave himself. His mother might post an obit in the papers but he couldn't imagine her—this one person who ought to care—doing anything to show other people that her son had been necessary on this earth. It almost stopped his heart. No one! No one to grieve! What a thought. No one! You could basically draw a sheet over him right now, lay a flower on his breast right now, and no one would come to grieve.

BACK IN HAMMERSMITH, delayed at another set of lights, Jess caught sight of a female parking warden she didn't recognize at all. Could this be her replacement? So soon? It was possible. How easily all traces of a person are erased. She tried to focus outward, even if it stung to do so. Gauzy objects floated, clarified, then became ghostly again. And she was ghostly herself, watching the living go about their business from this weird vantage point. So this *was* like death: the living close by but unaware of you as you drifted near, untouchable, as you went over your regrets. The new meter maid had found a car in violation. Two wheels on the curb. A Code 64. Or was it a Code 38? Jess had forgotten already.

Then, a small girl on the footpath waved. Waved right at Jess. The sweet little thing. A pom-pom hat and scarf. No parent in sight. Maybe ten years old. It awoke Jess from her daydreams, brought her back. This angel looked right at Jess and smiled. And Jess, surprised by this unexpected gesture of acknowledgment and the lift it gave her, did the most natural thing in the world.

She waved back, with the wrong hand.

INSIDE THE DISCO, Hatch lowered the Digicam and looked with his own eyes. Two hands only on the glass. Two hands. Two male hands.

TOM. HE HAD been looking straight ahead up to that point, in a deep daydream. The green-lending glass had given him back his own reflection and he'd been staring at it. But his attention was drawn by the movement of Jess's waving hand, a blur at the corner of his eye. Turning left he saw . . .

Jess waving. Waving with her left hand. On the glass. His hand. Matt's hand. And that was all. He couldn't believe it. His heart almost stopped. Words sprang to his tongue. Jess was out— she was out—she was out. He turned to his right? A little girl, waving back. Yes, a little girl. Again he turned left, saw that Matt was looking the other way, had noticed nothing. Only Tom had seen Jess take her hand off. The words rose in his throat but did not come out at once: ~~"SHE'S OUT!"~~

When the truck suddenly revved and moved forward, the lurch caused Jess to replace her hand on the glass. The flatbed pulled forward a couple of places in the queue, then stopped again.

Tom chose his words carefully, and directed them only at her. "You . . . you took your hand off." When she didn't hear him over the idling engine, he spoke louder. "You took your hand off."

She turned to face him. "What?"

"Just then. You took your hand off."

"What?"

"When you waved. You waved. Took your hand off?"

"What do you mean?"

Tom's voice rose louder. Surely she wasn't going to deny what she'd done? "The little girl. You waved at her, just before. I saw you, you took your hand off to wave back."

"I saw it too." Matt Brocklebank was now staring at Tom, his eyes even wider than Tom's.

Tom lowered his voice again—this was between Jess and him alone. Was meant only as a statement of simple fact. He hadn't made up his mind yet what to do about her oversight. In his mind, it was not yet a terminal error. He might overlook it. "You waved, that's all. To that . . ." Yes, he was determined now to keep this just between the two of them. Yes, this was for her information only. "That little girl, with your left . . ." He didn't even finish the sentence. He'd let it go. "Forget about it."

But the damage was done, for Matt had smelled blood. "Yeah. I saw it too. That's two of us. Jess? You took your hand off. You're out." Matt was shouting already and Jess had a frightened look that Tom ached to soothe somehow. But how?

Jess looked straight into Tom's eyes. What a look. No, it wasn't fear. He'd misread it. No, it was anger, hatred. With perhaps even a touch of pity. Tom lowered his voice even further, his own alarm growing, his own panic rising over his own error of judgment. "Actually, I . . . I could have been . . . mistaken. She's fine. I, I probably just . . ."

But he'd gone too far already, and Matt, completely alert now, was not about to let this go. "What are you talking about? I saw it too. Same time as you. Jess? That's it. You're out! Sorry." As Tom's voice had fallen away to an inconsequential murmur, Matt's now rose in triumphant excitement and aggression. "Jess, admit it! You know you did it. You have to admit it!"

Tom swung angrily. "You didn't see anything, so shut up! Shut up! You were looking the other way! I saw you, so shut up!"

But Matt was already shouting to the follow-up car driven by Dan, and then hammering on the glass to alert Hatch inside: "She's out! *She's out!*" and "We both saw it! Pull over! She's out!" and "She took her hand off!"

Tom had no choice now but to shout too, and across Jess the argument raged: "You saw nothing! She's fine. Leave it alone. Mind your own business."

"What are you doing? What is this?" To Jess: "You waved, right? You took your hand off, like he said. Own up."

The flatbed pulled out of the traffic and soon the remaining three were surrounded. "What's going on back there?"

Matt hotly told Hatch the story. "She's out. She took her hand off. We both saw it. Tom saw it first, then I did. She's gone."

Hatch was slow to respond and looked reluctant or unable to pass judgment. Finally, he asked, "Tom? Did you see anything?"

Tom turned back to Jess—and from her, still, the same entranced, searching, contemptuous stare directed right at him. He'd opened his big mouth and now she hated him again. Some informant reflex had driven him mad; some gamesmanship hardwired into him. "No," he said. "I saw nothing."

Matt was incensed. "You liar! You fucking liar!" Pointed an accusing finger at Tom. "You saw her. You can't change your mind now. Stop trying to protect her."

"I only saw—"

"You saw it and now you're changing your tune because—just because you two are—why? Getting all— What? Fuck you, man."

"Shut up! Last warning!"

"Tell the truth. Tell the truth. Tell the—"

"Shut up!"

"Tell the truth. Just tell the—!"

Tom was a hairbreadth from throwing a punch—which would be the first of his adult life—but Hatch stepped up onto the flatbed with them and held up two calming hands. "Calm down. Everyone just . . . calm down!" But it was too late. Soon all three men were shouting over one another, and were silenced only when Jess settled it all with her own, "STOP!"

In the sharp silence that followed, Jess took both hands off her ears, *both* of them, then said, very quietly, "Can you take me home, please? I just want to go home."

BEFORE DRIVING JESS home, as requested, the convoy honored a five-minute rest stop in a supermarket parking lot. Hatch took a call from the radio station and reported that the contest was now down to two people. Who had dropped out? He lowered his voice to give his reply.

Taking his chance, Tom joined Jess in the backseat of the Discovery. He closed the door behind him. On the luxury alpaca leather, they sat side by side.

"Can I just explain?"

But she cut him off, both with her voice and with those hurt eyes, those bloodshot eyes, no longer beautiful but even more vividly alive, forked with tiny lightning bolts of crimson. They narrowed and flashed at him as she said, "Okay, so now I see what it takes. What it takes to win. I guess you have to stop at absolutely nothing. Well, I hope it gets you what you want. I really do. But tell me: how do *you* stand it?"

"Stand? What?"

She turned her full, pale face toward him. "The hatred. The hatred that comes with it?"

Bull's-eye, he realized. She was right on the money here. His right hand began to tremble, and not just from the cold absorbed from the car. It was true. He had to soak up more hatred than she ever did on her city rounds as a meter maid, and to this he must now add *her* hatred, for she was telling him that she despised him too.

"How do you handle that part?" She shook her head. "Well, I hope it gets you what you want."

After that, and with Tom's *wants* forward and center and enlarged grotesquely and disgracefully before him, the motorcade, still six to eight cars in size, passed at a crawl into Jess's old White City neighborhood and rolled finally up her street to stop outside her address, that murky basement flat already dark inside behind its twisted vertical blinds, one or two blades missing and with no life visible inside.

Hatch helped Jess across the road, then let her go on by herself. She walked on wobbly legs up to her front gate. She looked injured, about to fall. But she kept going toward the flight of steps that led up the black-lacquered front door with brass ironmongery, then turned aside and descended to the right, and by a slow decline went down to the basement level and into darkness.

As the flatbed drew the Disco and Tom and Matt away, a light came on inside the flat.

Matt turned to the staring Tom and said, quite happily, "Just you and me now."

TWO LEFT, THEN, as the fourth night fell. Tom and Matt, ferried back and forth across London in endless little laps, from Hammersmith over to Hyde Park to Chelsea, from Ladbroke Grove north to God-knows-where. And it struck Tom that the sheer amount of sleep debt he owed himself was now not only to him but to almost every human being who had ever existed. Think of it. To live and not sleep a wink for such a duration—who had ever gone so deep into such territory as he and Matt were now going? Randy Gardner, yes, the world record holder, but who else? *Incredible. Who would have thought I'd achieve greatness this way?*

So Tom had become a test case now, and saw himself in such laboratory terms. As NASA put people in space, observing the human animal in a state of weightlessness, Tom had entered a condition as otherworldly as zero gravity: days which began with not getting out of bed, his body thus in trauma, his limbs twitching with miniparoxysms, muscle spasms, a frightening numbness growing in his swollen legs, symptoms of flu, growing irritability, a mouth ulcer, a sore on his bottom lip, a constant headache, blurred vision, slurred speech to add to the memory lapses, overall confusion and nausea bouts (the complaints of fifteen people bottled up inside his one body)—where would it end? With a mental breakdown, like the car thief, or permanently whacko like the insomniac, or dead like Walter? His symptoms were only the daytime warning signs. As this fourth night deepened, he could add growing hallucinations (imagining he'd won already, seeing himself alone, victorious, in the backseat) and psychosis (a desire to strangle and kill and then hide the body of Matt Brocklebank), as well as heart palpitations (making real the possibility his long-term health was now in harm's way). Also, Jess was preying on his mind, over and over, dragging his spirits low. She had really churned him up. Especially those words about hatred. Yes, being hated was the downside for treating the world as a battlefield. He saw in vivid flashes a fallen lock of her hair, her cheeks flushing in fright at something he'd said, those eyes that could domesticate any bachelor . . . yes, she came back to him repeatedly. And he wished again to tell her that he'd meant no harm. In actual fact his entire game plan had been to make her see the positive uses (sometimes!) of anger, of retaliation, of force, of not being afraid to make enemies. For Christ's sake, she needed such news. He'd gone out of his way to make her realize that in modern times you simply had to know how to raise your voice, to be able to drown out other voices. Otherwise you were left permanently in danger, doomed to be merely *a person*, yes!—as invisible as that—a speck, ignorable, hardly even warranting a name, human poultry to be shooed into any cage. This was all he'd been trying to convey. He'd wished to protect.

Okay, so now I see what it takes. Perhaps in the end she'd shown him that she'd understood this toughest of messages, even if she went on to shun the doctrine. Still, one day, Jess might yet realize that she'd once met a man who had told her the plain facts, who had said what he saw and no more, and who, in so doing, had raised her long-term interests high above his own chances of ever seeing her again in more romantic circumstances.

HATCH PULLED THE flatbed over, releasing the survivors for the next rest stop. Matt went to buy hot refreshments in the garage minimarket, while Tom, with his holdall of personal items, staggered off the back and almost into Hatch's arms.

"You okay?"

"My legs. One has gone numb. That's scary."

"What . . . what do you want to do? What are you saying? Tom?"

"I don't know yet. I don't think I can make it."

"Really?"

But then, without another word, Tom made himself walk off to the latest of the public lavatories that had served as havens for all the contestants throughout the entire event.

Alone in this tiled echo chamber, Tom looked around for somewhere to sit. Fat chance. Four cubicles only. And though this bathroom was vile, it was a palace compared with the canned hell of those Portaloos.

In the urinal he alleviated his bladder and a morsel of physical comfort returned. He washed his hands at the sink. Layers of grime—London pollen—came free; it flowed blackly down the drain. He splashed cold water onto his face and checked himself in the mirror. Red eyes, black ringed, looked depraved; they frightened him even. A jaundiced color had come to his skin. Bile must be crossing the blood barrier, discoloring him. Was his heart faltering? The beat seemed irregular. His ears were ringing. His legs, no longer able to bear his weight, made him slump on the edge of the sink. His sleep debt, underwritten till now by his self-belief, was being called in. He dropped to his knees, his chin came to rest on the porcelain edge, in a prayer pose. He was done, really had nothing left in the bank. And here, in this bathroom, was the only place he could show it. *So this is how it ends?* All his drives, secret hopes, his acumen, his wits (a Mensa mind!) plus his famous competitiveness, these had all been applied. And still he'd failed, beaten in the end by a kid with everything going for him, one who, in finding a girlfriend, had perhaps found the final energy-summoning excitements he needed. But what did Tom have left to be excited about? He sought Jess's face but saw again only her angry look of contempt. No, there was no renewing energy to be found here. Only a further (disastrous) subtraction.

With his unshaven chin on the sink, he let his eyelids close.

Didn't fight it. He certainly fell asleep then—but for how long? Only until a hand on his shoulder revived him.

He startled, looked up, saw a blurry Matt.

The younger man, when he came into focus, was as rudely fresh as when they'd begun four days ago, and he looked down on Tom with—was it pity? This awful freshness in his face mocked Tom's agony. Who was this kid? Some Recording Angel on Judgment Day, standing radiant over him, asking the last sinner in hell: "Are you okay?"

Tom confessed. The words, unedited: "It's over."

"Are you sure?"

When Tom didn't reply, the bathroom door soon banged. He was alone again.

Tom rose, then found the energy to stand at least. He couldn't sleep here. In the mirror, seeing his face once more, he checked his reflection. Had he really thrown in the towel? How would he live with himself now? Was there really nothing he could think of, nothing that might excite him afresh? No unvisited corner of his mind, heart or soul that he could now call into service? Was there no way left to bounce back?

DARK DIESEL, THE last suspiration of vanished forests fifty million years old, gushed into the flatbed, whose eight perfectly lathed cylinders would, if there was any justice in the world, keep a salesman's last hopes on the road.

In the superilluminated forecourt of the petrol station, Hatch held the pump's vibrating nozzle to the filler pipe, pretty much aware that his was a last-gasp effort too.

"I told you. He's pulled out," Matt insisted, shiny-faced.

Petrol backwashed. The pump clicked off. Hatch reset the nozzle in its home bay as the pump printed a receipt. "If you don't mind, I'd like to hear it from him. And he's still got a minute left."

"I'm telling you what he said. He's finished. He just told me. It's over. He's not coming out."

"Then who is *that*?"

Hatch pointed toward the bathroom door where a ghost in a fresh white shirt emerged. Tom walked forward, combing wet hair back, tucking in shirttails, ready again for battle, the limp in the numb left leg less pronounced.

It was a vision that Matt could only blink out. This was impossible.

"Come on! You've still got time!" Hatch shouted.

"But he quit. He quit!" Matt insisted.

"Are you in?" Hatch asked Tom as he came close.

"'Course I'm in. Let's go."

And with this, Tom climbed back up onto the flatbed and took up his old position.

Hatch waved to Vince in the cab of the truck. "All right? Let's take her out." Then he turned back to Matt. "Oh, he's finished, is he?" The younger man had no answer to this as he also retook his place. "Anyway. Just twenty-two more hours and you're famous. Both of you. Remember that. World famous."

MATT, HIS CONFUSION plain, stared at Tom as the convoy departed the petrol station, waiting, it seemed, for the return of the moaning, sink-kneeling, soul-defeated Tom who had said, "It's over," trying to resolve this image with the man beside him just now fastening the second-to-last button of his fresh shirt with sudden dexterity.

"So what's with the mind games?" Tom gave no reply. "A guy your age . . ." Matt shook his head in grudging respect. "What's your secret? Come on. What's the famous secret?"

"Just keep talking, doper boy. I'm going to win this thing."

"Fresh shirt as well," marveled Matt, shaking his head, incredulous. "Fucking hell. Slipped into something more comfortable, then?"

"How about *you* slip into something more comfortable. Like a coma."

As painful hour bled into hour, and as the two men moved toward the end of their fourth night, motoring through the fairy-lit city parks and the byways of West London, Matt's continuous sidelong gaze finally produced a comment: "You're a maniac. You're a total maniac. There's no point, you know. I can keep going like this for days. For *days*. You can't beat me. You're killing yourself for nothing."

"Let's just see what your blood test says," Tom replied.

MORNING CAME. THE mild excitement of dawn. Haze on the horizon over the Westway. London on its way to work. Matt wondering about Tom, and vice versa. Hatch wondering about . . . not much more than just keeping his eyes open right now. Vince, drained dry now too, filming occasionally, otherwise loosely keeping watch, as the Discovery was steered toward . . . toward . . . where?

Well, Hatch was still trying to work that out. They needed to settle down somewhere. Establish another camp where media excitement might build up once more. He'd been on the phone. ITV News had contacted him. Had an idea. A pretty good one. A photo op and a venue where they could film the big moment.

Tom heard bleeps. Looked aside. Matt's mobile phone sounding an alert. Matt looked at it, smiled. "Well, you're gonna have to beat someone who's in love."

What a faker this kid was. And a good one. You couldn't really tell he wasn't in love.

Matt shook his head. "Amazing. I thought you were finished

back in that bathroom. Man, you're one screwed-up ball of psychology. You can't win, you know. I'm twenty years younger than you. What is it? The secret. I'm going to get it out of you sooner or later."

As tired as he was, Tom expended breath to say one word:

"Secret!"

5

HE WAS ASLEEP. No, still awake. Just. For the next moment at least. Tom's eyes burned with the strain of keeping them open. But then sleep attacked again and had to be rebuffed once more. Wave after wave. For how much longer could he repel it?

And while Tom fought, the flatbed, like an ambulance carrying the sick, wove through the smoky, hooting, roaring morning of a great city, until Hatch found a place that would take them.

"Brent Cross. We got a mall," Hatch told them at a set of lights.

We got a mall? ~~"What kind of Yankee bastardization of beauteous English do you call that?"~~

They soon turned into the massive North London shopping mall that had agreed to host the contest either until its conclusion or until the police showed up again, whichever came sooner. The Land Rover was off-loaded and, with Tom and Matt walking slowly behind it, the luxury vehicle rolled into the high-domed mall forecourt. Officials waved them onward into the heart of the central concourse, gliding over the glossy, marble flagstones until they came to a stop by a fountain recycling its own watery froth.

Soon the Discovery was surrounded by shoppers. Families large and small. What was going on? What was up? Onlookers, men in suits, young mall rats who wanted to find out how they too could win a new car, pensioners in their electric carts, all pressed in, peered inside the car, blocked out light to the car's window, circling Tom and Matt, asking them questions. Vince drove them back, asked the mall manager for a cordon to be established. Soon, out came chrome poles and ropes. The car was corralled.

But Hatch wasted no time spreading the word. A world record was about to be broken. A world record. And when Tom and Matt were eventually released for their next five-minute rest stop, applause broke out. Great applause. Tom was astonished. Strangers! Saluting him! While Matt with his screen-star smile waved, at ease with the attention, Tom struggled to cope, turned away, lowered his head. No, he mustn't buy into this either, he told himself. Praise, in the end, was more destructive than being heckled.

The experiment is over. My spies tell me that at 9:30 p.m. last night Jess Podorowski lifted a hand and was eliminated. So the bad news is in. The selfish prevail. The greedy are stronger. To me, this proves once and for all that there's something very mean at the heart of things, that doesn't go according to the spirit of fairness, but to the antagonistic laws of perversity. Like Nero, let me hang my head and say, Qualis artifex pereo—"The artist in me is killed." Maybe I just need to grow up now. And that's what I'm going to do. This ends my last show . . . I'll never address you again. I'm gone. Like everything else. Gone, our innocence. Gone, Jessie Podorowski into the night. Humanity? We're a virus with shoes. The only music left to play? . . . Mozart's Requiem.

The crowd was little more than a blur now. Tom was seeing the world as a newborn: all haze and distorted noises. Sitting on the low wall of the foaming fountain, he focused his thoughts—and felt new determination enter him. Maybe the flowing water was helping him: weren't the negative ions it released meant to reinvigorate? He thought of Randy Gardner, the young kid who went eleven days. Was Matt Brocklebank a Randy Gardner? Well, even if he was, Tom would give it everything he had. In chess you tipped the king over when you were defeated, and Tom had toyed with laying down his king back there in the petrol station bathroom. But then, inspiration had come: a new plan—to go on till he dropped. Yes, *till he dropped*. There'd be no resignation. Let them hospitalize him afterward, but his ultimate limit had to be reached. What had he to lose? His health? His mind? Without victory in this contest, what was either worth? This was what had dawned upon him in that toilet. He'd make a last stand. And if he was eventually to fail, if it was Matt who turned out to be a Randy Gardner, then this wouldn't make him, Tom, a failure. He would at least have found his limit. This he could live with. And from this he could find some way to bounce back.

He summoned a series of dates that were crucial to him, and he recalled them easily, even in his state: lost job, 1832; defeated for legislature, 1832; failed in business, 1833; elected to legislature, 1834; defeated for speaker same year. Sweetheart died, 1835; had nervous breakdown, 1836; defeated for nomination for Congress, 1838; elected to Congress, 1846; lost renomination, 1848; rejected for land officer, 1849; defeated for Senate, 1854; defeated again for Senate, 1858; but in 1860 Abraham Lincoln was elected president of the United States. This story was a prayer in the life of Thomas Shrift, and he prayed it now in a public mall in North London.

THE CONCEPT OF a world record had taken a grip on the crowd's imagination. Numbers swelled. Noise levels rose as the big moment approached. Hatch had been waiting years for the fulfillment of this particular boyhood dream. And, barring a disaster, it looked like this moment was finally here: the moment when, on an overcrowded planet, one person rises high above others—and not above fifty other people, and not a few hundred, but above billions of others! And as unique as these record setters were, not many more people had actually *witnessed* such a breakthrough moment. No wonder the crowd was excited. Since the first catalogue of records, how many had stood as close to a Guinness moment as this Brent Cross crowd now stood to Tom and Matt and to the Discovery? No bloody wonder they pressed in tightly, wanted to be part of history being made, grabbed their once-in-a-lifetime chance to feel that they weren't absolutely pointless. No wonder they were right now giving Vince and Dan trouble, ignoring their calls to step back and pushing even closer, some laying their hands on the car as if *they* were the ones who had broken through the great barriers. "Hands off the car!" Hatch had to intervene. "Welcome to watch, but hands off the car!" But he too was ignored as one spectator after another set fresh new hands on the paintwork—two, five, ten, fifteen people, every second more, as if the contest had somehow been thrown into reverse.

Among those not so desperate, just happy to watch, stood Betsy Richards.

Having rested, she'd applied makeup, put on a dress and returned to help her new boyfriend. Looking glamorous again in a short skirt, high heels, a beaming smile, she made signs to Matt, a message anyone could read, that she was waiting for him, waiting to do his bidding, that she was his girl now.

Poor deluded girl, Tom thought. *You're in for a black eye. I've seen your gravestone, sweetheart, and it doesn't say* Brocklebank *on it, not anywhere.* The likely outcome of all her hopes would be . . . But he had to abandon this as a topic. His lids fell. His mind swam. Annihilation loomed, but in panic he drove his lids open again.

He turned his eyes off the girl, who represented another drain on reserves, and coughed. The nagging catarrhal bark had returned.

He bent double till the fit passed, then stood up again. When next his vision focused it did so on Hatch, standing right in front of him. "How you feeling?"

Tom nodded. It was the best he could do. "I'm. Good."

"You don't look too good. There's a doctor on the way."

"What doctor? What for?"

"Just to check you over. At the next break. Once we break the world record. No big deal."

"I don't need. A doctor."

"Don't worry. It's nothing. So tell me. How does it feel to be on the verge of smashing a world record?"

Tom could manage two more words. "Like shit."

Hatch giggled, said that this was a good line, and that Tom should remember it for the press interview after they'd crossed the line.

Vince then appeared. News for Hatch: "The Guinness Records man."

ONLY A MEAGER few world-class records had ever been set in the presence of Guinness Records man, Wally Korresh, though he'd witnessed a whole lot of attempts. To break a record of global standing now took some doing. It could no longer be done on a Saturday morning after walking the dog. These days it took super-human daredevilry, phenomenal bottle and—often, yes—stupidity. He'd seen people fling themselves off buildings, seen folks hold their breaths until they needed to be hospitalized, seen speedsters wind up in a twisted slug of metal. He'd watched people dive, memorize, lift, starve, brave, tolerate, build, bake, grow, freeze, contort, gulp, balance, strive, endure, conquer, destroy, basically torture themselves, basically treating their bodies as if tomorrow they'd be given a fresh new one, all in the hope of standing head and shoulders above all who'd gone before them. Was it a sweet job? Yes, his face told you that he thought it the best job in the whole goddamn world.

"How long to go?" he asked Hatch.

Hatch sighed with relief. "I was getting worried you wouldn't make it. Welcome."

"Traffic. Traffic. Murder. Anyway, let's go make history, shall we?"

"FIFTEEN — FOURTEEN — THIRTEEN — TWELVE —"

As Vince counted down, he was soon drowned out by the public, who lifted their voices to a booming chorus, thunderous in the vast, domed forum. Tom blinked, not greatly touched by this rising emotion, as the last few (and for him, strangely meaningless) seconds expired until, with a jubilant public cheer, he and Matthew Brocklebank stood on the other side of a world mark.

They had both broken a world record!

And now, what?

Fame? Was Tom now famous in some small way; justified in thinking—behaving—like a famous person? Was the rising sound he could hear different from any other sound he'd heard before? Yes, there was applause, and for Tom this was certainly new. But apart from this noise, this banging together of hands and, it seemed now, the popping of champagne corks, he felt nothing. This moment was a disappointment also.

Matt raised one arm in triumph. Accepted a glass. The public cheered again, louder, even higher, as he raised the champagne and drank it down.

But Tom, taking a glass with his free hand, had no wish to drink so set the flute down on the flagstones. As he straightened, a photographer's flash made his vision go blotchy, giving him deathly black zones of blindness. *So this is fame*, he thought, *the ultimate reward for being alive. This is what it is to be singled out.* And then he found himself flanked by both the Guinness man and Matt, who'd slid around the car to join him for the official victory photographs. More lamps flashed. Tom had to close his eyes.

Didn't even try to smile. His idiocy in standing around for over five days with his hand on a car was now documented history. He had only locked himself more securely into the henhouse.

Tom slid his hand around the car and went to the far side. The press had already decided that he was just a complication and that Matt, being a far better story, was unbeatable—the fallen aristo-crat on the brink of victory, still marvelously fresh, so handsome, well heeled, polite, charming . . . a model for a nation's view of itself, his accent alone a connection to the decorous traditions of an entirely other England than the one Tom represented. *Snap, snap, snap* went the moronic cameras. Tom, gazing back at Matt over the roof of the car, saw the guy putting on a show, still with the energy to do it, wrapping one custodial arm around Betsy as another battery of flashes erupted.

Lifting his eyes, Tom caught sight of Tayshawn in the crowd. He blinked heavily to make sure. Yes, the kid was back, and star-ing right back at him. But why such a sinister look? And then Tayshawn made a sign: his middle finger came up, the fuck-you finger. Tom blinked again. Was this happening? What had he done to warrant this? He could only think it must relate to Walter. Maybe the kid had just heard of the tragedy and held Tom respon-sible, not knowing that Tom had actually fallen to his knees, set his mouth to Walter's and done his best to save the old guy's life.

VINCE BLEW THE rest stop whistle.

Semidrunk, Matt stumbled off to the bathroom, while Tom found himself detained by a strange doctor. With professional concern, this man with a General de Gaulle nose asked, "Can you repeat after me: 'She sells. Seashells. On the seashore'?"

Tom opened one eye. "Yes. *Fuck off.* How'd I do?"

But the doctor insisted, made Tom sit with him inside the Land Rover. "This won't take a second. Thank you. We really need to see how you're holding up. These are unknown waters you're sailing in here."

What was the medic saying? Was Tom in danger? Perhaps it wouldn't hurt to let him run some checks. So he did as he was bidden. As the doctor took out instruments from a bag, Tom fumbled with his shirt buttons and allowed him to set a cold stethoscope over his heart. And in that moment the car door opened and a photographer snapped a picture of Tom, catching him just like that—*pop!*—with his shirt open, a doctor attending him, a wreck. "Thanks," the ghoul said, then shut the door again, happy he'd got the exact picture he wanted. *Oh, they'll love this shot,* Tom thought. It could appear beside one of Matt: the kid raising his glass, his other arm around a blonde, the perfection of the species.

Tom's pulse must have been very weak and hidden deep down because the doctor, in his hunt for it, moved the head of the stethoscope about like a chess knight. "She sells seashells. On the seashore," Tom intoned, obedient at last.

Seashells. On the seashore. It invited a memory and, jerked by a new hallucination, Tom was seventeen years old. Running back from a cold sea. Toward his first girlfriend. He saw her again, her name escaping him—zinc ointment on her bottom lip, the tip of her nose—opening up the towel draped around her shoulders and enfolding him in it, her sun-hot, one-piece nylon swimsuit heating him, the salt of the sea in her kiss, her ruby toenail polish clung to by sand. And beside her, a surprise. Waiting for him. Pressed into the sand a creation—a heart. In cockleshells. On the seashore.

Bliss. Had any other moment ever bettered this one? The girl had loved him. Proved it with a shelly message. And in return, he had responded with an early prototype of his *deep rapport*. A half-forgotten moment this one, so quick to pass by, it had come back to him now, giving him . . . what?

"I've got it," the doctor said. "There it is."

Heart.

Yes, concluded Tom, such moments as that one on the beach, they were the mint from which all future coin was struck. And this girl—what was her name, awful not to recall it—she could have found his pounding heart at once, with a cockleshell.

The doctor coiled up the stethoscope. "Okay. That's all still working."

Was it? Well, a doctor had told him so.

But then the quack added, "Just."

Just. He'd grown used to these barbs. *Still, ha!,* thought Tom Shrift. *Ha! Just.*

TAYSHAWN FOLLOWED MATT Brocklebank to the toilets. It had been a rough night on the streets for Tayshawn, who, as a member of a White City gang pretentiously called the Scrubs Lane Chapter of the Apostles of the Apocalypse, had been out selling drugs. His rationale for joining these drug peddlers and sometimes violent gangsters based in a poor West London housing estate had gone like this: *I'm sick of idiots telling me what to do.* So what had he done? Joined this semisecret society, the net effect being that even bigger idiots were now telling him what to do.

Dissatisfaction with the prescribed career path—from "grunt" to "foot soldier" to one day maybe being inducted into the "board of directors," where maybe (if you were aiming high) you might even become "president" yourself before being locked up at Her Majesty's pleasure—had been behind his attempt to win the Land Rover. But with this dream also busted, he'd had to make some fresh new decisions.

Sporting Walter's watch, he had told his gang mates he was out. He was saying good-bye. Had to. Was gonna move on. Was gonna go with his idea of somehow being a race-call commentator. The community center people had said he should write to the Prince's Trust. Who knew? A long shot, but what the fuck.

People he'd known since childhood stared back at him. Some of them said, "Fuck are you talking about, man?" No, Tayshawn wasn't going anywhere. First thing they wanted was the watch. For one thing. Seeing he was behind in his "payments." But Tayshawn refused to give it up. Said he just wanted to walk away. No. Wasn't going to be that easy. The exit strategy was complex. Either he paid his account, debts that amounted to—*hmmm, let's see,* said Demetrius the treasurer, computing the figure in his head— three hundred and fifty quid, more or less. So either Tayshawn settled his 'overdraft or his account would be closed, which Tayshawn knew full well meant that the balance would come out of his fat Afro-Caribbean arse.

And so Tayshawn, this servant of delinquents, an underling's underling's underling, had been up all night trying to sell crack to crackheads in secret meeting places dotted all over West London. On foot, by dawn, he'd taken in just a hundred and twenty-five pounds in crumpled notes. And that was gross takings. His cut, after his gang had extracted costs, would be more like fifteen quid.

Fifteen quid for a whole night out walking! Man, if only he'd won that car. Who had won it? Or was the contest still going on? Couldn't be. Had to be a winner by now. Curious also about the fate of Walter Hayle (the guy might even be good for a loan!) but lacking the legs to schlep all the way down to Olympia, he'd bought a morning paper in hope of spotting a story. And there it was. The people he'd met, and been one of, were now making the news! It could have been him in the paper! The picture was of the three remaining contestants: Jess Podorowski, Tom Shrift and Matt Brocklebank. Two of these people were okay by him, not bad sorts, but one of them he hated. And then he read on, and learned that the contest had been marred by the death of "a pensioner." Oh shit! And then, there was the name: Walter Hayle. In print. Walter Hayle. In the predawn light, Tayshawn had balled up the paper and stuffed it into a bin.

He now pushed open the public toilet's swing door and found the place empty. Where had Matt Brocklebank gone to? Of all the cubicles, only one, at the far end, had a closed door. Tayshawn moved closer, could hear a commotion inside. Uh-oh. He slowly put it together. He wasn't slow . . .

Matt had someone else in there. Tayshawn could hear the whispering. Matt was balling his girlfriend, no question. A nooner. A celebratory reunion bang with Betsy. The guy had just broken a world record and still had the energy for a toilet shag. What a cast-iron dude. Respect. Tayshawn shook his head. He stepped closer, saw the cubicle door posting: ENGAGED and smiled again: respect.

Then Tayshawn spun a little trick of his own. He slid back into one of the other cubicles and partially closed the door so that, through a crack, and via the mirror above the sink, he could still see the door of Matt and Betsy's cubicle. He wanted to see the door open. Had to see the chick come out. Just had to see this. *What a dude*, Tayshawn was thinking. *What a dude.*

One minute passed, and still there was furtive whispering. But then, before another minute could pass, the cubicle door opened and Tayshawn got his money's worth. More than his money's worth. Way more.

Matt—this king of all studs—walked out, straightening his clothes, hurriedly leaving the bathroom. But Betsy wasn't following, at least not yet. Tayshawn heard quite a bit of scuffling instead—man, she must have had all her kit off!—and then at last the cubicle door opened. But . . . no Betsy. *What the . . . ?*

Instead, a guy about Matt's height and size stepped out. A guy? A fucking *guy*? He was wearing a hat. Sunglasses. The hair under the cap was blond. Matt was in there with . . . ? No way! Was the dude really banging another dude? Or was it just a shady rendezvous? Plenty of times Tayshawn himself had conducted a drug score in a toilet cubicle. Could be just that. Sure it was.

But then the guy in the cap went and washed his hands and

when he straightened up, checking his reflection and tamping his face with cold water, Tayshawn saw his face in the mirror . . .

Fucking hell. The blond hair wasn't real. That was clear. The wig wasn't even *on* straight.

And then the guy took off his sunglasses.

No way! thought Tayshawn when he finally saw the guy's face. *No fucking way in hell.*

MATT HAD TO run to make it back to the Discovery in time. He shook his head, made a *phew* sound, then grinned at the onlookers: "Too much champagne."

Even the officials smiled back, relieved that their "winner" hadn't made a horrible slipup at the decisive hour.

Also back on the car, but wavering now, Tom no longer knew whether he was awake or asleep. He existed somewhere in between. If he was awake, it was purely a stroke of luck. If he was asleep, then in his dreams he watched through hooded eyes as Matt assumed the mantle of victor, playing to the crowd. And the crowd duly laughed at the young man's jokes. But Tom didn't laugh. He was the only one not laughing.

OFF TO ONE side, a reporter from *The Times* had a few questions for Hatch. Where had he come up with this whole idea? Had he ever imagined the contest would break the world record? What would this record *signify*? And how had the death of one of the contestants affected him? Was the contest to blame for that? Had he himself slept much during the last five days? (Hatch began to back away from these questions as they became ever more negative. It did not stop them coming.) How much further could these two men possibly push themselves? And if Hatch was to ensure against a second tragedy happening, was there a point where he would intervene, perhaps offer them *two Discoveries*? One each?

While Hatch picked his way carefully through each lethal question, barbed to wound him, he noticed Vince waving and looking distressed. With some relief, he excused himself but said he'd be right back.

Vince was standing beside the overweight young vagrant Hatch recognized as a failed contestant.

"What's this about?"

"You gotta hear this." Vince put his hand on the street kid's shoulder. "You remember Tayshawn here, right? He was with us till day three."

"I'm in the middle of something. If—"

"No, you have to hear this. Tayshawn here has just been telling me something and I think . . . I think . . . I think you'd better hear it from him, 'cos I . . . I dunno . . . I just . . ."

Hatch turned from his nearly catatonic sales assistant and looked piercingly at the boy beside him. "What've you got?"

Slowly Tayshawn revealed what he'd seen, but he was nervous, and every sentence was so insecurely stated that Hatch suspected the whole story a piece of make-believe.

"What are you on about?" Hatch finally said. "You on drugs?" What he'd just heard was insane. Hatch didn't have time for such rubbish. He told the kid he was dreaming; told Tayshawn—too clearly synonymous with drugs and criminality and deception anyway to be believed—to save it for somebody else. Getting overheated, he even pushed Tayshawn a little, a small brush aside, trying to sweep him literally away. "Go, or I'll call the police. What are you trying to do?"

And then Tayshawn said he knew where the other guy was, this other guy he'd seen, and that Hatch could come and take a look for himself.

"Just come and see for yourself. He's just over there, right now, just over there. I followed him, know-wha-I-mean? He's in that burger bar over there right now. But you gotta come now, know-wha-I-mean? If you don't believe me, jus' come and see for yourself, if you don't believe me."

DUTIFULLY, HATCH AND Vince and Dan followed the kid to the burger bar. And there, in a rear booth, what they saw froze them in their tracks.

The guy Tayshawn had seen earlier in the bathroom was slumped over a flame-grilled, triple-decked burger and driving fries into his mouth. He was still wearing the stupid cap and wig but, in his hunger, his sunglasses had fallen low on his nose so that his eyes could clearly be seen. And when those eyes eventually looked up over the rims of the sunglasses, it was to observe that he was being stared at by a party of four.

What Hatch and Vince and Dan and Tayshawn were looking at in amazement was an identical Matt, a double, a mirror Matt: the same build, the same face exactly, the same *person* as the Matt they'd just left behind out in the mall.

Burger and fries dangled from this duplicate's gaping mouth as the four slowly came toward him, cornering him, leaving him no possible escape route. He was trapped. Busted. The game was up.

"Shit," the young man mumbled, his face turning red.

IT HAPPENED THE way Hatch wanted it to happen—the only way he could afford to let it happen.

In a cramped Muzak-piped hallway outside the burger bar's bathrooms, Hatch stood over the crouching imposter. "Where you actually from? Bermondsey? Shoreditch? Where? No rich daddy, is there? No public school?"

"Actually, yes."

"Drop the put-on accent for a start."

"This is how I—"

"I said *drop it!*"

Matt shrugged. "We're college graduates. We live in—in Surrey."

Hatch stared into the kid's face. Had to accept that this was all vaguely possible—it wasn't as if the rich weren't as twisted as everyone else. "If that's true, then you make me even more sick. I ought to smash you one. I bet you brothers both make a nice little living out of pulling stunts like this? Acting the poor little rich boy. Name not even Matt?"

This identical twin found, for the first time, words hard to come by. "We didn't. We didn't mean any harm. It was just a laugh." As Hatch slowly shook his head, the young man added: "You could—you could just let us win it. Nobody would be any the wiser." Hatch's silence gave the fraudster added courage. He smiled. It really was an option.

"Get up," Hatch instructed. "Stand up." And as soon as Matt obeyed Hatch grabbed him by the lapels and forced his head violently against the wall. "Just a laugh? How many people you think are laughing? That guy out there?"

"We pushed him to a . . . a world record."

"Shut up and listen! Here's what we're gonna do. You and your brother are out. But the press can know nothing. I can't have the bad publicity. So here's what happens now. You are gonna find a way to lose that doesn't attract suspicion. And you're gonna do it fast. You think you can do that? You hearing me?"

The young man nodded. Had no choice. Fear in his eyes. "Yes," he replied with the same upper-class reading of the spoken word.

. . .

THROUGH THE FOG of his own troubles, and via a string of events impossible to work out, Tom observed a miracle take place—one that he found as bemusing and as anticlimactic as the annual stroke of New Year.

What actually happened was this: Tom saw Hatch walk up to the Discovery and whisper something into Matt's ear as he stood touching the car. Tom couldn't hear what was said, but even in his wound-down state he found this odd: Hatch had never done anything like this before and the act reeked of conspiracy. Had he gone over to Matt's side like all the others?

The second thing that Tom categorized as strange behavior was Matt's reaction. He began pacing up and down, gliding his car-touching hand from hood to roof and back to hood, red in the face, looking spooked, muttering loudly enough for Tom to hear: "Shit, shit, shit, shit, shit."

What was Tom to make of such things? And then something even more bizarre happened. The critical event, as it turned out. Matt sneezed.

He sneezed loudly. And then the crowd gasped. From these initial gasps rose raised voices, and from these voices a climbing pandemonium. Members of the public were suddenly shouting:

"Oh no!"

"Oh my God!"

"He took it off!"

"Did he?"

"I saw it!"

"Took his hand off when he sneezed!"

Tom looked at his own hand. He had not removed it. *Took his hand off?* He looked over at Matt, who was still standing there with one hand on the car, but people were pointing at him now, pointing and shouting.

Tom focused on Betsy in the crowd. He could see her face etched with loss and dismay as she stared at her new man from behind the string cordon. Her right hand was clamped over her mouth as Tayshawn (of all people) stepped up to her and began to whisper in her ear. *What's with all this whispering?*

And as Tayshawn whispered, Betsy's face turned from dismay to something like horror. Whatever the kid was whispering sure wasn't commiseration.

"He's out!" the crowd continued to shout.

"He took his hand off!"

"What happened?"

"He sneezed! Took his hand off!"

As the onlookers became increasingly noisy, Hatch walked back up to Matt and spoke quietly with him again until Matt began to nod and look lost, almost bereft. And then the most extraordinary thing happened. The young man took his hand off the car. In full view of everyone.

Applause broke out. Incredulity. Matt was out? Heads turned, looked briefly over at Tom, the winner by default, before turning back to Matt, the more dramatic figure, the unlucky loser. Many pushed forward to surround the younger man who had slipped up with victory in sight. As Tom watched all this, not yet fully certain how it related to him, he saw Betsy climb over the rope cordon slung around the Discovery, rush toward Matt—and proceed to hit him, hard, pounding him on the chest with her fists until he backed away, protecting himself from the blows. She had tears in her eyes and was shouting: "How could you?" and "Which one of you? Tell me! Which one of you was it?" Matt had to grab her wrists as she yelled: "You bastard! You *bastards*! Which one was it?" And when she called, "How could you?" over and over, the public could only presume that hers was an unprovoked attack, related to Matt's failure to win the car.

Tom closed his eyes. It was all too much. Too incomprehensible. He stopped trying to understand and instead cloaked himself in darkness. Distorted voices swelled, fell, then rose again: all of it easier to deal with in darkness. And when he next opened his eyes—just to check that he was not asleep and had not dropped out of the contest—what he saw made even less sense. The world was a chaotic place. Full of factions, each wanting to be heard. All shouting at the same time. The female protesters with their plac- ards were yelling, "Leave her alone!" and "Take your hands off her!" But the mayhem only seemed to intensify with their inter- vention. For some reason these two outsiders were trying to break Matt's grip on Betsy's wrists. *Why? Why?* Tom closed his eyes on this turbulence so that a form of calm engulfed him again. And he might have stayed like that, with his eyes shut, blotting out reality, if someone hadn't tugged on his free hand.

He worked open his eyes with extreme reluctance and looked down. A little girl. Sweet innocence looking back up at him. Munching something. A strap of licorice. Her other hand was holding something up to her face—a pink mobile phone. "Say cheese . . ." said the phone with a female American voice, before it went *click*! Oh yes, that's right, phones took pictures now. "You won," the child informed him as she lowered the phone and bit the end off her licorice strap and chewed it, regarding Tom as if he were a zoo animal. Black juice seeped around her teeth.

Tom turned his eyes back to Matt but couldn't see his last rival around the car. Where had he gone? He switched focus to the middistance. The noisy sideshow had slid some twenty yards away, with Matt now doing his best to escape the tearful Betsy as well as the two protesters, not to mention the snap-happy press, so that Tom, slowly and very dimly, realized he was the only one left with a hand still on the car. He must therefore be the winner. It was the only conclusion.

Hatch confirmed it. Came up to Tom and placed a hand on his shoulder. "Congratulations."

Tom nodded. Victory. He had done it.

He looked again at his left hand, still touching the metal, the last hand out of . . . how many had started out on this venture? "It's over," he said, as if to convince himself.

Hatch squeezed his shoulder. "You did it, buddy."

Tom nodded. But there was no joy in him. Instead, he felt like crying, and the tears rose, surprising him.

"You can take your hand off now," Hatch instructed gently.

There. It was done.

In this public space, this moment was uniquely private, one full of strange meanings for Thomas Shrift. Someone was clapping. Tom looked up, saw the car salesman still standing close by, smiling. Stirred by the moment, they shared a look, aware that something significant had been done here by both of them, though they were not sure what.

Tom forced his buckling legs to carry him the short distance to the far side of the fountain. There he found an open space on the polished marble floor, broad and cool and flat, and taking deep breaths he sank down and lay on his back, his ankles together, his arms at his sides. What immeasurable bliss, to give oneself over to sleep at last—to set down the awful burden of consciousness. The marble was cold and hard beneath him, and he lay there in the accidental pose of a mortuary corpse. But his open eyes then found focus on the great glass dome, hundreds of feet above. For all he could tell it was the fabled inner dome of heaven, sparkling up there with all its far-off and glittering promise, existing beyond the bounds of reason, purely out of hope—but wasn't this also a sufficient basis for existence?

And with this thought, the latest product of that peculiar Shrift mind, he shut his eyes. He slept.

6

TOM AWOKE. IN pain. Where was he? Twisted in the backseat of his victory car parked outside his flat in Barlby Road. His neck was stiff. His back sore. Not at all the recharge that he so badly needed. He'd forgotten how to sleep. Bursts of zonked-out unconsciousness followed by starts and fits, light shows behind the eyes jolting him awake—this was no substitute. The latest of these bouts saw him sit bolt upright in the morning light, blinking and finally seeing that he had three parking tickets stuck to his front windscreen.

The attacks never ended. You repelled one, the next arrived.

He'd completely forgotten that the Land Rover had no borough parking permit. He got out and unstuck each one from the glass. Jess's ex-colleagues had attacked him again, salaried vampires sucking him dry while he slept. Being rich, he saw, required not just the setup money; the status had to be fed and fed continually—it was expensive to be loaded.

Tom couldn't afford to run or maintain this car, couldn't afford a single day of ordinary ownership, but that was okay. He didn't intend to keep it. Despite all his efforts and suffering, he was still a champion chump, an insolvent world record holder, reputation rich perhaps, but pocket broke. Invisibly famous.

Had it been worth it? Yes and no. Profit and loss. You won with the left hand, lost with the right. He might have won the car but when Vince had chauffeured him home in the Land Rover the previous night, what he had seen from his passenger window wiped out that victory in a second.

A burned-out shell. A ruin. Fire had devastated both floors of the flat. Smoke and soot had turned the red brick black. Every window was broken, by heat or by firemen. The front door had been shattered by an ax. Inside the building, he knew, would be a version, in charcoal, of all his possessions.

His neighbor had struck. He had no doubt. This was no coincidence. It was a revenge act. As he looked at the wreckage he saw that both flats had been gutted. His neighbor had sacrificed his own flat in order to get even! The guy had really gone and done it, a madman theory response, doing with petrol what Tom had done with WeedKill Pro: like for like, blood begetting blood, until they wound up here, in a shared victory of ashes.

"Is this your place?" Vince had asked.

Tom parlayed this question. "This? No. No, it's not. I'm . . . I'm two doors down. I don't know who lives there."

"Christ! That was a helluva fire. Can't have nothing much left inside. You know them? Who lives there?"

"No idea. Never met them."

And it was not entirely a lie. He felt removed now from that lawn poisoner, his former self. Who had that nutcase been, creeping around in the dark, murdering another man's garden?

"Just as well," Vince had said as he handed Tom the keys and the Discovery logbook. "You're the man. Good luck to you." And then he had climbed out of the driver's seat and, signaling to Dan, who had followed behind in another car, left Tom alone.

Sitting outside his torched flat he had felt oddly buoyant. Tiredness had drugged him, and in this condition a thought had managed to rise and seize him—the meaninglessness of victory, the folly of it. His whole life's effort had been based around a single credo: that it was better to hate yourself in victory than love yourself in defeat. But was this right? He guessed that at some point everyone was more or less involved in the same quest to reach the top, to climb and do combat and overcome as to one day declare, "I made it! I am on top! I am the best!" But even while trumpeting all these "I!"s, and just when you're supposed to feel—as Tom now tried to feel—fantastically vindicated, content that victory's afterglow must now endure a whole lifetime, he found only . . . what? That you have to be a fireman to get in your own front door.

I hold a world record! his old inner voice wanted to shout.

But so what? came his new response.

I'm famous!

Big deal. *Get over it, you jerk. Just look at the blackened wreckage.* Just look at that, and learn.

He couldn't help but smile. Sitting there in his champion's car he started to laugh. The stresses in his aching face muscles eased. And he couldn't stop this laughter coming.

He shook his head; for a Mensan he'd been very dim. A truly intelligent person operates from the basis he could be wrong. Wrong! The wise stress their fallibility, not hide it—of course this was true. But how few wise people there were in the world by this measure: a half dozen per century that we heard about in the news. As for the rest of us, he calculated, the *un*wise millions, there was only this blind game of lying to ourselves simply because we draw a living wage from the life this lie allows; and not content with this deception, we forcefully *defend* this inner lie, which is merely the most convenient and self-serving thing for us to believe in. Tom beheld his own stupidity, plus the stupidity of millions, written for him in black charcoal against a gray London sky. Finally, it's not the lies we tell others that do the most damage, it's those we tell ourselves. From this all troubles rise.

Tom spotted Mr. Bombaum, the pensioner from two doors up, stopping in front of the gate.

"Mr. Bombaum! Hello," called Tom, scrambling stiffly from the back of the car.

The old man turned. Fright softened into recognition. "Oh, it's you. Nobody knew where you were."

"I've been away."

"People wondered if you was inside. During the fire. Hell of a fuss."

"Do you know anything? About how it started?"

"Don't you know? Didn't you hear? Been on the radio."

"What happened, Mr. Bombaum? I don't know anything. I just got back."

"Seems everyone's been away. Your downstairs neighbor, I mean. Seems he went away too. Left his Hoover on, didn't he. I ask you. Who leaves their vacuum cleaner going when they go away, leaves it going, with all that racket for days on end? No wonder it overheated. Caught fire, they say. Now look at it."

So, thought Tom, *a revenge act for sure, but a minor one.* Or did his neighbor know that vacuum cleaners, when left on, will overheat, catch fire? A cunning arson.

"I don't see what there is to smile at," Bombaum said, walking away. "I wouldn't be laughing meself."

Tom watched him go, then turned back to his flat. He wouldn't go inside. Yellow emergency tape webbed the doors. It might not be safe to venture any closer. His home. So full of the things he'd accumulated, prized, coveted and to some extent judged his own value by. Yet he felt no special anger, no desire to fight back or exact revenge, no urge to put a tube down his neighbor's throat and pour down it half a gallon of his own motor-mower petrol. (How crazy he'd let himself get!) He felt only a relief that the feud was over. He was, he'd found, desperate only to surrender. Defeat, in the end, wasn't so bad; at least, not half as bad as he expected it to be. He had his freedom back—this was the unexpected consolation prize. Released from the old ferocities, he could breathe again. Relief entered him.

He had an impulse to phone Lee Lerner's show and tell him about this turnaround. The broadcaster would appreciate such a story. Would laugh at the description Tom could give of the feud, the lawn (the four-letter word now dug up), the true outcome of the contest, and news of what he now intended to do as a result. His rage had gone. No, no more of that. And Tom felt a peculiar calm and lightness descend as he stared at the sight of the blackened ruins of his home.

A PERSON GOES to bed tired, wakes refreshed, in some ways reborn, seeing reality clear as day, suddenly *knowing*. It was magical, this process. Sometimes it felt like the best thing about life was the nightly escape from it.

Jess awoke.

Nat must go to boarding school—she saw it so clearly now. For the next few years she'd pass over care of her daughter to an institution. It was ridiculous for Jess and Val to struggle on like this, year after year, passing up this educational helping hand. And besides, who was a bigger advocate for the boarding school than Nat herself? Who had found the website, for example, ordered the brochures that pictured gardens, trees, a lake with clinker rowboats, happy students laughing on sunlit lawns "bowered by laburnum"? And who had once told Jess, "I want to go where I'm around people who don't think it's weird to piss yourself in public"?

Jess had never believed her daughter. Had discounted these claims, thinking only, *Typical Nat, sacrificing herself to make everyone else's life easier.* Two years of indecision had resulted. But today that debate was over. Nat would be better off around her own kind, in a properly financed institution, run by lovely people who could answer with greater knowledge and finesse Nat's heartbreaking questions, such as: "'Will I ever meet a boy who will still want to make love to me after he's helped me to the loo, helped me with my plastic knickers, waited while I empty my bladder and then cleaned me afterward? There's no such boy, Mummy! No such boy!'" What could Jess say to such a question? But the Florence Treloar Boarding School in Hampshire would know. And when Nat asked, "Mummy, will I ever be able to have an orgasm?" the staff of the Florence Treloar Boarding School in Hampshire wouldn't have to go into the next room and dab their eyes with a paper towel. No, Jess was going to do everything differently from here on. Was going to toughen up and be decisive. Go for what she wanted, and make sure she got it. Nat deserved expert care, and Jess had awoken with the certainty that she was no longer the person to provide it. Her fingers dialed the most familiar number she knew.

"Mumia? It's me. I'm fine. No, I just got some more sleep. Listen, I've just decided something. It's about Nat."

Jess made all the rational points—the Local Education Authority had confirmed they would cover all Nat's costs; the precious Disability Living Allowance would not need to be frittered on long-distance taxis; under this plan there would be enough money to go around for once.

But Valeria's reply made Jess hang up in shock: "How can you be so selfish?" Jess stared at the phone, back in its cradle. How dare her mother say something like this? How dare she? Selfish? How dare she!

On the table sat the school brochure Nat had ordered. Jess took a cup of coffee and went through this document again, trying to repair the damage done by her mother's comment. She read again one ex-student's touching testimonial. The girl was pictured in a wheelchair. "We understood each other. There I realized how strong women are, especially when we have to fight to overcome

something—in our case our disabilities. And how we fought. . . ."
Yes, this was it! How we fought! It was important to fight; Nat
hadn't yet learned this lesson, because she'd lacked a role model
all these years, but now she must learn this vital lesson as soon as
she could. Nat must learn how to be strong, how to fight back and
to face the hardest facts: among these, that she would never walk,
that she would always be funnily shaped, have droopy breasts, a
slack stomach, jelly legs, a body she could never, ever exercise.
Life, especially in relation to other women, would always be a
competition, one she would rarely win. Nat must learn to compete. Toughen herself in preparation for the world. This was what
Jess had awoken *knowing*. Education, happiness, financial inde-
pendence, a man, a great job, freedom—all of these had to be
fought for and fiercely if they were to be won. Jess had lost. She
had been—had always been—too soft, and she saw it now. It was
too late to change herself. But Nat could still learn these things,
and in beautiful surroundings. The school had a lake you could
row a special boat on.

A KNOCK AT the front door. Having just smoked four cigarettes
back-to-back-to-back-to-back, Jess went dizzily to answer it. Undid the multiple locks. A snib, a shank, a chain. The heavy fortifi-
cations of White City living.

And there, on the front doorstep, Tom Shrift. He stood gazing
back at her.

What a sight! He looked dreadful—today the trademark crisp,
white shirt was almost gray and very crumpled, the top three buttons undone, as if he had only half dressed, showing tufts of black
chest hair. His unshaven chin was almost a beard. His livid eyes
also, red lids and red underneath, showed no sign that he'd slept.
Quite the opposite. A vagrant, a lunatic vagrant—that's how he
appeared on her doorstep.

And he was a lunatic who had come here to tell her something. "I won."

At this she slammed the door. A fiery impulse. And she didn't feel even slightly guilty about it. How dare he, how dare he come looking for her now with his gloating news?

But she'd left the side gate open. Dammit. While pouring herself coffee in the kitchen at the back of her flat . . . a tap on the ranchsliders behind her. She spun around. There he was once more, his hair rooster-tailed, speaking muted words through the double glazing, a distorted picture, his outline double-edged.

How on earth had he found her? She remembered at once— Tom had been in the Discovery when they had dropped her off and he'd remembered the route. Outside the glass, this nutcase was suddenly a mime artist, all hand gestures, a moving mouth, shifting expressions. . . . He raised his voice: "We need to talk. You left your side gate open! A neighborhood like this, it'd pay to keep it locked."

Even now he was firing and reaching her with his little barbed darts. She drew the curtains on this Marcel Marceau performance.

Hurrying into her bedroom, she went to the window facing the street. From this room half buried below road level, she could see it . . . there it was. He wasn't lying. The blue Discovery. He never did lie though, she remembered. So, he had won. But how? How could he possibly have beaten Matt? Amazing. The power of selfish energy to smash down all before it. Well, she was learning this too. From her low angle she saw the Discovery's blue cabin. She shook her head. Matt had been right: Tom Shrift was a freak. A freak of nature. This man would have kept going till it killed him, such had been his determination to have the things that he deemed his by rights.

She drew the curtains.

Sleep. She needed much more of it. Fuzziness was returning. As for the man in her backyard, in time he'd give up and leave.

And so she lay down, pulled up the covers and let Tom Shrift do whatever he was going to do. She breathed deeply, let her thoughts calm down. And they did calm. She had done well in slamming her front door. She was proud of this act. And then sleep came. Like a car crash. *Boom.* Then oblivion.

An oblivion of sorts. She dreamed of Tom Shrift. In a fairground she had to run away to avoid him. But he had followed her onto the bumper cars. She urged the little car to speed up, but it had only one speed. And his car was simply faster. He could chase her down and bump her, again and again, ramming her even into smaller cars and into the walls. Finally she got out of her little car, walked over to his, pulled out a dagger and just stuck it in his chest. Stuffed it in there. And off he drove, bleeding, with the knife embedded, spouting blood, but bumping other people now, *bump, bump, bump,* somehow continuing to ram into others as his chest fountained . . .

She awoke. And felt calm. She felt so much better for the nap. She rose. Brushed her hair. Went into the kitchen to make coffee. Found it too dark. Drew back the curtains. There he still was.

The madman. He was still sitting there on her back steps, his back toward her, looking out at her backyard view, at the four-story council estate flats over the fence. A madman.

Tom turned as she came out on the concrete patio.

"You are . . ." she informed him, "you're probably the most stubborn man in the entire world."

A small smile. A shrug: "World champion."

No easy way of getting rid of him presented itself so she invited him inside. Made coffee.

Tom looked around. Drew his rapid conclusions. A poorly furnished flat, numerous items broken but mended—wires bound a chair leg, the teapot bore a long crack, a lampshade had been Sellotaped—life spans artificially extended, nothing thrown away.

But the place was clean, ordered. He discerned self-respect, even limited tastefulness, in the crisp white tablecloth, a cheap art print, two tall-stemmed candlesticks. On the window ledges cacti with intense purple flowers grew in old yogurt containers. The smell of the coffee reached him. A fresh pot on the countertop needed only to be plunged. He sat on a stool beside it. Her obedient servant.

"I just want to ask you one thing," she said. "One question. And I want a short answer. And then I want you to finish your coffee and go. Deal?"

He nodded.

"Your big secret. What was it?"

"My secret? Simple. Make people think I had one."

"There *was* no secret?"

He shrugged. "Not really. Well, maybe . . . the conservation of energy that most people spend on being nice."

"You must conserve a hell of a lot of energy, then."

"I do. I won, didn't I?"

"Okay. Now you can go."

"I can't. I haven't told you why I came here."

Silence. "So?" she finally said.

He held up the Discovery keys. "Here. It's yours. Take 'em. It's yours. You won it."

She stared at him, then at the keys, then at him. "What are you talking about?"

"I'm giving you the car. It's yours. I only won it by thinking of you and your daughter, so really, it's yours anyway. Couldn't have done it any other way."

Her temper exploded then, suddenly and spectacularly. "Get out. Get out. *Go!*"

"What? What . . . what's the matter? Take it! It's for you!"

"What an arsehole!"

"What!"

"Do I look like someone you can *buy*? Well, you might be surprised to know, I'm not for sale."

"I'm not trying to—anything. It's for you. And your daughter."

"Get out. I'll call the police."

"Will you hold on a second?" Her speechlessness gave him a second to speak. "At some point . . . toward the end of the contest, I knew I couldn't win. I was finished. And then, I was in this toilet, and an idea came to me, this wild—it came from nowhere—of winning the car for you. And . . . I don't know . . . it was weird. Adrenaline started flowing again. I got this new lease on life. I got excited. As tired as I was, as dead on my feet as I was, I started to wonder . . . what it'd be like . . . to come to your house, stand in front of you, and just say, 'Here' "—he held up the keys again—" 'it's yours.' "

Silence from her now. Her oval, pale face of hidden unhappiness staring at him.

" . . . And that was all that kept me going. In the end."

Silence.

"Of course, when I finally won, I thought of keeping the car myself, but something weird's happening to me. Well, say something."

Her cheeks finally pinked with passion as she shouted, "Sex, that's what kept you going!"

"No!"

"People don't just give each other cars."

"Christ, you're a complex woman."

"*I'm* complex? Listen, you've made a mistake. I wouldn't go near you for all the . . . T-shirts in China!"

Now he was stunned, simply stunned by her. His voice was now as loud as hers. They were both shouting now. "I don't believe this . . . after everything I went through? I don't believe . . .

this is unbe— So you're telling me . . . you don't want this car?"
He stepped toward her and held up the keys.

She stepped close enough so that the keys touched her chest.
"I don't want *anything* from you."

She had cut him off, excluding him now even from her pity.
He hadn't counted on this. She was . . . she was meant to have
been delighted. He'd seen her delight in his mind all through that
endless fourth night and fifth day. The excitement it had generated had been the deep resource he'd called upon to get him
over the line. But now she'd told him what she really wanted from
him. Nothing.

He stepped back from her, turned, saw a darkened hallway leading away, at the end of it a lit-up bathroom. Without asking her permission, he stumbled toward it on stiff legs. Shut the door. Ran the
cold tap. Scooped chilled water onto his face. In the basin mirror
above, droplets ran down his face. Did the pain in his chest actually show? No. And the cause of this pain? Not just the slap and
sting of rejection but the recognition that she was probably right.
His offer of the car merely masked some demand: affection, kisses,
some order of payback—some reward he hadn't put a name to. How
low he was—even at his most admirable, he'd been unconsciously
working the angles. He toweled his face, returned to the lounge.

"Well, you're—you're . . . no way, no way—you're taking it."
His voice had lost its earlier resolve. No strings attached now. Yes,
even the invisible ones were cut. "Just . . . take it for a drive, then
decide." He placed the keys on the broken-tiled countertop and
prepared to exit.

"Over my dead body." Her arms were knotted tightly across
her chest. "You couldn't make me even touch it."

She snatched up the keys and threw them right back at him.
He had to catch them to stop them striking his face.

"Don't be stupid now. You know you need it." He raised his

eyes. Looked at her. He hoped they told her that he expected nothing in return. "Just . . . just take it. Please." He set the keys back down, gently. The keys lay on the tabletop. "It's yours. It really is yours."

For the first time she saw that this man looked lost. She lowered her voice also, sensing an advantage, possibly a climactic victory. "No. Go find Tayshawn. Give it to him. Someone else. Or sell it. Spend the twenty-five grand on a therapist." A last stab wound: why not finish him off?

In full retreat, he stopped as he prepared to pass through the ranchsliders. "It's, uh . . . it's . . ." He could barely string these words together. "It's not . . . it's not worth twenty-five grand."

"Fifteen grand, then, whatever."

"It's not worth even that. The car is . . . is . . ."

"It's worth—it's gotta be worth . . ."

"No . . . it's secondhand."

"Secondhand?"

"It's secondhand. The . . . Land Rover is secondhand."

"Second? No. It's—it's new . . ."

"One previous owner. Had an accident in it. It's a rebuild. Twisted chassis. The car's probably worth, right now, six grand, tops. Anyway."

For a second time he moved to leave.

"We—! But we—*it said, 'win a new car*'! The blimp thing! All along, on the brochure, they said . . ."

"I phoned the yard after I read the ownership papers. Spoke with Mr. Mouth to Mouth. They're saying they never said it was 'brand-new.' They only meant 'new' as in 'new for us.' They never meant 'new' as in 'brand-new car.' Like a new girlfriend, they said. You can say 'new girlfriend,' but it doesn't mean she's never been someone else's girlfriend beforehand."

Again her voice stopped him from stepping outside.

She was absolutely enraged now—reeling: "They can't—"

"They got us. Nothing we can do. We fell for it."

"You're just going to . . . let him get away with it?"

He shrugged. Looked at her brokenly. "And I wasn't lying. What kept me going was giving the car to you. I'll try not to park on any red lines so you never have to see me again."

Too late she understood that he was gone. That she would never see him again unless she quickly called, "Don't go!" It was on the tip of her tongue.

"WHAT?" JENNIFER BACK said as she looked up from her magazine.

"Nothing." Hatch came in the back door. "Everything's fine. I . . . I just didn't get much sleep last night. How are the boys? How's Ronny?"

News awaited him. Ronny hadn't slept last night. Insomnia. Night frights. Post-traumatic shock was a possibility. The gunshot might be manifesting itself in unpredictable ways.

Hatch received all this news with a climbing sense of entrapment. For want of anything else to say, he told his wife he was going up to take a nap.

Her left eyebrow rose. This was strange. "You haven't had a nap in ten years!"

"On the seventh day he rested."

Half an hour later Jennifer Back pushed open the door of the master bedroom and found him sitting on the end of the bed, a suitcase open on the floor, his packing of it suspended. "Terry?"

He was studying something in his hand. He unfurled his fingers for his wife to see. She stepped closer: it looked like a small piece of twisted metal. "Where? Where are you going?" she asked.

"It's over."

"What's over?"

He took some time to reply. "The business. The business is.

It's going into receivership. I kept it from you. I owe money. Tens of thousands. And there's more. I haven't—"

"Stop—Terry—"

"I've been a fuckin' worm. Lied, cheated. I haven't told you a lot of things."

"I know. I'm not dumb, Terry. I know." It was the way she said *I know.* "About everything," she added.

He stared at her. She knew. There was no doubt now. His infidelity had been her secret too. "You didn't say? All this time? Jen? I don't understand. How? How did you . . . how does a person . . . I mean . . . *why* would you say nothing?"

She shrugged. Not even teary-eyed. "To hang on. To keep going. Because we have four children."

Hatch had just arrived at this conclusion too, but by wildly separate means. "I stopped trying. We both did." He closed the fingers of his left hand on the bullet and looked up at his wife whom he'd just remembered how to love. But did she love him back? No. How could she? It was impossible.

"I want to keep trying." He managed to say this much. *I want to keep trying.*

And then he bowed his head. Tears came, welled up inside him, and in the midst of his aching self-pity, as sobs made his chest heave, a miracle: he felt a hand touch the crown of his head, touch it where he was balding, just where all the Back men went bald; and he felt by this gesture anointed, a decision confirmed between them without either saying a word, an old contract reissued, no loopholes, no fine print or wiggle room, an ironclad warranty, one that said: "I will be there for you. For as long as I live." And such a covenant was not to be handed over to a social agency, not to a stepfather, or a caregiver, not to a lover. No, the original text read, "*I* will, *I* . . ." and the dishonoring of this assurance, the transference of this "*I,*" was not to be contemplated unless every possible effort had been made, every drop of strength exhausted unto the outer limits of endurance. Under such cover Hatch had grown up. He was an old-fashioned kid. He understood finally that any lesser guarantee was simply not worth issuing.

THERE IT SAT. The grand prize, the blue Land Rover Discovery. What on earth was it doing here, still parked at the curb outside her flat?

Tom was bullying her again. She looked up and down the road quickly, semifurious, scouring for him, but saw only a delivery-man, a kid on a bicycle, far off a parking warden. Where was he, what was his game? And then, *What an arsehole!* Leaving it to her like this. What was he up to now? She'd been very, very clear about not wanting the car. He was taking a huge liberty. Leaving it behind was an insult.

She approached the Discovery gingerly, as if it were booby-trapped, and shook her head in anger: what was she to do about this? Perhaps nothing. Just ignore it. This might be the best thing. Just ignore the huge, gleaming vehicle. Sooner or later, someone would come and take it away.

She circled the car, just as she'd circled so many cars in the last few years when trying to tell if they were in violation. Ran a hand over its sun-warmed body. And couldn't help but remember all the other hands that had touched it in the last seven days: Tay-shawn, and poor Walter especially (may he rest in peace), Matt and Betsy, the car thief, the insomniac, the soldier who wasn't a soldier, Team McLusky, the truck driver, the gentleman from Zaire, all losers, like her. And she, the Central Loser.

The paintwork was still perfect. Hard to believe this car had been in an accident. Was Tom perhaps lying about this? No. He never lied. This clean-shaven man with his pressed white shirts, a bank teller's furled cuffs, his unbounded confidence and belief in himself, even despite a whole lot of evidence to the contrary—she was prepared to give him this: he was not the type who made things up.

Looking in the back window, she saw again how roomy the vehicle was. Nat's chair would fit in there easily. She'd even heard of chairlifts that allowed the disabled person to be hoisted up and then slotted straight in the back, locked in place, traveling by road without ever having to leave their own chair.

Going around to the driver's door, she saw also that the front door was open. The keys, however, were not in the ignition.

Should she? Would she dare?

With Tom still nowhere to be seen, she opened the driver's door, then did what no one had been allowed to do during the contest—she sat behind the wheel.

She shut the door and sank into the leather that the car thief had told her was genuine alpaca hide. (She had tried to picture an alpaca—conceived of a tall goat.) Her fingers tested its softness, then ran across the smooth, mahogany-trimmed dashboard before finally taking hold and gripping the leather-bound steering wheel with two hands. Beautiful. A beautiful car. Luxury leaked into you. Armrests even for the driver. A coffee cup holder. A satellite navigation system. Lexus freedoms everywhere. And such luxury didn't depreciate; it survived, cast its glittering spell right till the end. *Well, cast it on me,* she prayed.

And then she heard a murmur from the backseat. She squawked, just about jumped out of her skin, turned. In the backseat, alive under coats, something moved. And then a head appeared. The now familiar face. He looked at her. Matted hair, unshaven, a white shirt.

With a pounding heart she tried to catch her breath. "What? What are you doing?" she gasped.

"After giving the car to you . . . I had no plans."

He sat up. Saw her white-knuckle grip on the steering wheel. Then smiled victoriously.

"So," he said, "where's your dead body? *Wouldn't even touch it,* I thought you said."

She blushed. Oh yes. He had a point, this infuriating man.

THEY DROVE DOWN to Back-to-Back Cars together through the noonday traffic. So many cars everywhere. Tom complained about them, called it a metallic pandemic. "Once the Chinese and Indians have got one each, we're fucked," he told her. If humanity hadn't perfected the hydrogen-cell engine in the next twenty years, it was all over. "The only hope then is to decamp and head for Gliese Five eighty-one C, the closest habitable planet."

Jess listened. Smiled at the ongoingness of this man's voice, spouting his cranky opinions as usual, but suddenly she felt consoled by them. Was pleased for once to listen. Tom was back on form, insinuating, reeling off facts, theories, solving the most complex problems with solutions that sounded so simple to her ear and that appeared, on the surface, to be rational and obvious. Lucky man, she decided, to need an audience of only one to be in heaven. He truly lived by his own rules. What had he once said? *As long as the thread on the nut holds, tighten it.* Well, this guy was certainly born with a spanner in his hand.

The yard, when they reached it, looked closed. The chains hung in slack crescents, blocking off the drive-in entrances. They parked on the street and walked up.

At first they agreed that this looked like being a giant waste of time until they saw Dan slinking between the autos. Jess hailed him first. Tom trailed in her angry wake. This new stridency of hers hadn't been lost on him.

Dan smiled. Said it was nice to see them again, and with some color back in their faces. He told them the footage he'd taken looked really neat and then added, with Mormon-level politeness, that Hatch should be down in an hour or so, because he'd phoned ahead and said so. Dan nodded. A simple man. He knew nothing about this. When he asked Jess if he could do anything to help in the meantime, she said, "No," softened by his bumbling, high school dropout ineptitude. She said they needed to speak to Mr. Back personally.

"Okay. So. He'll be down soon then. So. If you wanna wait. How's the car working out anyway?"

"Oh, it's just great," Tom chimed in. "Wonderful."

"I'm really pleased to hear that. Really pleased. If you wanna wait in the waiting room inside, then, yeah?"

So Tom and Jess went inside. Sat side by side on the bench seat in the little room off the showroom.

"This is a waste of time," Tom muttered almost immediately.

But Jess was determined. "He's not getting away with this."

"Fine. But it's still a waste of time."

"Sorry to take you away from the front line," she said, "but this is important. What he's done is wrong."

Ten minutes later Dan popped his head in. Asked them if they still wanted to wait. Maybe he could take down a message and get Mr. Back to give them a call back?

No. They would wait. "We're going to wait as long as it takes until we get satisfaction."

"Oh," Dan said, made nervous by the conviction in the woman's voice. "Anyway, he'll be here soon."

"Not bad." Tom nodded with approval.

"What?"

"Go get 'em."

"Watch this space," she replied.

IT WAS ANOTHER whole hour before Hatch pulled up outside in the street. Dan rushed toward him from the dealership yard. "What is it?" But before Dan could answer, Hatch spied for himself the Discovery parked on the forecourt. "What's *that* doing here?"

"It's . . . it's, um . . . it's Tom and Jess. They're waiting for you inside."

"Oh Jesus. What do they want?"

"They seem . . . uh . . . pretty angry about something. They said they were gonna wait for you. 'For as long as it takes until they get satisfaction.'"

Hatch nodded. This news didn't surprise him. In fact, the sentiment even seemed to move him. "That's what we're all waiting for, isn't it?"

He walked toward the garage, but furtively now.

Inside his office, Hatch kept quiet, went to the venetians, pinched two blinds and peeked through the widened slit into the showroom's waiting room and saw the couple.

He released the blinds, slunk quietly back to his desk, opened the cardboard box he'd brought. The paper shredder couldn't be turned on until these two diehards were gone, so he set the shredder on the desk and just looked at it. Minutes passed. Tom and Jess were now holding up the dissolution of his family business, becoming a serious inconvenience. With the receivers due as early as tomorrow there were large volumes of papers begging urgent destruction. But what could he do?

The wall clock ticked. Defiant at first, fairly confident that he could wait however long it took for these people to leave, he soon began to wonder if he had what it took to win a waiting contest against such extremists. He began to doubt it strongly, being unwilling to submit to the kind of animal suffering that was clearly their specialty. He must not let this become a waiting game—he was doomed to lose such a thing—and yet he did not know how to prevent it from turning into one.

. . .

OUTSIDE IN THE showroom, exhibiting a patience born of long practice, Tom took a risk. He looked down at Jess's left hand at rest on the seat between them and made his move. He laid his right hand upon hers and awaited rejection. . . .

But it didn't come. Instead, miracle of miracles, she eventually—and without looking at him—spread her fingers slightly wider so that his thicker digits fell to fill the soft spaces she created. Wonder of wonders.

They both sat in silence after that, a deep-reaching silence, just holding hands; she feeling all the things that two people feel when they hold hands for the first time, he trying to think what one is supposed to feel when two people hold hands for the first time. *Tick, tick, tick, tick, tock.* Two foiled and divergent types, then, side by side, neither even daring to look at the other, but enjoying a shared peace disturbed only by the noise of traffic rushing, ever rushing by, outside. And Jess, who had always been too slow her whole life, possibly because she had never made enough noise from the moment she was born, and Tom, too fast his whole life, perhaps out of his desperation to become someone who mattered—neither felt any desire to rush anywhere at all. Instead they silently admitted to a world that was as it was, that finally had to be taken on its own terms. Born into it, you had no choice but to rise to the daily challenges as they arose, to be capable, when called upon, of feats; usually ordinary feats but every now and again extraordinary ones also: such as keeping your hand on a car without sleep for five days and eleven hours and twenty-two minutes, or holding your breath for eight minutes and fifty-eight seconds, or else eating fifty-three and a half hot dogs in twelve minutes, or memorizing pi to a fantastic number of decimal places, living for a hundred and twenty-two years and a hundred and sixty-four days, and learning to love despite the pain. Yes. All of the above were tough. But, as the record books now showed, not impossible.

Writing NOTED "Damage Noted"
fine Paid 9/1/09